KLOTSVOG

RUSSIAN LIBRARY

R

■ □ ■

For a list of books in the series, see page 247

Foreword by
Lara Vapnyar

Translated by
Lisa C. Hayden

KLOTSVOG

MARGARITA KHEMLIN

Columbia University Press / New York

Published with the support of Read Russia, Inc.,
    and the Institute of Literary Translation, Russia
Columbia University Press
Publishers Since 1893
New York   Chichester, West Sussex
cup.columbia.edu

Library of Congress Cataloging-in-Publication Data
Names: Khemlin, Margarita, author. | Hayden, Lisa C., translator.
Title: Klotsvog / Margarita Khemlin ; translated by Lisa Hayden.
Other titles: Klot´s ˘vog. English
Description: New York : Columbia University Press, 2019. |
    Series: Russian library
Identifiers: LCCN 2018061305 (print) | LCCN 2019003061 (e-book) |
    ISBN 9780231544146 (electronic) | ISBN 9780231182362 (cloth)
    | ISBN 9780231182379 (pbk.)
Subjects: LCSH: Jewish women—Soviet Union—Fiction.
Classification: LCC PG3492.54.H46 (e-book) |
    LCC PG3492.54.H46 K5613 2019 (print) |
    DDC 891.73/5—dc 3
LC record available at https://lccn.loc.gov/2018061305

Cover design: Roberto de Vicq de Cumptich
Book design: Lisa Hamm

CONTENTS

FOREWORD

Klotsvog: *Notes from the Jewish Underground*

LARA VAPNYAR

I have to start with a confession. It's not unusual for me to cry over a book. I choke up when I reread the scene of the old Prince Nikolai's death in *War and Peace*. I tear up when Ennis calls Jack "little darling" in *Brokeback Mountain*. I start weeping when I read about dying children squabbling over an orange ball in the oncology ward in *People Like That Are the Only People Here*. I dab my eyes with the tip of a tissue and go on reading. What is unusual for me is to bawl over a book for hours. To bawl, to sob, to go through an entire box of tissues, to feel devastated for days afterward. And yet this is what happened when I finished Margarita Khemlin's *Klotsvog*. And these weren't sweet tears of empathy either—I cried from shame, from horror, from the deepest self-loathing. I felt like I needed to go to a house of worship and beg for forgiveness, except that I'm not religious and had no idea who to beg or how.

I'll try to explain why this book affected me so much, but I need to get my bearings first, so I'll start with some literary context.

Dostoevsky's *Notes from the Underground*, a classic of the "confession of a bad person" genre, opens with a direct statement by the narrator:

"I am a sick man ... I am a spiteful man. I am an unattractive man. I believe my liver is diseased."*

The novel proceeds in the same vein. The Underground Man lists all the slights, all the humiliations, all of the instances of his being spiteful, cowardly, and dishonest, going into the tiniest details, savoring them, almost delighting in them.

Margarita Khemlin's *Klotsvog* also opens with a direct statement by the narrator:

> My first name is Maya. Patronymic Abramovna, maiden name Klotsvog. My surname's very unusual but I don't know its literal meaning. If anybody knows, please tell me. That's not important to me, though, because what's important is how somebody made life's journey, not what their surname is. I was born in 1930 and—like my whole generation—saw too much, things that weren't pretty.

The tone of this opening is similar to the Dostoevsky opening, but it's hard to imagine a more startlingly different narrator. Even though *Klotsvog* the novel is framed as a confession, the main character, Maya Klotsvog, seems unable to see herself for what she is, to judge her actions correctly, or to understand their effect on other people: on her mistreated and abandoned lovers and husbands, on her neglected children, on the mother that Maya banishes from her life.

This striking lack of awareness is introduced early on in the seemingly innocent sentence where Maya talks about her profession. "Field of work: mathematics teacher. Retired, of course. But I don't consider myself a former teacher. Like a lot of other

---

* All Dostoevsky translations quoted are by Constance Garnett.

professions, a teacher's profession doesn't exist in the past tense. Acknowledging that sustains me tremendously." Later we realize that even though Maya does hold a teacher's diploma, she has never worked as a mathematics teacher. Save for a short stint managing a special education class, she has never worked as a teacher at all. How then can something that is obviously not true "sustain her tremendously"?

Some readers might be tempted to see Maya as an unreliable narrator. Others might even go so far as to see her as a self-serving monster who is lying in her confession in order to dupe the reader into thinking that she's innocent. After all, she does have a tendency to sacrifice her loved ones for material gain, and she's very successful in upgrading her housing situation and her wardrobe from one husband to the next. But taking Maya for an antihero would be a grave mistake. Unreliable narrators are there to confuse the reader. Maya is confused herself. What she has is a sort of blindness of perception, which prevents her from realizing that she is often the cause of her own and her family's suffering; but she's not aloof to that suffering, she feels it deeply; more than that—she suffers herself. "Fima [Maya's first husband whose life she basically destroys] recognized something scary and began crying, too, half-asleep. I sobbed out of pity, confusion, and an uncertainty that had covered me from head to toe." What we have here is rather a case of an "unreliable author" who hides raw emotion behind Maya's stilted language, steeped in imperfections, and influenced by Soviet bureaucratic clichés. Just look at this sentence: "We gradually learned that our husband and father had perished during the forcing of the Dnepr." (Kudos to the translator! It must have been really hard to get it right.) This strangeness of the language serves to distance the reader from the characters, so by the time you experience the shock of recognition (Oh, shit, this is me! This book is about me!) you're completely unprepared and it overwhelms you with its emotional power.

Hence the hours of bawling.

But that's not the point.

Which is another strange expression that pierces the *Klots-vog* narrative from time to time. I used it just now, because I was afraid to start crying again, and I suppose Maya uses it for the same purpose.

Dostoevsky's Underground Man claims that extreme self-awareness is a sickness: "I swear, gentlemen, that to be too conscious is an illness—a real thorough-going illness." Well then, the extreme lack of self-awareness must be a sickness too. And it looks especially disturbing if you consider its origins in Maya's case.

The Holocaust is barely mentioned in *Klotsvog*. We know that the thirteen-year-old Maya and her mother managed to escape right before the German invasion, and there are no descriptions of the atrocities, almost no discussion of their toll on the survivors. And yet the entire narrative is saturated with allusions, like the detail about bags filled with clothes and toys that used to belong to Fima's first wife and first children, who perished in the Holocaust.

It's easy to frown at Maya for her deep aversion to Yiddish, until you realize that the entire Yiddish-speaking population of her hometown was murdered. And it's tempting to mock Maya for her ruthless pursuit of her two obsessions—better living conditions and nicer clothes—until you remember that her childhood house was "razed to the ground" by the Germans, and that her best dress likely burned along with Maya's best friend, who had taken it for safekeeping. And it's hard not to cringe at the dishonest, immoral, and sickening arrangements Maya makes when she finds herself pregnant by her married lover, until you remember that her actions are guided by rumors of Stalin's own "final solution," his plan to dispose of the Soviet Jews who survived the Holocaust. There is a good chance that if not for Stalin's death in 1953, his plan would have been realized.

Not that emotionally blind Maya understands any of that. Later in the novel, when Maya's daughter renounces her Jewishness, Maya comes to complain to a wise old Jew, Beinfest. Here is what he says: "She's scared because she ended up Jewish. All children are afraid of the dark. And Jewishness is akin to the dark for children if they don't engage with it."

Maya refuses to process that thought, but it sticks with the reader. Jewishness is akin to the dark. Jewishness is akin to the fear. Unless you engage with it.

A lot of Jewish writers have engaged with the theme of survivor's guilt, but none of them has handled the question of survivor's *fear* quite as Margarita Khemlin does. The blind inexplicable animal fear that makes you do unspeakable things. Dostoevsky, who despite being a recognized anti-Semite managed to influence and stir several generations of Russian Jewish writers, probably comes the closest. Here is the passage from *Crime and Punishment*:

> "Where is it," thought Raskolnikov. "Where is it I've read that someone condemned to death says or thinks, an hour before his death, that if he had to live on some high rock, on such a narrow ledge that he'd only room to stand, and the ocean, everlasting darkness, everlasting solitude, everlasting tempest around him, if he had to remain standing on a square yard of space all his life, a thousand years, eternity, it were better to live so than to die at once! Only to live, to live and live! Life, whatever it may be! . . . How true it is! Good God, how true! Man is a vile creature! . . . And vile is he who calls him vile for that," he added a moment later."

In that sentence, Dostoevsky is being clear-eyed about the weakness and despicable nature of human beings. He passes judgment while simultaneously negating it with empathy. And this is exactly what Margarita Khemlin does throughout her novel.

I started with a confession, so I'll try to end with a confession too. Why did this book affect me so much? The thing is that I've always prided myself on my presumed extreme self-awareness. I considered it my best skill as a writer. I thought that I completely understood my deepest fears, desires, and motivations, and that this understanding provided me with amazing insights into my fictional characters. After reading *Klotsvog*, I saw that I'd been blind just like Maya. I discovered that my consciousness has been harboring so much more of the dark, shameful, despicable stuff than I'd ever known. Here is one example. I'd always thought that my inclination to distance myself from all things Jewish was a cultural one, an aesthetic choice more than anything else. I realize now that it stems from that sticky shameful survivor's fear even though I am a whole generation removed from the Holocaust. There were plenty of other discoveries, some of them much worse than the existence of survivor's fear, but those are too painful and too private—I'm not ready to share them.

Margarita Khemlin's *Klotsvog* has been a revelation. I hope it will affect other readers in the same way. But in order to let it work, please, approach it with maximum empathy and a maximally open mind.

TRANSLATOR'S NOTE

I last saw Margarita Khemlin on September 6, 2014, at a translation award ceremony in Moscow. She came to the ceremony to return an amber necklace, a gift she'd made for me a few years before, and then restrung during my time in Moscow—the necklace was such a favorite that I wore through its soft band of leather all too quickly. She handed it to me, telling me she'd fixed it for all time; I thanked her. And then she vanished, emailing later to apologize, though the apology was utterly superfluous because I knew she didn't like ceremony or ceremonies.

Margarita vanished from the earth altogether a little over a year later. I learned of her death on a gray October day and went outside to dig potatoes because fried potatoes make for comforting medicine. And perhaps, too, because she and I had talked about kitchen gardens and vegetables one night in New York City a few years before—the garden still makes me think of her. Although I'd only translated two of Margarita's stories before her death, she was, for the translator in me, a sort of first love. Her "Basya Solomonovna's Third World War" was the first work I chose myself, translated, and then published, in *Two Lines*. I wanted to translate *Klotsvog* as soon as I read it, too, having loved the voice that Margarita channeled for her title character and first-person narrator, Maya Klotsvog. I'm grateful to Columbia University Press and the Russian Library for supporting my translation of *Klotsvog*.

Margarita wrote about a vanished Soviet Union, where she was born and lived, and where I first visited in 1983. *Klotsvog* conjures up a very specific corner of that world, and Maya's language in the novel often includes phrases and vocabulary typical of the Soviet era. The narrative that Margarita creates for Maya is written using the *skaz* technique, mimicking oral speech in written form. Timing, pauses, momentum, word order, and a myriad of other factors take on tremendous importance in *skaz*, making it particularly crucial for a translation to capture a narrative voice that's unlikely to sound literarily smooth. Maya's voice is very distinctive: she loves to call herself a pedagogue and sometimes sounds likes a petty bureaucrat, plus she has a way of emoting, in somewhat purple hues, when describing the many twists and turns of her love life.

I can't claim that my English-language rendering of all Maya's tortured phrasings—sometimes she tries a bit too hard to make her speech sound elevated—will evoke in English-language readers the reactions that Maya's original does for Russian readers. Experiences are just too different, though I can say that learning (and later teaching) Russian during Soviet times and using textbooks published in the USSR taught me some of the rhythms and peculiarities of standard, often rather formal language, along with phrases, for example, about cities being "cultural centers" or Soviet peoples standing "shoulder to shoulder." Maya often uses similar types of expressions, so I felt right at home.

As a student, I also learned of institutions like Pioneer Palaces, places where children—Young Pioneers—went for lessons and activities in their leisure time, just as one character does in

Klotsvog, to work on his checkers game. A note on checkers: the novel includes mentions of the "Chapaev" variation, which involves flicking pieces (this certainly makes it worth looking up online for details!) and is named for Vasily Chapaev, a Red Army commander during the Russian Civil War. Chapaev has other mentions in the novel: there's a Chapaev cinema, and Maya even recalls the film *Chapaev*—specifically a scene where the White Army mounts a "psychological attack" on the Red Army but is forced to retreat.[1]

There are two other historical references in the book that I'd like to mention briefly. Though neither Pinya Mirochnik nor Menahem Mendel Beilis plays directly into the novel's action, both are part of the antisemitic atmosphere in which Maya lives. Beilis was accused of killing a boy in a blood libel murder in Kiev in 1911 but acquitted in 1913. Pinya Mirochnik, however, was Maya's contemporary, albeit as a figure in a notorious feuilleton that played on xenophobic and antisemitic propaganda themes: In a piece written in 1953 by Vasily Ardamatsky for the satirical newspaper *Krokodil*,[2] he was accused of embezzling state property, as well as having relatives overseas. Although the reference to Pinya Mirochnik is, technically, an anachronism in the novel—the scene in which Maya references it predates its publication—this only serves to highlight further the fears that Maya feels during a very stressful time of pervasive antisemitism.

The Beilis accusations from before Maya was born and the Mirochnik accusations from her lifetime—along with the nationality question on official government paperwork—contributed to the survivor's fear that Lara Vapnyar mentions in her beautiful foreword to this book. Her essay offers both historical context and her own, very personal, reactions. I can't thank Lara Vapnyar enough for writing this foreword—it's no exaggeration to say that I couldn't have even dreamed of such a fitting piece, which left me with tears, too—and mentioning the sorts of discoveries that *Klotsvog* can inspire in readers (and in the novel's translator: I'm grateful for the new perspectives her foreword gave me).

So many people played parts over the years in bringing this translation into the world that I can't list everyone and all their help, though I want to list many because noting their contributions will reveal certain technical aspects of the book (without spoiling the story) that readers might like to know about. Christine Dunbar, my editor at Columbia University Press, has been encouraging and patient from start (when I suggested *Klotsvog* as a potential book for the Russian Library) to finish (when last-minute text issues came up). It's a pleasure to work with an editor in whom in-depth knowledge of Russian, Russian literature, and translation blends so well with both an ear for English and a willingness to allow a translation to be a translation so a book can possess its own very unique textual logic in English.

Anonymous peer reviewers offered very helpful comments that were both tactful and candid. I'm grateful for their assessments of the novel itself, which helped me see *Klotsvog* from other angles, and of my translation. My Russian colleague Liza Prudovskaya, who has read a draft of every novel I've translated, answered, as usual, hundreds of questions and saved me from at least as many careless mistakes. Other people helped, in various ways, with individual words or lists of words: Olga Bukhina, Ian Dreiblatt, Mikhail Krutikov, and Sean Bye. I'm especially indebted to Olga Radetzkaja, who translated *Klotsvog* into German, for sharing her correspondence with Margarita: Olga asked Margarita many of the same questions I would have, so her generosity is much appreciated. Michael Klimov helped me translate the Ukrainian speech that comes up in the novel. After much deliberation about how to handle the bits of Ukrainian, I decided to transliterate a few key words, to give a taste of Maya's multilingual environment rather than either erase the Ukrainian completely or break the flow of the *skaz* narrative too much with a lot of transliterated Ukrainian words and footnotes with English translation.

Finally, Margarita's twin sister, Alla Khemlin, and Margarita's husband, Vardvan Varzhapetyan, both helped me tremendously by answering questions and giving me articles and support after Margarita's death. To say it was a bittersweet pleasure to meet with them and Christine in Moscow in September 2018 to talk about the translation feels inadequate because I miss Margarita so much. Margarita, of course, is the person I am most grateful to, both for trusting me with her stories nearly a decade ago, when I was just starting as a translator, and for becoming a friend. Translating Margarita meant serving as one of her voices in English (I'm not her sole English translator; I'm part of a chorus, along with Melanie Moore and Arch Tait) and I can only say that losing an author, particularly someone like Margarita, whom I knew and felt such affection for, has been a deeply heartbreaking experience. I think of her every day and I'm still thankful for her trust, which helped me gain confidence. And then there are her stories, which have taught me so much about writing and life and the world. And then, of course, there's her amber necklace, strengthened for all time and ready to be worn again and again, as a sort of talisman and a reminder of literature, loss, and love.

Notes

1. As of this writing, in late February 2019, the scene can be viewed on YouTube here: https://www.youtube.com/watch?v=8v9U7v3telo.

   Georges Sadoul's 1965 *Dictionary of Films*, translated, edited, and updated by Peter Morris and published by the University of California Press, includes a description of *Chapaev* and the scene. The listing is online on Google Books: https://books.google.com/books?id=_CL5zCKR2PgC& pg=PA59&lpg=PA59&dq=chapaev+psychological+attack&source=bl&ots =EzcYq1nUQ9&sig=ACfU3Uohcy-LCQbucw9kI1waveQl-fzA-g&hl=en&sa

=X&ved=2ahUKEwi8tPSal9fgAhUK7qwKHXveAGoQ6AEwAnoECAcQA
Q#v=onepage&q=chapaev%20psychological%20attack&f=false.

2. The *Krokodil* piece is contained in *The Soviet Government and the Jews, 1948-1967*, ed. Benjamin Pinkus, Cambridge University Press, 1984. It is available online, through Google Books: https://books.google.com/books?id=V7
g8AAAAIAAJ&pg=PA135&lpg=PA135&dq=pinya+mirochnik&source
=bl&ots=YI3L47Yrbb&sig=ACfU3U2wOmmEc1W6E13lZNxxohDoN8gl-
Q&hl=en&sa=X&ved=2ahUKEwj4mJH5qdfgAhVCj1kKHTpoAjIQ6AEwC
noECAgQAQ#v=onepage&q=pinya%20mirochnik&f=false

KLOTSVOG

My first name is Maya. Patronymic Abramovna, maiden name Klotsvog.

My surname's very unusual, but I don't know its literal meaning. If anybody knows, please tell me. It's not important to me, though, because what's important is how somebody made life's journey, not what their surname is.

I was born in 1930 and—like my whole generation—saw too much, things that weren't pretty.

Field of work: mathematics teacher. Retired, of course. But I don't consider myself a former teacher. Like a lot of other professions, a teacher's profession doesn't exist in the past tense. Acknowledging that sustains me tremendously.

Place of birth: the city of Ostyor in the Kozeletsky region of the Chernigov region. Very few people know the place now, but it was an important center of the Jewish nationality at the time I came into the world. Almost all the authorities on the regional level were Jews who toiled hand in hand with other nations and peoples. First and foremost: the Ukrainian people. And nobody was keeping tabs.

But that's not my point.

People lack the persistence to live. Especially certain people. I have always had persistence and understanding.

My memories of early childhood on are filled with the beauty of my native places: the Ostyorka and Desna Rivers, the Ostyor-Kiev trip on the boat *Nadezhda Krupskaya*, beautiful forests, nice architecture around town. The old synagogue building on the least crooked street—Pervomaiskaya—stood out. There was a movie theater at the other, opposite, end of the same street, toward Soloninovshchina. A Jewish-language theater operated in the synagogue right up until the mid-1930s. The theater was still there later, too. Enthusiastic amateurs acted there on their own initiative; my mother, Faina Leibovna, was among them.

On Soloninovshchina, they turned the estate of an important landowner unfamiliar to me into a stadium, but we rarely went there because it was far away. The museum of local history has been famous throughout the entire region since 1906.

We lived comfortably. We loved gathering and boiling clams. We got in a bad way if we ate up a lot of clam innards. Tempering the digestive process was useful, though.

The skills I acquired in childhood helped me overcome adversities later on in life, too.

I remember my grandmother, who was a virtuoso at twisting a stocking below the knee so it lay properly on the leg and didn't droop. There were no elastic bands or other accessories. My stockings always looked excellent. I taught my girlfriends, but only a few of them could do it, though that was later on. Anyway, we didn't have those problems as children because in the winter everybody went around in comfortable wide, baggy pants made out of any kind of fabric; people tied newspapers over their legs for warmth.

Mama, my grandmother, and I spent the period of the Great Patriotic War in evacuation, in the vicinity of Atbasar Station in the Kazakh Soviet Socialist Republic. My grandmother died of pneumonia.

Mama and I worked in a train carriage repair factory. I made strides in the metalwork field and the foreman treated me with particular respect. He was an ulcer patient, so we agreed that I would give him my portion of alcohol, he would give me his milk. That's how I received the supplemental nourishment necessary for a thirteen-year-old girl of my age.

We gradually learned that our husband and father had perished during the forcing of the Dnieper. I don't remember my mother's reaction.

My father was a caring and kind person in every way. After the Polish campaign, he brought home a piece of fabric for a suit for himself: gray fabric with small fuzzy spots. Mama decided to burn a thread to verify the quality. The thread burned instead of smoldering and the wrong smell spread. Mama came to the conclusion that the fabric wasn't wool, as my father'd thought. But she didn't say anything to him. So as not to upset him.

He brought back pieces of fabric for dresses for Mama and me, too: dark brown with a silky stripe and with a thin, broken stripe; my mother didn't verify their content. At least I didn't see her do it. They were sewn into plain, severe English styles. I should note that since the material was expensive and the responsibility was great, it wasn't Mama who sewed them but a good tailor, Ilya Mordkovich Kheifets, who Mama had to hire through connections because he had so much work and she requested they be sewn quickly, hiding from Papa that she'd paid way too much.

When we were leaving for evacuation, Mama laid those dresses out on the bed so she and I could be clothed in them over our summer dresses. We forgot to do it, though, because we were hurrying. Of course, someone who stayed in Ostyor wore them out. I dreamed that my dress would make its way to my close childhood girlfriend Bellochka Ovrutskaya and that she'd give the dress back when we returned.

Their family, which had a lot of children, stayed in Ostyor: they refused to evacuate. They were given one cart, but Bellochka's grandfather asked for two so they could take everything they needed. It wasn't given to them, though some people got extras that they could have done without if they weren't hauling away enough junk for the next hundred years.

Bella's grandfather took the position that "I don't plan to lend my conscience to those lacking in that area. That's not why I've lived my life honestly. Let them be as ashamed as their conscience allows." He was principled in matters of justice. They were shot with the other Jews in the ravine on the Desna; a friend of Mama's told us that in a letter in 1944, when we were planning to return after receiving permission. My dress had definitely disappeared into the unknown, and I cried out my childish soul over it.

I don't know the fate of my father's piece of fabric.

We lived in Ostyor for a while after the war even though it turned out our house had been razed to the ground. We rented a small place with some nice people we hardly knew. Families hired my mother as a nanny. I successfully graduated from night school, eighth grade.

Then we figured we needed to move to Kiev to look for jobs. My mother's younger cousin Lazar, a highly qualified pattern maker, lived in Kiev's Podol district with his wife, Khasya, and adult son, Motya. Lazar helped us rent a small place from an old lady not far from his house, and he always helped us with advice.

My mother could only find nanny work, though the pay was higher and she could even take meals with one family. Beyond that, Mama often brought me something delicious, too. This was sometimes a matter of chocolate.

In Kiev, I worked at a savings bank and looked at so much money belonging to other people that I had fainting spells and bad dreams. The big responsibility wore on me; I just couldn't get used to it. Figures with zeroes spun in my head. It seemed like the zeroes were always throwing themselves at my neck and suffocating me.

In an environment like that, the work almost finished me off. Mama, who saw it all, suggested I quit the bank and consider another line of work.

Uncle Lazar spoke out against that idea. I can't rule out that he was afraid of having to contribute material assistance. He was under the strong influence of a wife who was greedy and unpleasant in all respects. Especially with respect to my mother.

Their mutual dislike dated back to before the war.

My mother wasn't a true dressmaker, she was simply able to sew a little. Her stitching always came out a bit crooked, which wasn't especially important, though it spoiled the overall picture on the insides of garments. Mama hurried and had a bad eye for measurements. But Uncle Lazar lavished her with praise to his Kievan Khasya, who asked my mother to sew her a dress out of dark blue crepe satin. Khasya never had a figure but she had a large stomach. And she requested that my mother make a small belt with a button to go on that stomach. My mother explained that she needed to hide her stomach, that she should even make a style without darts instead, not something with a belt. Khasya was offended.

Mama sewed the dress as Khasya dictated, but there wasn't enough fabric for the belt. Khasya turned our whole place upside down searching for the material Mama had allegedly set aside so there wasn't enough for the belt.

Of course the dress didn't turn out too well, but a little belt wouldn't have prettied it up.

Khasya spun and spun in front of the mirror, all red and sweaty, and told my mother off in Jewish for her lack of skill. My mother was silent for some time, then said something to her. Khasya turned pale, tore off the dress, and scurried around, like she was going to run out of the house in only an undershirt with straps and a bit of lace trim at the hem, but she came back from the hallway and bashed the mirror with her fist. The mirror cracked. Khasya was in tears; my mother was crying. Each one stood in her own corner and nobody made a move to reconcile.

They cried, they blew their noses, Mama into her apron and Khasya into the new dress, which she balled up in her hands and used as a handkerchief. I don't know how things were left when they parted.

Mama later wore that dress for a long time, she just changed the style to fit the line of her own figure. And Khasya didn't set foot in our house after that. Lazar either. It turns out Mama told Khasya then that Khasya could hang herself out of spite, using that little belt that didn't exist. And then Khasya bashed the mirror. The mirror stayed in Ostyor when we left for evacuation. Our neighbor Khvoshchenko brought it back to us as a sign of gratitude when we returned. We were prone to irrational beliefs but we hung up the mirror because we lacked means, so it didn't cross our mind to heed bad omens.

I should say that whoever took possession of the sewing machine because of the German occupation never returned it to us. The explanation is obvious: a sewing machine isn't a mirror and it can provide substantial supplemental earnings for somebody's day-to-day life.

And so. We started from zero again after the war and somehow or other we grew close to Lazar and Khasya once again. Though due to sad necessity. In any case, we weren't thinking about any kind of help at all from their side—there was no reason for their worries.

I enrolled in evening classes at the pedagogical technical college. At the same time, I forced myself to continue working at the savings bank.

Back in school, my arithmetic and geometry studies were graded "*vidminno*"—meaning "excellent"—presenting me with no real choice. I didn't relate deeply to humanities subjects, they went in one ear and out the other. But I loved children. Looking at them and, well, just in general.

And this is where my first feelings overtook me.

Viktor Pavlovich Kutsenko taught our major subject to us. He was young and handsome. A soldier from the front with medals and decorations. Everybody was in love with him, but he started singling me out, personally, right away. Of course this wasn't a matter of my abilities or the baggage of my knowledge. I understood that I appealed to him as a woman.

Viktor Pavlovich's wife, Darina Dmitrievna, worked at the technical college, too; she taught history. But that's not my point.

"You can't operate with infinity the same as with finite quantities. Got that, girls? And did you lads get that, too?" And we'd all answer "Got that" in chorus. Viktor Pavlovich had established that greeting and always began his lectures in a similar way, regardless of the actual topic. Naturally, with our lack of specialized knowledge, we didn't completely understand what he had in mind, but we happily responded to any humor he offered.

We didn't have anybody's examples to follow for love. At the cinema, we saw pure relationships and one kiss the whole movie. Life brought its own corrections, though.

Life's crowding, crampedness, and striving to share our knowledge led to learning about the physiological side of interactions between a young man and a young woman from various sources that didn't always warrant confidence. After all, nature constantly prevailed.

I won't say my relations with Kutsenko were despicable from the very beginning. But we soon started meeting at his house on Saksagansky Street, after calculating exactly when Darina Dmitrievna was teaching.

Of course you can't keep secrets in a communal apartment, and everything came out in the open. Darina Dmitrievna reacted calmly, she just asked us not to let much show at the technical college and to find another place to meet since this was awkward because of the neighbors. That's what Kutsenko conveyed to me.

What could I offer? Mama and I rented a small space partitioned off by a curtain.

There was no doubt whatsoever that this was love. Even without the possibility of close contact, we wandered Mariinsky Park among the ancient chestnut trees and stood, embracing and looking from above at beautiful Kiev, which was rebuilding itself at a headlong pace after the barbarous wartime destruction.

Only once did Kutsenko and I meet at the apartment of one of his pals. This turned out to be very unpleasant because we later had to treat his pal to drinks and to talk with him for a long time.

One day Darina Dmitrievna caught up with me at the technical college and asked me to walk to the tram stop with her. She spoke politely and quietly, as was always her way. There was an eight-year difference in age between her and me, like between Viktor and me. They were twenty-eight and I was twenty.

I really felt that difference. Various doubts were tearing me apart, but Darina Dmitrievna and Viktor Pavlovich maintained a surprising evenness, both in their behavior and in other things. I thought at the time that they resembled each other a lot but I was different.

Darina Dmitrievna said:

"Maya, you know that I know everything. I'm not blaming anyone. And I'm also not judging you harshly. But I'm appealing to your feminine conscience. A very small amount of time will go by and the question of the future will come up. Love runs its course quickly and people have to either separate or live together. Viktor Pavlovich shared his thoughts with me, that he wants to marry you. Don't think he loves you so very much. He simply wants to have children. For reasons beyond my control, I can't have children. Of course, you're a beautiful young woman. And your children with Viktor Pavlovich would most likely be good-looking. But I'm concerned about something else. After all, you're Jewish and your children would be half Jewish. And you yourself know what the situation is now. You read the papers, listen to the radio. And then that shadow would fall on Viktor Pavlovich himself, too. Anything can happen. Don't you agree? Babi Yar over there is full of half-bloods."

"That was fascists, Darina Dmitrievna, and they're not here now," I said, answering as well as I could since I wasn't very interested in the newspapers and only looked at the tables showing government war bond figures.

"That's right. It's the damn fascist occupiers and their hirelings who were to blame. But that was about something else. And now there's a different twist. You haven't seen this with your own eyes so aren't in a position to imagine it in actuality, but I've seen it. Just so you know, history develops along a spiral. And what difference would it make to you if your loved one or children suffered, particularly if they're nice and pretty, too? Think about it. He's the type who wouldn't leave you at the edge of the grave. He'd follow. And if kind people held him back, how could he live then? He couldn't. I've studied him well. I beg you not to tell Viktor Pavlovich about our conversation. He might be a strong person but he has many wounds. Both in his head and on his whole body. Did you see the scars? He'll have nothing but sorrow from you later. And you'll suffer because of it, too."

The tram came right then. Darina Dmitrievna stepped up on the footboard and waved to me.

The challenge Darina Dmitrievna presented me with turned out to be awfully difficult. There was nobody I could ask for advice. The girls at school were young, inexperienced, and always ready for gossip and jealousy. I wasn't friends with my female bank coworkers. But a decent relationship had come about between me and a manager, Yefim Naumovich Surkis, first of all because it was through him—a second or even significantly more distant cousin of Aunt Khasya—that Uncle Lazar arranged for my job. And second of all, Surkis always smiled and was the model of a cheerful person who could resolve any kind of misunderstanding easily and on his own.

Yefim Naumovich assured me he'd keep everything in confidence and in secret.

In answer to my description of the situation, he was quiet for a long time, then answered:

"You were given solid advice. That's painful, of course, but forthright. I'm not inclined to baby talk here. My family, they all perished. I'm alone, without kith or kin. I save myself—though very badly—with jokes and banter. I think it would've been easier if I'd perished with them. One piece of advice: tell your problem to Viktor Pavlovich. Share the uncertainties as your own, without betraying Darina. Let his decision be final. Things are starting to happen in our country here so it's possible he'd have to follow you to the end of the earth. The situation is serious. One of my relatives works in a barbershop on Bolshaya Zhitomirskaya and nobody will sit in his chair for a shave. A Jew with a razor, that's a big deal! Funny? Well, they asked him to leave his job."

I sat silently and tried to imagine the depth of the situation. And I couldn't.

Surkis noticed my state and patted me on the shoulder:

"You know what, lass? You could marry me. I'm a person who's been through things and seen things. And I'm not old yet, either. You can't scare me with death and Siberia. I wouldn't allow you to feel lost, either."

And he started laughing. He started laughing in a bad way, without the right zeal, as if he had to.

I ended up completely confused. I got an earful of unnecessary information from all sides: someone on the tram would say something offensive directed at Jews, at work they'd be talking about an article in the newspaper about cosmopolites and Pinya Mirochnik from Zhmerynka, and all this as they cast sideways glances at me.

As bad luck would have it, Viktor Pavlovich got sick at that time and another instructor replaced him in class.

I went around like a ghost for a week. I couldn't stand it so I dropped by at Saksagansky Street to call on Viktor Pavlovich and find out how he was.

I ran into Darina because she opened the door. Darina started waving her arms around:

"Go away, you brazen girl, a person has a fever and can't get comfortable in bed, but you trot on over!"

I ran home in tears. As it happened, it was December 31 and a new year, 1951, was on the way. Mama was planning to go to Uncle Lazar's to celebrate. I was supposed to go, too, but I didn't feel like it.

Mama was curious and asked me what happened. I asked her if she didn't know what was going on and what planet she was living on that she couldn't find an explanation for my tears. And I told her about the newspapers, the radio, and so on.

It turned out Mama was aware of events but was too tired to attach any significance to them. And she advised me to do the same, otherwise I could lose my mind. And I still needed to go to school and keep leading my life.

So as not to spoil Mama's mood on the holiday evening, I pretended I'd calmed down.

We went to Uncle Lazar's.

Surkis was among the other guests in attendance. He periodically winked at me in a friendly way and when I was adjusting my hair in front of the mirror—my hair was pinned high on the sides by my temples, and locks of my hair were starting to frizz, like I'd curled them specially, but it was natural—Surkis embraced me around the shoulders, from behind, and quietly whispered: "So, have you decided to marry me?"

Surkis had been drinking so I wasn't offended. Quite the opposite: I took his words as support at a difficult moment.

Surkis and I went to stroll around nighttime Kiev and then came to his apartment. He told me he'd fallen in love with me at first sight but couldn't bring himself to admit it because of our age difference. When I asked what the difference was, it turned out he was thirty-six years old, he just didn't look very good because of all he'd been through. We laughed a lot. The unpleasantries dropped to the second or third level of importance.

Nobody should think that one night—especially a New Year's night—resolved the matter. Frivolity is not in my character. All that happened between us were conversations related to the future.

It was as if scales had fallen from my eyes. I saw the unenviable position I would be in even if Viktor Pavlovich left Darina Dmitrievna. Where would we live? Of course it would be possible to partition off their current room, people did do that. But what would come of it? Nothing good. Viktor Pavlovich didn't have another place in Kiev—his living space had been destroyed during the course of the war—and Darina Dmitrievna was the primary occupant because her father lived there until his death in the war, as did her mother, who was also deceased, from illness and grief.

The specter of homelessness hovered over me. And Surkis had a large, one-room apartment on Bessarabka Square. His family had lived there happily until the war. It was from there that he went off to the front as a volunteer without any second thoughts. Then his children and wife perished.

Yefim Naumovich openly declared: "My dream is to fill these walls with children's voices and a wife's laughter again."

And so, dear friends, that moment in time affected my future fate.

The point is that I had a very attractive appearance. As time passed, some people even told me I was the spitting image of the actress Elina Bystritskaya. An unquestionable resemblance.

But that's not my point.

I was extraordinarily indignant that my situation didn't allow me to completely reveal my feminine essence. I was often sick because of the conditions where my mother and I rented our small place: we lacked conveniences, heating, and good nutrition. My hair was dulling before my very eyes, my figure was losing its definition, and inferior sleep on a daybed offered no tranquility. Beyond all that, I wore unprepossessing clothes, although I tried to embellish them with little collars and cuffs.

My romantic infatuation with Viktor Pavlovich had overshadowed my thinking, leaving me with just enough awareness to think only of my love for him, especially since this was my first love. But the horrible assumptions hovering all around literally drove me into a corner and forced me to return, again and again, to the days in evacuation that had brought so many deprivations.

Of course, the problem of the future fate of the Jewish people— of which I was a constituent part due to my birth—rattled me. But things were working out from that angle, too: I could live pleasantly and with dignity alongside a reliable person, at least for an allotted time, until new ordeals. Be that as it may.

I told Mama about Surkis. She was elated: she couldn't have dreamt of more. She expressed certainty that she would finally find her own indispensable corner of the world alongside her beloved daughter.

I answered Yefim Naumovich in the affirmative three days later.

Then I purposely ran into Viktor Pavlovich (who had recovered) at the technical college and told him everything was over between us, to the last drop. He demanded an explanation but I hinted that there was nothing to explain. Our love had dispersed like smoke.

At that same time, I realized I was pregnant. Intimate relations had not yet begun with Surkis and I'd made a firm decision about marriage so I needed to hurry with either a dangerous underground abortion or the other obvious choice. I chose and moved—along with the insignificant items constituting all my property—to Yefim Naumovich's. Meaning, put more simply, to Fima's. Mama followed my advice and stayed at the old place for now so I could get used to my surroundings calmly, without an extra set of eyes.

Something completely unexpected awaited me. Every day counted, but things just weren't happening for Fima. And weren't happening and weren't happening, to the degree that one time he started weeping. I began weeping, too, since I was losing hope for my future with him. Fortunately, though, Fima loved to have a drink and that solved the problem in the sense that he didn't remember anything in the morning. And I convinced him there'd been intimacy after all during the night and that we were finally husband and wife in the full sense. Fima was very elated and cheered up, though really with no grounds at all for the long term.

We registered our marriage. Following the practices of the time, I left the savings bank so as not to cultivate nepotism; I continued my studies at the technical college. I switched to day classes and diligently devoted myself to housework, too, since I was preparing to become a mother.

I listened to Viktor Pavlovich's lectures and thought only about the subject under study.

My pregnant condition had become obvious. Kutsenko somehow found a moment to ask how far along I was. I answered that it didn't concern him.

Pretending to joke, he said: "We'll see about that when the little one comes into the world."

Time was moving along and the worrisome Jewish rumors weren't quieting down. My personal apprehension added to it: the possibility the child would undeniably resemble Kutsenko. At horrifying moments, I wanted the deportation to take place as soon as possible, before the baby's birth.

That's the stifling atmosphere I found myself in. Personal and public overlapped and didn't let me breathe freely.

But that's not my point.

A problem came up with my mother. As a daughter, I wished her solely the best, but she had a strong personality. And Fima's and my apartment was one room plus, of course, a kitchen. Yes, the ceilings were high—nearly four meters—but that's height, which had nothing to do with width here. The space seemed decent even so. Depending on how it was used.

My mother moved in with us. Her personal property included the mirror from Ostyor, particularly notorious because of the crack. Thanks to Fima's laxness, Mama mounted the mirror in the entryway, announcing its importance to family history.

Well, yes.

Mama loved cooking various dishes and was especially keen on garlic. The smell spread beyond the door, through the whole building. Considering the circumstances that had arisen, I gently reprimanded her, saying she could use a little less garlic, hinting that the neighbors were joking about the particular habits of Jews. Mama was offended and asked Fima for his thoughts, if I was right or not.

As my husband, Fima was on my side but evasive: "I like it. My late wife was keen on garlic, too. For its flavor qualities and for its healthfulness. But we have to be more careful now, especially with the little things."

And I was in a condition where I took every little thing to heart.

My relationship with my mother served as an example of what can happen in life. It's one step from love to hate. No matter what she did, she did it from spite. She proposed partitioning off the room using a chiffonier but could have set up her sleeping area in the kitchen. Fima let her push him around and partitioned off plenty of space for her. Except the chiffonier didn't reach the ceiling, so no isolation came of it. And my entire spousal life with Fima was within her earshot. It's true that even proved useful for me. No special feelings of any kind had formed for Fima and—since he himself showed no initiative of his own in that particular sense—Mama's presence behind the cabinet played no real role. But I had my principles.

And then. Fima loved giving gifts. He bought me pretty clothing and shoes and inexpensive jewelry to lift my mood. And something for Mama at the same time, so as not to offend her with inattention. But money doesn't stretch forever. And only he was working. Mama was so happy for any surprises and fussed over them so much that it provoked Fima to do even more. It got to the point where my husband wouldn't bring me anything but would bring Mama a scarf, stockings, or new saucepan.

The building had a basement where some residents had maintained enclosures for their household necessities since forever. They brought down their pickles, preserves, unneeded old clothes, and junk, for just in case. We had one of those compartments. Shortly after Mama moved in, she expressed a wish to put things in order there and manage it her way in the future. Fima presented her with the key to the lock and heartily approved her intentions.

And so Mama got under way.

But there were Fima's late wife's things, children's toys, and clothes. All covered in dust, mouse residue, and the rest.

I waited and waited and waited and waited, but no Mama. I went down there: Mama was lying on some sack of old clothes, with no apparent signs of consciousness. I tugged at her and even beat her on the cheeks so she'd come to.

She opened her eyes and said: "Forgive me, daughter. I made you marry Fima. But he has such a past, he'll hang around your neck like a stone."

And she was crying.

At a loss, I answered her: "Get up, let's go home. We'll talk in a normal place."

We came back.

I told her:

"What is this silliness? What kind of 'made you' are you talking about? Fima and I have a mutual fondness. Well, maybe it's not love to the grave but that's still no small matter. And with regard to you, dear Mama, since it's come up, there's basically no reason for you to be here at all. If you pricked up your ears less at night, there might be more use for this marriage."

Mama responded hostilely:

"What're you talking about? You're shameless! I sleep so soundly I don't hear anything at all. Let alone what you're thinking about. And in case you'd like to know, I know how to count, too. I see my own kinds of signs, maternal ones. What's your due date? The real one, not the one you're shoving on Fima? Nothing escapes your mother. So get used to it. You and I could put the child on its feet. Without the unfortunate Fima and his apartment with the little basement. I'm guilty in this, too. I pushed you, I didn't explain how difficult it would be to live with someone you don't love. And I ask forgiveness for that."

The thought ran through my head that Mama was right and her guilt was beyond question. She could have warned me. On the whole, though, it's not my nature to compromise. Besides, life is life, and what could you say if she hadn't figured that out by her age?

The situation was intensifying.

With all that going on, my annoyance was growing. The question boiled down to: Either Mama or me.

Nevertheless, time was moving along swiftly. I took an academic leave at the technical college to prepare to give birth.

Fima continued to be in excellent standing at work, but his personal behavior was becoming more and more difficult. And alcohol was the primary parameter. He was embarrassed about this and tried to leave the house for those kinds of events. He'd found a drinking buddy, Leonid Petrovich Yashkovets.

I can't help but note that Yashkovets wasn't working officially anywhere using his employment record book; he considered himself an artist working under private arrangements. His artistry consisted of drawing questionable little posters for cinemas, primarily the Chapaev Cinema. To make trouble, he depicted women on the posters so they looked more like me than the actresses who were actually in the movies. I know he adored me because he worshiped beauty in and of itself. Fima liked that: it flattered his masculine vanity.

As far as my mother went, she'd sniffed out something unsavory. She went to Ostyor a few times with the goal of establishing herself there with some of her relatives or acquaintances instead of living with us.

She spoke of it like this: "So you'll give birth, I'll take care of the child, and go to Ostyor. It calls to me. What can you do? You won't be offended, Mayechka?"

"Of course I won't be offended. Just so long as you're happy, Mama."

No, this wasn't easy.

But that's not my point.

Fima's attention was slipping away like sand between your fingers. There was no enjoyment for either me or him. And the gifts ceased, in competition with the damn vodka.

My maturation and coming into being as a person fell at a difficult time. It worked out that I had to come to decisions about my life on my own. Without advice, without support.

One time, right before I gave birth, Fima came home very late, in the dark, and started lamenting that he couldn't forget his previous family and kids, and that he'd wanted to discuss them a little, but I'd never offered him that. That I was an insensitive woman and should be selling salted cucumbers on Bessarabka, not preparing to give birth to a new person.

I answered Fima in full about the salted cucumbers. And about his outward behavior and his hidden deficiencies. In conclusion, I sealed things by saying I was afraid his child will be ashamed to see a father like him every minute.

At heart, I had no problems with my conscience because the father is the one who raises the child, not the one who conceives the child.

Fima took my remarks into consideration and didn't drink for two weeks. On the day I gave birth to my son, Mishenka, though, Fima showed up at the maternity hospital drunk, and he wasn't alone, he was with Yashkovets. And without flowers, without anything. How very shameful in front of the doctors, nurses, and other women on the ward!

Despite all that, my heart was still pleading for real, true love. But all my strength was taken by my precious child, Mishenka.

A year went by with the child's screaming and diarrhea, plus constant efforts to get even a moment's sleep. Mama helped as much as she could. Nobody can replace the birth mother for an infant, though I had setbacks with milk and we improvised to feed the baby.

The situation around me was hardly changing, and I'd learned to distance myself from both Mama and Fima. Most important, I completely lost track of the political circumstances because I was absorbed in caring for my child. Since I was officially considered a nursing mother, I believed that at least the law would be on my side and I personally had nothing to fear. Uncle Lazar served this idea up during one of his visits. He repeated reliable sources from the highest circles, that the Soviet authorities weren't fascists after all and would only send certain people away.

I must say that Uncle Lazar turned out to be better than I'd thought of him. He became a different person when he conversed in social settings without the influence of his wife, Khasya Tovievna: we often drank tea in the kitchen with him, and he consoled me about many things. Mama was always glad of him and sighed, remembering their difficult childhood.

One time Khasya called on us along with Uncle Lazar, though. She'd seen Mishenka before, of course, but now he'd grown a little and was almost a year old. Khasya was fussing over the child and then, by the by, she noticed his face didn't look like either mine or Fima's and said to my mother: "So who does your grandson take after?"

Mama was flustered but answered as wittily as she could muster: "Khasenka, you should think instead about who your son Motechka takes after. He's greedy and sharp-tongued."

Khasya didn't lose her cool: "Not greedy but thrifty. And anyway. I'm not talking about character but appearance. Leave my son alone, anyone would want a son like him."

Then we switched to unrelated subjects, then a tipsy Fima came in and there was a small scene over that, and then we put it to rest.

It didn't escape my attention, though, that Mama was looking at me with great alarm and even sorrow.

These days there are lots of Brazilian and other television series, and everybody's knowledgeable about how things happen in life. At that time, though, I had only myself and my son, Mishenka.

After painful reflection, I said to Mama: "I'll kill you if you ever blab to anybody that Mishenka isn't Fima's son."

Mama recoiled as if I'd turned my threat into action that very instant. And a few days later she announced she was leaving for Ostyor, for the distant relatives. They'd found her a job as a nanny at a day care there, and she'd be better off in the fresh, familiar air.

For my part, I breathed a sigh of relief. Mama's health was weak and she had manifestations of asthma. Maybe something more serious. Including carrying Koch's rod-shaped tuberculosis bacteria. It was yet another risk for the child, but who was tested then?

With all this, however, Mama laid all the housework, care for Mishenka, and everything else on me.

But that's not my point.

The house became much brighter and roomier after Mama left. One side of the chiffonier had blocked part of the window before, but now Uncle Lazar moved it to its normal place; they put Mama's daybed in the kitchen and Fima brought in a child's bed, too, so Mishenka could develop freely in his own place instead of constantly being in a baby carriage or at my side. We took Mama's notorious cracked mirror to the basement. We didn't hang anything in its place since we had no means with which to purchase anything decent and I didn't want to bring in new junk.

The time had come to resume my studies at the technical college. Day classes were out of the question because Fima'd been transferred to another position with a significant reduction in salary.

I put Mishenka in day care. Fima used some old connections and found me a secretary-typist job at a shoe factory in Darnitsa with the plan that I would transfer to correspondence studies. I quickly learned to type and became indispensable on all issues.

And everything would have been good other than, naturally, Fima's behavior. He systematically pestered me with conversations about his family that perished. He tormented me about whether or not I understood him.

In the beginning, I answered that I understood and shared his everlasting grief. I gradually stopped reacting, though, because he elaborated on the topic of death even more forcefully after I answered.

When he'd finally gotten to me, I said:

"You know, Fima, a marriage stamp in a passport isn't a verdict or a sentence. Keep that in mind. This is a difficult time, but I won't hang on to you. I'm registered here. I'm a mother. And you're a drunk and nothing else. You'll be fired from work soon, then you'll be a social parasite."

As a result, Fima moved to the kitchen to sleep. I greeted that development with considerable relief, but without hope, either.

As I've already said, nature prevails. I wanted true, mutual love. And here I turned my gaze directly on my supervisor: Miroslav Antonovich Shulyak, the factory's head engineer. He paid me no excess attention. Always stern, presenting a good appearance. A very interesting man. And young.

Of course it troubled me that he was my supervisor. I nipped my growing feelings in the bud. Still. Two people of the opposite sex who find themselves in close quarters every day inevitably fall under the power of certain thoughts.

To celebrate International Women's Day on the eighth of March, there was a gathering of all employees, particularly the female staff, and then another in the factory cafeteria with a more selective management circle. I realized then that something would happen between me and Miroslav.

Misha was a sickly child in his early years—my tense condition during the pregnancy was showing its effects. It was hard and inconvenient for me to get frequent doctor's notes, as objective circumstances required. I worried tremendously over Mishenka. Beyond that, Fima had absolutely distanced himself from the little boy, and everything fell on my shoulders.

Fima got to the point where he thought this up: "Mishenka isn't to blame for anything. But I just can't come to love him. I feel like he's living instead of my other kids. And they want to live, too."

You can't go very far with ideas like that. There's a child growing but there's a person like that in the house. Under the influence of that alcohol on his breath, he could poison the child's existence at any moment. But where would I put Fima if I were to divorce him? Where would he live? I even prayed to God he'd meet another woman with her own living space who could take him in.

But that's not my point.

Something pleasant and unexpected happened at just the right moment: a letter arrived from Mama, from Ostyor, that she was getting married. Beyond that, she was marrying a good man, with part of a house. By the name of Gilya Melnik. Mama wrote that I should remember him, since he'd lived fairly close to us before the war. I recalled him. Mama was forty-five at the time of her new marriage.

Gilya's family perished in the occupation, and he and Mama had come together happily. Gilya was a procurer of leather by trade and wasn't at home much because he mostly traveled from village to village. Well-off. But Mama intended to continue working so that, as she wrote, she could set something aside for a rainy day, regardless of Gilya's money.

This turn of events prompted me to think I could send Mishenka off to Ostyor, to his grandmother. There were fresh dairy products, meat, and so on.

Mishenka and I headed to Ostyor the next Sunday.

Of course my poor but happy childhood arose in my mind's eye. And the small Ostyorka River. And the clams on the grassy shore. Mishenka was surprised at how little the houses were, he pointed his small hand and pronounced it "wittle, wittle." A very smart child, even though he was only a bit older than two then. He'd started talking early, distinctly.

Gilya made a good first impression on me. Reserved, modest, thorough. Mama had even gotten younger with him. Love or no love, a woman should be with a man.

A serious discussion took place. I hinted to Mama about Mishenka. She made the decision to take him for temporary rearing. I should mention that as soon as Gilya took the boy in his arms, he didn't let him go right up until I left.

I left Mishenka and a suitcase of his things with them.

Now that I had made temporary arrangements for my son, a period of personal rebirth began for me.

By 1953, I'd reduced my classes at the technical college to nothing. I quit my studies because I was physically exhausted from being a nervous wreck. Episodic chance meetings with Viktor Kutsenko had completely worn me down. He didn't ask anything: he just looked, questioning. Only once did Darina Dmitrievna take me by the elbow and demand I leave her husband in peace. I answered that I had no need for her husband and that I didn't talk with him.

She expressed her disbelief and declared, in an insulting tone: "Little snake."

And that was after everything that happened that was exclusively her fault, not mine. I quit my studies.

Beyond that, expectations of new Jewish ordeals that didn't come about gnawed away at my consciousness. As Yashkovets said in a drunken state:

"Don't be afraid, Mayechka, maybe they won't bring all your people to Siberia: they could just build sheds here on the bank of the Dnieper. At least it's your native land here. I'll bring you red lipstick, you can count on me."

His jokes always struck me as being pointless. But Fima laughed. Yes, I'm a woman and I tried to look good every minute.

Nevertheless, just as I was headed toward complete despair, it became clear that nobody was going to touch anybody. Stalin died. So many wasted nerves.

Fima and I had a weighty talk. There was much to discuss.

In the first place, my relations with Shulyak were developing in a natural direction and where could we go if not to my own house, where I was registered as a resident? Particularly because nobody was being taken away now. The question of divorcing Fima arose.

Yes, it's easy to come to that kind of decision, but living space was a sticking point.

Yashkovets helped here. He took Fima in, with curses on my head, of course.

But that's not my point.

It was then that Fima fully developed the idea of taking Misha and going with him to the State of Israel. Many Jews—and Fima in particular—had hopes for Golda Meir. He kept a newspaper clipping in his wallet that announced Golda's visit to the USSR.

This was a matter of days long gone, autumn 1948. The clipping had become unsanitary over five years but Fima read and reread it, like a classic work. And stuck it under the nose of anyone who happened to be around when he was in a condition of heavy alcoholic intoxication. It's too bad he didn't show me that filth immediately when we became close. My life would have taken a different turn.

And here Fima said:

"Good, I'm going to live at Yashkovets's temporarily, may God grant him health, but I'm taking my son Mishenka and we're going to Israel. I don't need anything here: not the life, nothing. But it's different there. Stalin's dead now, that's all allowed now."

Yashkovets played along with everything.

In order to close out the unpleasant topic, I said, keeping my eye on the future but not at all agreeing at heart:

"Good, good. Just let Mishenka grow up a little. Let him stay at his grandmother's and get stronger for at least a year."

So that's what we agreed.

I took back my maiden name after the divorce. That's how I wanted to mark the freedom of my new life.

After a little time had passed, I wrote to Mama about the divorce so she could look after Mishenka a little longer. This time I wrote with a light heart because the moment had come when there was nothing to fear, which meant I had to live my life.

Fima kept his promise and didn't show up to see me at the apartment. One time I ran into him on Yaroslavsky Val, during the winter. That's a tricky locality: it's slippery, and he was walking, drunk, and fell. Children were sliding down the smooth path on their satchels and they bumped into him—his body blocked them. They resented it and started mocking him, "Yid, Yid, Yid." And by now he barely resembled a decent person: that's how much he'd taken to drinking.

I observed from across the way, then walked past because it served him right.

But that's not my point.

It's interesting that relations with Miroslav Shulyak remained the same after my divorce from Fima.

We met calmly at my house and went to the movies and theater, where people always paid intent attention to us, a handsome couple. But no family life came about.

Loneliness weighed on me. At our workplace, I inadvertently, by chance, told Miroslav that people were talking about us behind our backs. And that they'd hinted to me in the Komsomol organization that it would be good for a Party-oriented person—and Shulyak, of course, was a Party member in a mid-level post—to marry and not fool around in plain sight of the collective.

I said that, in a womanly way, for no particular reason, to indicate my mood. But Miroslav came to his own conclusion.

"Mayechka, why is it you're telling everybody you and I are in love. That's our personal matter."

I answered in the spirit that I wasn't telling them, that people saw it themselves and thought that if there was love, then there should be a family, too.

Shulyak seemed offended at my straightforwardness. But then, as it happened, I sensed I was pregnant. My joy was boundless. I announced it to Miroslav. A couple of weeks later we registered our marriage.

It somehow worked out I hadn't told Shulyak about Mishenka. My true family status remained out of reach for many people. I myself didn't expand upon it. I justified my divorce to Shulyak as caused by character differences with my former husband. But conversation about Mishenka didn't come up. And what of it.

Everybody has their secrets. Mine was a wonderful, beautiful, healthy little son: Mishenka. Shulyak's was a paralyzed elderly mother. That's not subject to any sort of comparison. Her heart was healthy and she'd live another hundred years with good care.

It was my fault. Mine alone. I'd been thick-headed. It moved me that Shulyak would hurry home to his mama after our dates. And—with the details—that turned out to be the trouble.

There's a reason for the existence of the ancient folk custom of the bride and groom meeting parents and relatives before the wedding. But I really couldn't have supposed such a cruel and dirty trick on Miroslav's part.

Even so, despite my youth, I made a rational decision that didn't come to me especially easily or simply.

For a fee, a particular woman visited and tended to Miroslav's mother. I hinted that she could be paid more in order to move in and continue her noble work around the clock. And we'd find someone else if she didn't agree. In light of my pregnancy, I couldn't devote fitting attention to Miroslav's mother. He agreed. We found a nice old woman for all the functions.

An unforeseen and irritating malfunction came about. My pregnancy went amiss at a very early stage. I don't know what served as the reason, most likely it was alarm about Miroslav's mother. He was very upset.

I was forced to leave my job, again so as not to cultivate nepotism. But I didn't despair.

I met Miroslav's mother. She turned out to be a very old woman. Miroslav was her youngest son, a late one, and the other three had perished on the fronts of the Great Patriotic War. Her husband died in 1943 from an unsuccessful medical operation. The most annoying part is that Olga Nikolaevna had fallen ill literally a year ago, as it happens when Miroslav and I met.

The meeting with Olga Nikolaevna was short, so it wouldn't be difficult for her. Of course she came away satisfied. She said that as someone backward who'd grown up in a family of very religious people, she read the Bible and knew a lot about Jews, but wasn't at all against her son living with me. I smiled cheerfully in response.

Miroslav insisted I resume my studies in day classes at the technical collage and I easily achieved a diploma for myself. He especially insisted since all that was left were the gov exams.

Yes, the government had given me an education. So would I really not take some kind of government exams in exchange for that?

And then, after several years of mandatory separation, I ran into Kutsenko again. Life experience prompted me that I needed to be tolerant of human weaknesses and so, with open heart, I gave him a break.

Darina Dmitrievna had gone to western Ukraine to teach Russian at some educational institution or other. There was a noticeable shortage there in that particular specialty. Things were moving toward divorce for them. Victor was in low spirits.

My maternal heart thought constantly about my dear Mishenka and once, in a moment of weakness, I told Viktor: "You have a son. Mishenka."

He displayed interest but as far as I could tell, it was evident that the news did not genuinely excite him.

"It's too late now, Maya. If only you'd told me before. I've suffered so much. You can't ruin the little boy's life—he has another father."

Viktor remained indifferent, despite all the tenderness I displayed for him. Nothing came about between us because we were already different people. Viktor constantly helped me with my studies, though, with term papers in all subjects, not just mathematics. He had particular success with history and other humanities subjects.

Uncle Lazar and Aunt Khasya ceased all contact with me after my divorce from Fima. Only my mother treated me with understanding—she even wrote me a warm letter about it. That's also where she informed me of touching details about Mishenka and invited Miroslav and me to visit for the summer.

It was true that I hadn't seen Mishenka in a long time and missed him very much. Furthermore, the time had come to introduce Miroslav to the full complement of my dear family since Miroslav had been starting conversations with his own mother regarding all of us moving into one apartment with more space. I hoped that after seeing Mishenka, Miroslav would abandon those unsuitable plans and speak out with an initiative for Mishenka to move in with us. Because it was very clear: the choice was either an old lady who couldn't walk, or a small child.

And there we were in Ostyor: we'd arrived on the river route, over the Dnieper and the Desna, on the hydrofoil *Nadezhda Krupskaya*.

I caught sight of a horrifying image. Mishenka was in some sort of unsightly cast-off clothing and his hair had been cut with electric clippers.

I asked Mama right away why the child had been neglected, but she answered with an air of incomprehension: the child's growing fast, and why buy expensive things when the neighbors' boy is a year older and good clothes were handed down? It's not easy to buy things at the store and there's not enough money anyway. As far as the hair went, it was a real benefit for hygiene because Mishenka's hair was so thick there was always screaming during combing: even the shortest hair tangles, and you couldn't reach the roots with a comb. And this way you could always see his whole little face.

Yes, Mishenka has my hair. Only mine is chestnut and Mishenka's is almost light brown with ash tints. As it is at birth so it shall be for life.

Of course, I personally hadn't sent money for Mishenka since I had justifiably considered my mother and Gilya's material position to be satisfactory enough that they could ensure order for the child. But it turned out Gilya wasn't traveling to the villages now because of his health status: he was working, sitting, at a local craft cooperative and the earnings were different there.

And all this was whispered, hastily, so Miroslav wouldn't hear.

He heard something else instead, though: Mishenka had grown used to calling my mother "*mamele*" and Gilya "*tatele*." Furthermore, the three of them tossed Yiddish words around amongst themselves. Yes, Ostyor is Ostyor and the surroundings mean a lot.

Miroslav wanted to pat the boy on the head, but Mishenka didn't understand the gesture and started crying.

Mama rushed to console him:

"Moishele, Moishele, don't cry! He's a nice man. Uncle Miroslav won't hurt you." And she was looking at Miroslav as if he were an unrelated acquaintance who'd popped in for a minute rather than coming to visit his mother-in-law and, one could now say, his own son.

Miroslav showed no bewilderment and, to the contrary, quickly got into the swing of things:

"I know a little bit of Jewish, I was born by the Zaitsev factory in the Podol district, it's almost Jews all over. We used to play Beilis in the caves. For old times' sake, you might say. Come over here, little guy, you're small and I'm large. I don't quarrel with the small guys."

And he smiled so cordially that Mishenka believed him and went to sit on his lap.

Well, fine, I thought, the main thing now was contact between Miroslav and the little boy, and I'd somehow join them later.

We ate lunch peacefully.

Gilya and Miroslav found a common topic—leather processing and new developments in shoe technology. Gilya asked intelligent questions, despite lacking an education. Miroslav gladly answered intelligibly. Particularly since both had fought at the front. And there's nothing to say here about reminiscing: just you try and stop them.

Mama told me the following when the men and Mishenka headed to the Desna for a walk.

Surkis had turned up about a month and a half ago. Sober. He'd come and taken a seat in the middle of the room, with the demand that his son be given to him right now.

Fortunately, Mishenka wasn't home at the time—he was running around outside with the neighbor boys. Mama calmly explained that Surkis had no right to make orders about the child. That even though Fima was the father, there was still a mother, too. And you had to start with the mother. And in a nice way, too. She somehow calmed Fima, fed him, and poured him a little glass of liqueur. He mellowed and asked to doze off.

After he'd gone to sleep, Mama sent Mishenka off to distant acquaintances at the other end of Ostyor for the night. An entirely different conversation got going with Surkis after Gilya came home from work.

Gilya straight-out threatened the police and explained that he wasn't going to mollycoddle and would let Surkis have it in the face, even mortally. He wouldn't even be sorry to go to jail over Mishenka.

Surkis went through the roof:

"Ah, so you wouldn't be sorry over Mishenka, but you'd be sorry over my ruined life? Beat me because of my own life, not because of Mishenka! Well, come on! Why're you standing there like a post? Beat me, you Yid ass!"

Gilya hit him, but not hard. Mama assured me that if Gilya had given it to him with all his strength, Surkis would be applying for disability later. No way around it. Fima fell headfirst on a stool and much blood flowed. Mama bandaged him.

Surkis sat for about half an hour, until his head was back in place, then went running out the door.

And he hadn't shown up since.

I was horrified. This sort of behavior was evidence that anything could be expected from my former husband.

Mama justified herself by saying she hadn't wanted to trouble me by reporting the incident. I understood, though, that she mostly had herself in mind. After all, how could she have allowed that disgraceful fight to take place? Beyond that, she'd sent Surkis directly to me instead of explaining the pointlessness of his claims once and for all. Particularly since she'd been under the protection of her husband, Gilya. My life with Miroslav had just barely begun, and an unsightly conflict could ruin the impression.

Such was reality.

Our parting with Mishenka was heartfelt. He eagerly hugged and kissed Miroslav and said goodbye to me in words, without tearing himself away from his grandmother.

We'd agreed that toward the end of the month, after it warmed up nicely, Miroslav and I would come and take Mishenka home to Kiev. Miroslav was the first to raise the issue and I said only that since he'd made the decision this was how we had to proceed. As the mother, I'd always dreamed of getting Mishenka.

But another decision had also ripened in Miroslav's mind.

"Mayechka, I liked your mother and stepfather very much. They're simple working people. Not to mention Mishenka. Unfortunately, it's extremely rare that I see my mother now. Even though she, unlike your family, doesn't live far away. Here's my opinion: we'll combine my communal apartment room with your apartment so we can trade for a two-room apartment. Maybe in Darnitsa, but even so. There's more natural surroundings there. If we don't hurry things, it won't even be too far from the center. So we don't need to change our roads and routes. And Mama would be with us. At least she'd fully feel love and respect at the end of her difficult days. She's earned it."

Yes, she'd earned it. And I'd earned it, too.
But that's not my point.

It lay ahead to resolve a small task more complex than the apartment trade.

I'd carved out time to visit Yashkovets. Not at his house, of course, where there was the risk of catching Surkis, but at his workplace, the Chapaev Cinema.

Yashkovets was drawing something for yet another motion picture and greeted me absentmindedly. He was set to meet me halfway, though, after seeing I'd brought a bottle of *horilka*.

I asked him directly how things were with Surkis, about his health and what he was doing.

Yashkovets described Surkis's situation in brief as really bad. He'd been irrevocably fired from his job and he was lucky he'd just been asked to write his own resignation, but his health was hanging by a thread. He was drinking a lot, whatever came his way. He was panhandling for kopecks by a store.

I was horrified. How shameful! But Yashkovets shook his head and even noted approvingly that that's what many former men from the front did. And it was fine. They'd earned the right and nobody could dare condemn them. And they also had the right to their own living space, where they were registered.

Then, for no apparent reason, he started singing, "The enemy burned my family home, did in the entire family . . ."

Alcoholics have a surprising tendency toward singing.

I noticed Yashkovets was almost sober and wasn't opening my bottle.

I let the part about living space pass, but was curious about Fima's plans regarding Mishenka. It would be good for him to renounce Mishenka, so my new husband could adopt the child.

I said that with a goal: for the information to reach Fima, first through Yashkovets, then later, when I'd personally add the hows and whats.

Yashkovets shrugged his shoulders.

In parting, I expressed my surprise that he hadn't touched my gift: "Do you really not like it?"

He answered that he was afraid to drink—what if I'd poisoned it?—but then he opened the bottle and gulped right from it:

"How about that. I'm joking around. It's great nasty stuff. I'll share with Fimka. Me and him haven't *bachily* anything like this in a long time. Good for the health, *bude*. And don't you be sad. Everything'll work out on its own. On its own."

I'd promised to drop by on Viktor that same day, to pick up my thesis. As I walked down the long corridor to the door of Kutsenko's room, my heart hinted at something disagreeable.

And that's how it turned out.

I found a woman who didn't belong there at Viktor's. She was wearing a robe and washing the floor. And based on her whole sloppy appearance—she wasn't even wearing a slip—I realized she was there as the woman of the house.

I asked her directly: "When will Viktor be back?"

She answered the question evasively: "And who are you to inquire about his comings and goings?"

She went for conflict right away. Without hiding anything, I announced that I'm a close acquaintance and perhaps even more, and that I was seeing her here for the first time. She burst out in cynical laughter at that and wrung out the dirty rag right on the floor as she said:

"I'm the one seeing you for the first time and you can be sure it's the last. You're Maya. I recognize you. Viktor told me about you. Goodbye."

Yes, betrayals are brought on by the people closest to you.

Of course I caught Kutsenko (literally by the sleeve) at the technical college and looked him intently in the eye.

He took the paper intended for me from his briefcase and said: "That's it. We're even. You've worn me out to my very soul."

And he took off so fast it was almost insulting.

Now it lay ahead for me to draw some distressing conclusions.

In saving Surkis's good name, I'd twisted the matter for Miroslav in such a way that my former husband had gone to live with some other woman, everything was in complete order between them, and he had no use for the apartment. And Surkis had renounced his very own son Mishenka.

And now it was turning out that my whole life was under threat because of that drunkard.

Of course I could tell Surkis that Mishenka wasn't his son. But I couldn't appeal to Kutsenko for support on this sensitive question. For some inexplicable reason, he'd become embittered and completely turned me away, something I could tell, based on how he looked at me. And it was also unclear what would follow after sorting that out. I'd turn out to be who-the-hell-knows what kind of woman: Surkis could show up and make a scene in front of Miroslav. Of course you couldn't delve into all the details, but the basic picture was unflattering. Under narrow-minded reasoning. The main thing was that Misha was legally Surkis's son, according to the documents. And, really, documents are a serious obstacle for everything.

It was obvious Surkis could say and do things because of his past and present position: not just things I couldn't disentangle myself from, but also where the police would turn out to lack the power and means for having any effect.

I fell into despair. I expected Fima to arrive at any minute so was searching for a way out, but didn't find one. Even so, I successfully defended my pedagogy degree and enveloped my husband with constant love and care.

A decision finally came to me, literally in my sleep. Surkis and Mishenka needed to change places. Mishenka should be picked up from Mama's as soon as possible and Fima should be sent to Mama. Gilya would keep after him and find him some kind of work. And there would be air, healthy food, and no drinking buddies. Let him change his official residence to Ostyor. Perhaps some sort of woman there would stick with him out of good intentions.

Miroslav was rushing me on Mishenka's arrival. Beyond that, Olga Nikolaevna was getting worse and Miroslav intended to intensify the selection of a new apartment.

My crucial meeting with Fima took place.

I made my appearance before his eyes rather early in the morning.

I was standing there, silent, looking him right in the face. For a minute. Another. He was silent and I was silent.

Then I sat on a chair and started in: "Fima, I'm so glad to finally see you."

Fima, who was of course hung over, fumbled around under the table—there were empty bottles lying around there.

I took a good half-liter bottle out of my purse and held it out to him:

"Drink. Otherwise this conversation of ours won't come off. It's best not to drink, but you decide for yourself: either drink or don't drink. I can't tell you what to do."

Fima opened the bottle like he wasn't hurrying, but his eyes were in a big rush. There were two glasses on the table: dirty, with cigarette butts in them. Fima turned toward the workbench where Yashkovets daubed his paint and grabbed a glass from there—it had red paint in the bottom. He splashed some in there without a glance. It looked like genuine blood. He drank it without looking. It ran down his beard, to his shirt. Then Fima poured a second time. And it was blood again. I felt scared, even pitied him.

"Give me the glass, I'll wash it for you. For old time's sake."

Only then did Fima see what he'd been drinking from and what color it was. He fell on the bench and started moaning.

At the hospital, during evacuation, I'd heard the moans of injured people without arms, legs, and tongues. The only thing left from the entire person was the moaning. Oy!

I sat down next to him, embraced his shoulders, and started crying. He moaned, I cried. He moaned, I cried.

Fima said: "You thought I'd die. But I want to live. I can't stand myself. But I want to live. Why did you show up?"

And I was crying, I couldn't stop.

"I don't trust your tears. Talk without tears," Fima grabbed me firmly by the shoulder.

And I was crying and sobbing through and through.

He stood and splashed some vodka into that same bloody glass and held it out to me: "Here, drink it, you'll calm down."

I wanted to push Fima away, but was afraid of making him mad, so I drank.

I wiped my lips and said:

"Regarding Misha. That's in the first place. Regarding your future life. That's in the second place. Or you can count however you see fit."

I was wary of one thing: that Yashkovets would pop in and interfere. I described the situation in brief. And offered him a chance: Fima leaves for Ostyor, to fresh air and Gilya's influence. He'll straighten out there and come back to life. A year, two, whatever it takes. Influence works wonders—as a pedagogue I was aware of that. And he'd be a new person there, entering a new life.

And indeed, this was when Yashkovets butted in: he stopped by from work, for lunch. It was obvious he stopped by for a drink; apparently it was gone at his workplace. The bottle he saw was more than half-full. He was glad.

"Ah, the instigator in person! *Zdorovenki buly*! What're you agitating about?"

"I'm agitating for Fima's life. And you're getting him drunk, Lyonya."

"Uh-huh, I'm getting him drunk. Right. You brought good *horilka*. Can I give it a try? Or is it just for you?"

Fima was silent.

I said: "Fima and I are having a crucial conversation. Drink fast, let us get through this."

Yashkovets folded his arms on his chest and sat theatrically on a stool. He even neatly moved the stool away from the table.

"I don't give a damn about what you brought, but I care about Fimka. I'm not going anywhere. Everything here's mine. It's me that saved Fimka here, when you took him out of his own house. Don't you *movchi*, Fima. Tell her to her face, what you're thinking."

Fima was silent.

"Tell her what you'd told me, when we'd drunk her damned *horilka*. It's her that offered that bottle so I'd talk you out of your own son. You tell me, was I bought for a bottle? I couldn't be sold to that broad for a case of it. Especially because she'd be sorry to spend money on twenty half-liters."

Fima was silent.

Then Yashkovets grabbed a bottle out from under the table and whacked it on the floor. Because of the earthen floor, it didn't smash; this was the first floor, it was a shack, what could you expect? And as the vodka was flowing out, Fima and Lyonka's terrifying eyes were looking at it. But neither moved from his place.

My patience had come to an end.

"Yashkovets! It's either you or me. Fima, you decide right now, which one. Your whole future life is at stake. Watch out or I'll leave and there won't be anything else. You won't see Misha. You won't see anything."

Yashkovets seemed to have come to life. He'd been grinding at the puddle with his boot for a long time, sniffing the air, and shaking his head. Then he walked up to his press, gathered up some brushes and cans, tossed them in a rucksack, and silently left.

And here Fima started talking:

"So it's like this. That I wouldn't see Misha, I understand that. Don't think I don't understand. I understand. That it's my death here, I understand that, too. I wanted to enlist somewhere, but they wouldn't take me. There's my age and the rest is no better. I don't know Gilya. He doesn't know me. You thought all this up beautifully. The question is how it will turn out."

"There's no question. I'm giving you an opportunity. Take it if you want, don't if you don't. Mishenka will live with me, his mother, and with his stepfather. It doesn't matter if you renounce him or not. I wanted what's best for my son. He doesn't need you in this shape, even as a temporary phenomenon at holidays. But if you get better, then of course I won't have the power to forbid you to meet. Now, about the apartment. You have rights. Let's exchange it for two small communal apartment rooms on the outskirts. That's very wonderful. Then Mishenka and I and my husband will live in seven square meters. If you'd like to know, my husband's mother is paralyzed and I'm obligated to help her. We're taking her with us. My husband doesn't have an apartment. His mother's literally occupying a bed with kind people, sometimes for a month, sometimes two. Well?"

Of course I'd laid it on thick with the facts and changed the truth a little. It's extremely complex to get through to a consciousness fogged by alcoholism. I was, however, able to do that anyway.

Fima said: "When do I go to Ostyor?"

"In a week."

I gave him a deadline and was already weighing how to organize the trip to Ostyor without Miroslav, bring Mishenka to Kiev quickly, and convince my mother and Gilya to take Fima in.

I told Miroslav my heart was breaking from missing my son and I couldn't wait any longer. And so as not to distract him from work, I'd go alone and bring Mishenka back. Of course Miroslav expressed the desire to go with me anyway, the next Sunday. But I categorically refused. It was impossible to accomplish everything in one day, but this way I'd move forward on Wednesday and, as it happened, be back home on Sunday with my son.

Mama and Gilya greeted me with surprise. I quickly put everything in its proper place, though.

Fima was done for. Only they could save him. Fima was as dear to me as ever, and I was indebted to him for so much that it was impossible to cast him adrift. The main thing: how would I look Mishenka in the eye? He hardly knew Surkis, but the documents recorded him as Fima's son. And here I looked intently at Mama and she nodded ardently to me in response.

I was waiting for Gilya's reaction. As master of the house, he was the head of the family.

And so I told him:

"My dear Gilechka, my fate and Mishenka's, not to mention the unfortunate Fima's fate, depend on you here. I don't need to explain to you what he's endured. He's been beaten to a pulp. He's a war hero but there's no place for him in the world. I began a new life. And what am I to do if I know Fima's perishing right in front of everybody and nobody cares?"

Gilya responded that there was no question. Fima wasn't a stranger, all Jews are relatives, and this was one of those things. Completely indisputable. For Mishenka's sake, he was ready to do anything, including sacrifice.

That required only a half hour.

Things turned out differently with Mishenka, though. Mama and Gilya were mentally preparing to say goodbye, but then they got completely unhinged at the crucial moment.

Gathering up Mishenka's little things, Mama bathed them in tears, caressing them as if they were tiny pieces of Mishenka and she was laying Mishenka himself in the bundle. An unbearable spectacle.

Mishenka was glad, though, to go to Kiev to Uncle Miroslav's home in a big building.

Mama was curious about Fima's material position. I waved my hand in a negative sense.

During lunch, Mishenka huddled up against Gilya and his grandmother, said things to them in Yiddish, and looked at me with interest.

Mama laughed:

"He says you're very pretty. That you're much prettier than Gilya and me. And is it true you're his mother?"

I couldn't bear the tension, and embraced the boy.

When I was alone with Mama, I told her about my plans and that Miroslav would adopt the boy for the sake of his future, meaning his "nationality" box on his paperwork. Mama regarded that with as much understanding as she could and assured me she'd take appropriate measures with Fima.

"The main thing, daughter, is for you to have peace of mind."

Mishenka and I were standing on the deck of the hydrofoil boat, looking at the Desna's waters. Then at the broad Dnieper. My son was holding my hand.

I applied a pedagogical technique. I addressed Mishenka with a serious question: Could he endure two days without speaking Jewish? He and I were going to play at him forgetting every one of his Jewish words.

As a pedagogue, I knew two days was a huge period of time for a tot and that it would be possible to break that acquired habit later and gradually wean him from it. Especially in a new setting.

Mishenka was surprised: "What language is that, Jewish?"

"The one you speak with your grandmother and Uncle Gilya."

"I speak with them in all kinds of ways."

"Well, the one where you say 'mamele' and 'tatele' and other words."

Misha was silent.

Then he said:

"Let's do this instead: I'll talk however it comes out and you tell me yourself what words are Jewish and what ones aren't. Because I don't know."

A smart boy.

Yes, a pedagogical ordeal lay ahead for me. But I wasn't afraid of anything then.

Miroslav was happy. He didn't leave Mishenka's side. The day after we arrived, they went to Kreshchatyk Street for toys. I wanted to buy the clothes myself: Miroslav and I had brought to the basement the junk I took from Ostyor so as not to offend Mama.

I rushed off to Fima's after they left.

Fima greeted me warily. He was sober, but in a gloomy state.

"Well? It's not working out or something?" He asked this angrily, as if I owed him.

"It worked out. You can even go tomorrow. Mama and Gilya are awaiting you with open arms."

"Where's Misha?"

"Misha's with me."

"Well, fine. So then he's with you."

I was anxious about the question of Mishenka popping up again. Why stir up what's unfixable?

"Fima, that's my condition to you. And I'm not changing it. Misha's living with me and my husband. Either you go today or I don't know what will happen."

Fima nodded and decisively added:

"Yes. I'm going. Thank you. I'll just wait for Lyonya, to say goodbye. I hadn't told him anything, just in case. You go. I'll pack my things without you."

But how could I go? Yashkovets would come, start sweet-talking Fima, and maybe vodka would pop up.

"No, Fima. I haven't invested all this energy to abandon you halfway. There's no reason for you to say goodbye to Lyonya. You're not leaving for the front or jail. You're leaving for another life. And he can drag you into the old one. Write him a note if you want. I'll give it to him. And the keys and the rest. The last boat today is in an hour and a half. I'll see you off. So there's no more incidents. I have money for you, for the beginning. You'll earn money yourself later. You're not an invalid, thank God."

Fima looked at me plaintively. But I had no sympathy for him, not a gram.

He sat at the table, wrote a line on a scrap of paper, didn't fold it, and put it in my hands just like that.

"Give it to Lyonya. And the keys, too."

It turned out he'd been putting on a show: he grabbed a little suitcase he'd packed long ago. And we left.

The Krupskaya departed, half empty. Fima was standing on deck with his suitcase; he didn't wave.

But that's not my point.

I hurried home.

Mishenka and Miroslav were setting out their purchases and enjoying each other's company. Miroslav was walking around the apartment, through the hallway, kitchen, and large room, measuring something with a tape measure. He was writing on a notepad.

We couldn't fall asleep for a long time. We were listening to the boy's breathing—he was on the little daybed in the kitchen. He didn't fall asleep for a long time, tossing and turning, and crying out. I was glad to notice it wasn't in Jewish. And later he clearly called me in Russian: "Mama."

I heard it just fine. But I didn't go to him, so as not to condition him to it. Night is night.

A few days passed.

I was overflowing with feelings and exhaustion as a result of the changes. I just needed to talk to someone. To someone who knew Fima and our whole difficult history.

I went to see Lyonya Yashkovets. All told, he was Fima's closest friend, but he wasn't up on everything.

I bought a bottle of expensive Georgian red wine—some Khvanchkara—a cake, and some meat. I wanted to make Lyonechka happy.

And there I was on Bolshaya Zhitomirskaya Street, walking through the familiar gateway. I saw a big fire site. I even felt a scratchiness in my throat. Smoldering wood, cinders, wooden beams. A bed burned to blackness.

It smelled strongly of smoke. And nothing showed from the street, out from behind the big buildings. Just think! I hadn't suspected a thing until the last second!

People said a fire broke out in Lyonya's shack three days ago. At night. And Lyonya had oil paints, kerosene, and turpentine inside. He'd poured it into a vial for me so many times, for spot removal! Thank you to him, of course. Be that as it may.

Lyonechka burned to death.

And Fimochka would have burned to death, like a candle, if he'd stayed.

And right then Lyonechka's words sounded in my head: "Everything'll work out on its own. On its own." Yes. By the force of things.

I'd expended so much energy! Transportation, moves, persuasion. Fine.

I took Fima's note out of my purse and neatly tore it up.

"Farewell friend I'm leaving forever"

And not one punctuation mark. Not one.

But that's not my point.

I approached Miroslav tactfully regarding the adoption. He asked if Fima had renounced his son. I assured him it was a matter of formalities. Then he assured me that everything would fall into place as soon as Fima wrote the necessary paperwork.

We needed to work on the apartment question. The swap involving his mother. And while we were swapping, he thought about where to accommodate Mishenka with us in the large room and where to put his little bed. And he pointed out the chiffonier to me: it needed to be turned perpendicular to the window to partition off the room.

A familiar picture. Either Mama was behind the cabinet or Misha would be there. I objected that we had a kitchen, a large one, thank God, bright and with a comfortable daybed so the boy was content and separated from the adults. So nobody was bothering anybody.

Miroslav snapped:

"Why are you allowing yourself to even say 'bother' in your thoughts! How can parents bother their own child?! He needs to be within sight at all times. Suggesting things to him, looking at him yet again—it's a pure delight. And the kitchen's no place for a child. There's the stove, there's the water faucets. A downright danger."

Beyond that, there was our dream of installing a bathtub in the kitchen right where the daybed was, as it happened.

Forceful arguments. I agreed right away so as not to make Miroslav nervous over little things. I remarked only that we needed to make the swap with his mother quickly. In the first place, that would be helpful for Mishenka. Let him see and learn to understand another side of life. Chamber pots, smell, aging's deadly outcome. Otherwise children grow up in hothouse conditions and don't distinguish where things are good and where they're not so good.

Miroslav fell to thinking and cut off the discussion.

Mishenka stayed in the kitchen.

In order to put all my time and all my energy into my husband and son, I didn't look for work.

We enrolled Mishenka in kindergarten and I was always one of the first to pick up my child, so he wouldn't feel abandoned for even a minute.

One time, after yet another visit to Olga Nikolaevna's, Miroslav came home upset and told me she'd gotten significantly worse and needed more care, but the current helper was old herself and couldn't cope with everything. He saw a solution in my going to visit Olga Nikolaevna at least several times a week, doing laundry, and cooking food to last several days.

As it happened, I'd come to the conclusion at that same time that I needed to work in my field. And I'd found a good position at a night school. Beyond that, there were the pressures of extra expenses because of clothing and other necessities for Mishenka. Putting that decision into practice in life, though, was delayed since it was better to start with a new school year.

Miroslav regarded my decision respectfully and himself began going to his mother's several times a week after work (as well as definitely on Sunday) to do laundry and cook. Naturally, he sometimes spent the night, too.

Matters related to the move were not progressing. We were offered complete hovels in exchange for our living space—either without running water, or too far away, or losers by all parameters.

And Miroslav had cooled somehow, too. He'd been drawn into taking care of his sick mother and announced at one point that it wasn't worth moving in together. It would only be harder for everybody.

I didn't grouse.

Transportation to Ostyor was cumbersome in the winter. The chilly bus that went as far as Kozelets was so-so, and then you still had to hitch a ride. I was in no hurry so set Ostyor aside until spring, in order to go by water. I was staying on top of events anyway. Mama wrote long letters that made it possible to piece together the state of things.

And it was like this.

Gilya was exerting a positive influence on Fima. To the extent that Fima had only gotten drunk one single time in two months. He'd found a job at a local savings bank, in an unimportant, even rank-and-file position, one might say, but was in good standing. He actively helped around the house, split wood, touched up things that needed it. Gilya had lengthy talks with him and Fima had returned to a new life as a result. Of course that wasn't simple, though. Sometimes he lost hope. Again and again, Gilya emerged with his strong character and unambiguously said, "It's either/or." Fima would calm down and even try harder and harder to become a human being.

Mama and I agreed I'd send letters to her at the post office, to be held for pickup, so Fima wouldn't read them. Not everything they contained was for his eyes. I described my circumstances with Miroslav, wrote about Mishenka and about Miroslav's ardent wish to adopt the boy so we'd have a full-fledged family. And so, Mama and Gilya would activize their work in that complicated regard. No matter what, paperwork for his renunciation of Mishenka had to be drawn up by spring.

And then, toward the end of March, a long-awaited letter arrived from Mama, announcing that Fima had arrived at the independent conclusion that Miroslav should adopt Mishenka. His behavior had worsened sharply, though. It's possible that the question wouldn't make headway without me. So I had to go and apply proper pressure.

Little time remained until first open water but I went anyway, catch-as-catch-can.

To my surprise, Fima truly had changed. He'd gotten younger. He talked about his work, how they appreciated him, and how in the future he was planning to strive for respect and a new position that took his work experience into account.

Gilya nodded and Mama chimed in after every word Fima said. I thought he'd become a child to them, though in terms of age, he was old enough to be their younger brother.

He asked about Mishenka. But as if he were in a fog. As if he weren't asking about his own son but someone else's boy.

We formalized the necessary paperwork the next day: all Gilya's acquaintances everywhere greeted us welcomingly and treated us with understanding.

Mama kept after me with questions. But I'd been setting forth the whole truth at the table for everyone to see, so there was nothing to add. Misha's growing, Miroslav's working, Olga Nikolaevna's sick.

Mama's eyes filled with tears:

"Oy, daughter, she's not sick, that's just the way she lives. That's her life, until the very end."

Of course she asked, directly as a mother does, if Miroslav and I were planning to have our own child. I assured her that we were very much planning on it but it was not yet time.

"And who's determining the time for you?" Mama couldn't hold back.

I didn't begin to go into detail.

Fima hitched a ride to see me off in Kozelets.

He talked endlessly along the way:

"I'm another person now. Gilya completely remade me. What had I been thinking? All my people are gone. And all around me they'd made so much sickness, out of themselves! And that damned sore spot presses at me from every side. But Gilya taught me. You have to roll that sore spot up inside your own self. And the big thing is, he showed me how with his own hands so I can picture it! You, he says, you roll it up inside yourself and it'll shake into wherever it needs to go. And then it's okay. Then you can somehow live with it. But when it's all around you, you're just turning to keep from hitting it. But when it's inside, it's okay, it mixes in, blends in all right in the end. Against the bones, against the tendons. Yes. That's what Gilya says."

Fima was waving his arms around as if he were placing—stuffing—something in his heart, guts, liver, throat, and head. Eyes. Ears.

"Well, I did it. Not right away, that's obvious, not right away at all. But it worked out. You can see."

I didn't see anything.

"Fima," I said, "You've undoubtedly set off on a good path. You're not drinking, your face is nice now. If things go well, you'll get married!"

Fima gladly chimed in:

"Of course. And I'll even have more kids. There's this one woman. She moved here. Blyumochka Tsivkina. She's actually from Chernigov, but she moved here to be with her relatives. She doesn't have anywhere to live in Chernigov, but it's the more the merrier here. Gilya introduced us. He didn't tell you?"

"No. It's too bad it's time for me to go, otherwise we would have definitely met."

We'd arrived. Of course everybody at the bus station noticed me. I was wearing a sand-colored coat that was wide open—it was warm. My circle skirt was of thin wool. It was sewn strictly on the bias and definitely worn with a wide belt. Otherwise the silhouette didn't come out.

Fima didn't ask about Yashkovets. And I didn't say anything. I figured Fima no longer had anywhere to put Lyonya: every place was full. The ears and brain and liver. And then Gilya and Mama would have to pick up the pieces later. And I would, too.

Fima announced, on his own initiative, that he'd personally come to Kiev very soon to officially change his place of residence to Ostyor, at Gilya's, since he'd been hired at work—against one of the rules—and needed everything to be legal.

I practically let this go in one ear and out the other, wrongly so.

Now about Mishenka.

I have to say that his behavior was not always sunny. He displayed a tendency toward solitude and listened to me inattentively, though he eagerly played with Miroslav and went on long outings. As a pedagogue, I worried very much about the absence of established contact. I tried to repair the indissoluble bond characteristic of a mother and son. At first, though, I only got as far as Misha calling me "Mamochka" instead of "Mama." He called Miroslav "Papa." That's quite a lot, nonetheless.

Then I slowly and systematically started pointing out table manners, personal hygiene, and various other little daily things to Misha, since they hadn't trained him in the proper way in Ostyor.

At first Misha didn't eat well: he was paying attention to differences in the food, between mine and in Ostyor. It was tastier there. I explained that on no account could it be tastier than his own mamochka's cooking. And that he had to eat every last crumb and not be picky. The little boy would leave his plate three or four times, run out into the hallway, press himself against the apartment door, and cry. I consoled him and kissed him all over because who will feel sorry for a child if not his mother?

We gradually grew closer and he began entrusting his childish secrets to me. For example, he liked kindergarten a lot but couldn't understand why the children laughed when he inserted common Yiddish expressions in conversation, things like "*tshepe nit*" (leave me alone), "*nakhes*" (pleasure), "*fishele*" (little fish), "*farkert*" (the opposite), "*nebbish*" (poor thing), "*eylik*" (hurrying), and "*berkitser*" (in short).

I explained to him that people didn't talk that way in Kiev, only in Ostyor. And Ostyor was a village. Backward compared to the capital. And if he didn't want to be backward among good children, he needed to speak Russian. Ukrainian, at the very least.

Jewish words Mishenka picked up from Gilya and Mama sometimes burst out of him at home, too, but he blushed and corrected himself each time and always sought my gaze for approval. I would praise him and make him repeat the word in Russian several times.

That happened once in front of Miroslav. He didn't let on that he'd noticed. But he reprimanded me after Mishenka left the room to go to his spot in the kitchen.

"Why are you pestering the child? Maybe he has a liking for languages and you're ruining it. It's development. And development's the most important thing in a growing person."

"There are various kinds of development. Languages, fine. Be it German, be it French. But my child will never speak Jewish. That's for his own benefit. And don't pretend you don't understand. Jewish words cost you nothing. But oh, they could cost him so much. They could bring him death."

Miroslav went silent. And didn't bawl me out in similar situations later.

That incident pushed me to the thought that it was time to find a place for Mishenka in a hobby group with a developmental focus.

Miroslav loved playing checkers during free moments. He most often played against himself. Sometimes he invited Mishenka to play against him, for fun. Mishenka made good progress for his age.

I brought the boy to the Pioneer Palace for the checkers hobby group. The leader immediately noted that Misha showed promise. Though he was only six years old.

And so I brought back the documents with Fima's renunciation. I presented them to Miroslav. He was glad. The story of the adoption had commenced.

The chestnuts were blooming. Like little white and red candles. Like always. Nothing in nature changes. Unlike in a human.

But that's not my point.

On Sunday, Miroslav, Mishenka, and I strolled around the Mariinsky Garden. Mishenka mastered his new two-wheeled bicycle. I was nervous, but he only fell three times and it didn't hurt. Miroslav constantly stayed beside him as a safeguard.

We came home late that evening. Miroslav was fussing with the bicycle downstairs, so Mishenka and I were the first to come up to our floor.

Fima had made himself comfortable under the window in the stairwell. He saw us, flung his arms wide open, and knocked over his little suitcase with a loud clatter—his elbow had pushed it off the windowsill.

"My dear people, you're finally here! And I was just about to leave! I think I'll go to Lyonya's, then come over here first thing in the morning. Mishenka! You're so big! Mayechka! You're so beautiful! Well, let's have a hug!"

I hugged Fima so as not to bicker with him for no reason. I took a sniff. Sober. Misha didn't hug him: he grabbed at my arm and started pulling me toward our door.

"Fimochka, it's a good thing you came," I said, "my husband, Miroslav Antonovich, will be here in a minute, you'll meet. And it's way past Mishenka's bedtime." I stared into Fima's eyes, not changing direction for a second.

He made a calming gesture to me, as if he were treating me with understanding.

I introduced Fima and Miroslav. Yes, it had an official feel. But all the better.

We sat down to supper. Fima looked at Mishenka and absent-mindedly answered the polite questions Miroslav and I asked. He patted Mishenka on the head. Mishenka almost choked on his tea. I took away Fima's hand, sharply but with a smile. With a smile.

He asked about the boy's interests. I answered that he showed great promise in checkers. Fima was glad.

"Oh, *shashkes*! *Shashkes* is a big thing! A lot of people dismiss it, they think you can only flick them around in the game's Chapaev version. But the boy figured it out. Smart kid!"

Mishenka tossed me a glance and buried his face in his cup. He had a special cheery children's cup.

Once we'd quickly sent Misha off to sleep, Fima shared the news from Ostyor. Everybody was healthy and they'd sent gifts: preserves, homemade potted meat, dried raspberries. He took them out of his little suitcase and displayed them right on the white table cloth.

He started saying goodbyes:

"I'm going to Lyonya Yashkovets's now, that's my friend from the front," he explained to Miroslav as an aside. "I'll spend the night, haven't seen him in a hundred years. And then I'll go to the housing office and the police at eight in the morning to officially change my place of residence. I have the change of address papers and all the other forms I need. Don't worry. Thank you for your company."

And right then, without a break:

"So you're not surprised, I have government bonds in my suitcase. I often spent my whole salary on them when I was single. These are for you and Mishenka, for the future."

And he pulled out a packet wrapped in newspaper. The newspaper came loose and obligation certificates scattered over the whole table.

Miroslav raked them up and, all serious, stuffed them back into the little suitcase. He clicked the locks.

He laid his hands on Fima's shoulders and said:

"Thank you, my dear Yefim Naumovich. But we aren't in need of anything. Right, Mayechka? And they'll come in handy for you in the future, for getting yourself established."

I nodded in agreement. Though I'd expected objections from Fima's side.

Fima cheered up, though:

"Of course I see you don't need anything. Just wanted to present a gift. I thought and thought and came up with it. Don't be offended."

I offered to walk Fima to the end of the yard.

Pounding in my head was: He'll go to Lyonya's now, but Lyonya's not of this earth. What a blow! He'll rush to the neighbors and who knows what nonsense they'll talk. And he's in an imbalanced state. He could get carried away in any direction.

"You know, Fimochka, I didn't tell you, but there's good news. Even joyful news. Lyonya got married. And he and his wife went off to the North somewhere, recruited for a job."

"How's that? I didn't know. That Lyonya! He gave me quite the scuffle over a woman. Was this long ago?"

"Just after you left, I stopped by to call on him and give him your note. And that woman happened to be there. They admitted they were planning to go. They were just waiting for you to settle things in your life. You found a place and they left."

"So that means I was holding everybody up. You. And Lyonya. Can you forgive me, Mayechka?"

"What kind of question is that, Fimochka, I forgive you a hundred times."

I had no other way out so it worked out sounding authentic.

"And they let the shack burn down. They're going to build something there. I went, saw it. I thought maybe I'd see them again, but they'd already left. The neighbors told me in the yard. Are you happy for them?"

"Of course. I'm happy so I need Lyonya to be, too. That means I'll head for Lazar's now. Your mother's always dashing off letters to him and I add postscripts. He's on top of things."

Fima was all wound up. Given his situation, though, that was right and raised no suspicions at all for me. If Mama was corresponding with Lazar and Fima didn't know anything about Yashkovets, that meant Lazar didn't know about it. If he'd known, he would definitely have written. What an event. Even so, the danger remained. There was Khasya, with her wicked conversations. No, I couldn't let Fima out of my sight until he'd officially changed his place of residence.

So this is what I did.

"Fima, wouldn't you like to spend some time alongside Mishenka? Until about tomorrow morning? You can sleep in the kitchen. I'll bring Mishenka in with us: Miroslav and I will make room. It'll be nice for us and a big delight for you. We'll all have breakfast together in the morning. After all, you're saying goodbye to your former home. You have a lot connected with it. You and I may be divorced, but we're friends. I'm asking you as a favor."

Fima thought for a brief second. And agreed.

I won't hide that I wanted to correct the tactlessness Fima committed. Things like bonds are handled in private. If he'd wanted to give them to Mishenka and me, he should have done so when Miroslav wasn't there.

We came back to the apartment. Miroslav approved the plan. He said:

"It's inhuman to throw a person out of his home for the night. I'll say more than that, Yefim: if you can't get everything processed in one day tomorrow, stay with us as long as you need. Converse with your son. If you reason it out, he's a child to both of us. Well, there's the paperwork, birth certificates, and all that. But you sired him. You didn't do anything bad to him. He should consider you one of his own. And life is life, after all."

Fima's eyes filled with tears. There's the vivid power of the word. And where it leads.

Mishenka was already sleeping so we carried him, drowsy, to our bed. We perched ourselves around him.

I wanted to change the linens on the little daybed, but Fima asked me to leave them so he could warm himself with Mishenka's heat.

In the morning, we all ate breakfast together and talked about insignificant things. Miroslav lingered so he could take Mishenka to kindergarten, and Fima and I headed to the housing office and wherever we had to go after that.

Fima was silent along the way. To distract him, I told him about my life with Miroslav, and about his mother, Olga Nikolaevna. Fima didn't answer and wasn't even truly listening.

Then he opened his mouth anyway: "Tell me, Maya, if I hadn't agreed to this, what would you have done with me?"

I stopped, confused.

"And what could I have done? Not even with you, but in general? You're strange, Fimochka. You're living in the past. And you're asking questions from the past. Thank God everything's resolved between us, only the last step is left. And here we are going to do it, the two of us, with a good mutual agreement. That's how it is, right?"

"Yes, yes. I was just wondering. Lyonka used to tell me you could even kill, that's how you are. He said you're passionate. But I'm not passionate. I'm not even jealous. We're different, that's where the problem is. I've been pondering about why things didn't turn out well for us. It's not because I was a drinker. And oh, do people live with drinkers. You, Mayechka, are made from a different dough. Like matzo. Unleavened and hard. And a lot can be made from you. Under certain conditions, of course. You never know. My wife made matzo brei. And little pies. The children loved them. But I'm stale. Like something you can't soak in water. If you soak it in water, you won't eat it. Because it's disgusting. So you can't do anything with me."

I kept quiet. Naturally, Fima was taking stock of his life's path in Kiev while on the path to changing his residence. There wasn't much for an observer to say.

"You, Fimochka, are making idle conversation. You have to look ahead."

"Yes, Mayechka, yes, you're right. Let Mishenka be happy. That's at the root of this."

And so we reached our destination. They did everything quickly, even at the police station's passport desk. Fyodor Grigorievich Tarasenko, the station chief, was an acquaintance of Fima's from the old pre-war times.

He made a comment about me: "Fimka, why didn't you hold onto this sweetheart?!"

And Fima answered with a smile: "Her decision. I'm not going to keep her on a leash, you know that yourself."

Of course, the remark was tactless. And obviously neither one nor the other could keep quiet.

Then, to smooth the situation, Fima asked: "Fedya, do you remember Lyonya Yashkovets? The artist at the Chapaev Cinema."

"How could I not. Poor guy. Did himself in drinking."

"What's that?" Fima gave a start.

"That's how he burned up without a trace. Right in his own shack. It's the next station's territory, their guys told me about it. You know Sashka Krutovsky? He's the one who told me. Went out to the scene. Went through the coals, put together the protocol, and closed the case."

"What case?"

"It's obvious. Drunken fire."

Fima jerked his head.

"Did they find bones? Well, a skeleton?"

"There was so much junk there—metal and stones and antlers— Lyonka loved to carve figurines. Nobody really investigated. Seems like there wasn't a separate skeleton. You understand fire makes no distinctions. Anyway, he was declared as burned. Nobody was sad about him. *Nema* and *nema*. And don't you be sad. You have your life at a starting point, you might say."

Fima looked at Tarasenko with understanding, but there was nothing behind it.

The chief assured him they'd send the documents to Ostyor by mail without delay, that they'd be in place within two or three days and he'd be able to register.

We walked down the street at a leisurely pace. I was thinking about how to show my reaction about Yashkovets.

Fima beat me to it, though:

"See, Mayechka. You were wrong. Lyonya didn't leave. He burned up. Though it depends on how you look at it. Maybe he actually left. Departed to his place of permanent registration. And nobody will move him out of that place now. Neither the police nor a woman nor his stray little friends. Nobody."

And he stated that so calmly it gave me a chill in my nerves.

Fima didn't even look in my direction. I shortly answered that I had other information. And I'd already set it forth. But the police were looking on the outside of things. Maybe they were wrong.

Fima grumbled: "Be quiet, be quiet. I knew it. I knew it."

I'd made a plan.

After the matter of changing the official residence was finished, I wouldn't leave Fima until his departure. I'd see him off at the river station. I'd already offered. He'd refused and said he was planning to go to Lazar's.

I didn't like that, particularly in light of the new report on Yashkovets. But there was no way around it. I just offered to go with him.

Fima agreed, as if nothing had happened. He seemed to pull himself together.

"Exactly. Enough pouting. You have to make up. How long since you last saw Lazar?"

"I'm not counting."

"Then you especially have to go. As families do."

By all indications, it worked out that there was still a lot of time before Lazar came home from work. Fima wanted to buy some sort of toy for Mishenka. We stopped at a store and found success: Fima bought an interesting metal train set with five little red railroad cars that should go around in a circle if you put the rails together right. Fima asked to take Mishenka with us to Lazar's; we'd need to pick him up early at kindergarten.

We came home to our house so we could leave at five to pick up Mishenka along the way to Lazar and Khasya's.

Mishenka was very glad we came, and he walked holding Fima's hand. Misha told us how things were going at kindergarten and recited a new verse.

Fima praised him and asked him to repeat it several times as an encore. When Misha said it the third time, he forgot the last line and Fima cued him.

The tail end of a line was sticking out of the cake shop on the corner near Lazar's house. Fima asked the last woman in line what they were selling and she said it was Kiev torte. It had just come into being at the time and had immediately become famous and terribly hard to come by. I told Fima we had to buy one as a treat for Lazar and Khasya, come what may.

We stood for about forty minutes and bought two; it was one per customer.

It was already nearly seven in the evening. And as warm as if it were summer.

Fima abruptly said:

"I don't feel like being inside. Lazar and Khasya aren't going anywhere. We'll come later, that's even better. We'll definitely catch them at home. Let's go sit in the public garden. Enjoy what's around us."

To be honest, I didn't really feel like going to Lazar's, with all those conversations of his I've known by heart since childhood. And that's not even counting Khasya.

We sat down on a bench. Well, there were chestnuts and green grass. Children running around, mommies with baby carriages.

Mishenka settled in and sat.

I suggested to him: "Go over there to those boys your own age, introduce yourself, and play."

He refused. Fima abruptly tore the twine off a torte box, pulled a jackknife out of his pants pocket, and started cutting the torte into big pieces right on the bench.

"Mishka, let's eat up the torte. Don't be bashful. Go to it."

And he grabbed the first piece himself. He stuffed it in his mouth, practically without chewing. Mishenka was looking at him and pinching little crumbs off the torte with his little fingers.

I should say that the torte was of fairly brittle composition. There were nuts, candied fruit, and a fragile base: it was like meringue, but not meringue. Fima was covered in crumbs, his face was smeared in crème. People had started paying unpleasant attention to us. Fima didn't care, though. He didn't even eat the next piece, he gobbled it down like a pig. This was no longer a matter of manners, I didn't know what it was.

Mishenka felt uneasy—he wasn't used to this. I'd trained him for tidiness. He placed the piece of torte back in the box and looked down at his feet, at the ground.

I reprimanded Fima:

"Behave yourself like a human being. You don't have enough patience to eat. People are watching. Your behavior's disgusting them. And you're waving your knife around like a drunk hooligan."

This was where I realized Fima didn't hear me. He was stuffing and stuffing himself with torte. But the torte didn't fit. It was crumbling on his shirt, jacket, pants, and the bench. In a hill on the ground. Very, very white. Looking like chestnut flowers.

Mishenka steeled himself and steeled himself, then he started crying.

I grabbed him, cupping his face in my hands and pressed him to myself.

"This is the last time I'm setting a condition, Fima. Be a human being. You've created a circus act. What are you trying to accomplish?"

Fima answered extremely unintelligibly because his mouth was crammed with torte: "Go home. Take the second box. I'll eat this one myself and go to Ostyor."

This is where I understood he was definitively out of his mind. I didn't know how that got through to me.

So as not to make him nervous, I picked up the second torte and very, very quickly, both running and walking, left with Misha. I looked back once and Fima was cleaning out the empty bottom of the box, scraping it with his nails like a dog. But nobody was looking at him anymore. They'd all scattered.

I don't remember what condition Mishenka and I were in when we reached the house. He looked warily at the box with the torte and squeezed my hand very, very firmly.

It wasn't late yet. Miroslav was at his mother's after work.

Mishenka asked to sleep in our bed, something that hadn't happened before. He whimpered and complained he was scared. And he's a big boy.

I lay there next to him, understanding I'd need to handle this new problem on my own. Without involving Miroslav. He'd decide Mishenka had a bad genetic inheritance and in the end there'd be a shadow cast on a boy who wasn't guilty of anything.

Miroslav came home very late that night. He was glad when he saw Mishenka on our bed. I didn't let a word slip about Fima's horrible display. I said the documents had been squared away and Surkis had set sail for Ostyor.

When Miroslav was having supper, he noticed the box with the torte on the windowsill. He was surprised and wondered where I'd managed to buy it. I said we'd been lucky by chance. Specially for his mother. Only one had come our way.

Miroslav asked:

"But what about Misha? He should definitely eat some torte. Let's divide it in two. One in the box for Mama, one for Mishenka."

And that's what I did in the morning. Miroslav took half the torte with him to work, to bring to Olga Nikolaevna later. After Miroslav left, I crumbled the second half into the toilet while Mishenka slept.

The memory of the previous day haunted me. The thought popped into my head that Fima's little suitcase hadn't been on the bench in the little public garden. That he'd left it somewhere. I took a look at home; not there. That meant it was either in the store where we bought the train set or at the police station. But what's the difference? The difference is that his passport was either on his person or in the little suitcase. If it was on his person, there was hope Fima would pursue the matter of the residence permit to its conclusion. But if not, well, I'd be waiting for him to visit and then fussing all over again. And I hadn't planned to take those obligation certificates from him as a sort of buyout anyway, so I didn't care about them. Even if they were government bonds. Although, of course, that's not good household management.

I decided not to embark on anything since there wasn't much I could do.

That evening, Miroslav assembled the train set and he and Mishenka played for a long time, despite the late hour. The little red train cars rode along the circumference. It felt like they'd never stop. My head even started spinning.

Mishenka laughed, and Miroslav laughed and loudly shouted: "Toot-toot!"

Mishenka repeated after him and stretched his little arms up in the air.

Yes, children redirect their attention quickly. They have short attention spans and they direct it at one thing. I couldn't redirect mine from Fima for anything.

And just as I thought. A telegram arrived from my mother two days later. During the day, when Miroslav was at work and Mishenka was at kindergarten. "Why is Fima delayed worrying."

I answered with a telegram, too: "Don't worry paperwork delayed."

In the meantime, I went to see Tarasenko at the police station. I described the situation to him and asked him to get involved. He laughed at first; he said, what, can't a free man have some fun? But then I reprimanded him, saying this was no laughing matter since Fima's temperament was unbalanced and urgent measures needed to be taken for Fima's own sake. I mentioned the little suitcase and the passport that was either in the little suitcase or on Fima's own person. Moreover, without a residence permit.

Fyodor Grigorievich promised to do everything he could. But only a bit later, in approximately a week, if Fima didn't turn up on his own. For now, he advised me, go make the rounds of all Fima's friends in Kiev if I want and send telegrams to everybody possible outside the city. There were frequent situations where a person prone to using alcoholic beverages attached himself to acquaintances and drank to his heart's content in a state of stupor and the police wasted their energy. He also offered to make an immediate call from his office to the information line on casualties. I requested that he personally do that. After all, they'd treat a police chief differently. He called. Yefim Naumovich Surkis had not come through the lists. There was nobody unnamed. If you didn't count two gypsy-looking women without documents and one legless invalid on a wheeled dolly.

And so. There was nowhere to send telegrams other than my mother in Ostyor. But they weren't suspecting Fima of anything there. I didn't know his Kiev acquaintances other than, of course, the deceased Lyonya Yashkovets.

I went right away to see Uncle Lazar at the plant. As it happens, he was working away on some frightening-looking thing—Lazar was scratching away with a file at a piece of iron squeezed in a vice, back and forth, back and forth. Amid the hubbub, I attempted to explain, but Lazar just waved his arms around. Of course, he'd already been nurturing his fury at me for several years. And here I'd finally turned up, without an invitation, to ask a favor. He grasped that immediately, though he'd been deaf for a long time and had apparently grown even deafer during that period. Which did not excuse him. Beyond all that, he—as a well-known model worker who loved exhibiting himself in front of everyone—allegedly feared abandoning his high-precision metalwork for even a minute. He forced me to mill around until lunch. I stayed to wait by the guard desk. It's good it wasn't a long time.

As I stood, I drafted up an outline for the conversation. Nothing detailed. Only the question of when Lazar last saw Fima.

Lazar started right in, though, deluging me with reproaches for ingratitude.

"So you came running, little niece! On your own little legs. Didn't stumble on those heels? Your little skirt too tight? You should have worn one even *korochshe*, so you'd walk better. It's shameful to look at you. At least Khasya's not seeing this."

And he was looking around proudly: had everyone understood he was speaking with his own niece? Because this was pleasant for him, after all, since I'm not some dimwitted bumpkin girl.

I calmly heard Lazar out and loudly asked him my necessary question: "When did you last see Surkis, my former husband?"

"I saw him a long, long time ago. Before you'd even kicked him out. What, you're impatient to get married again, nobody will have you without the dishonesty?"

"Just so you know and can tell Khasya, I married a decent man long ago. Didn't Mama write to you? That doesn't matter, though."

"Obviously not. It's just I haven't seen your former Fima in recent days past because I've been attending late meetings at work. Labor union and open Party meetings. And social obligations. But my son saw him. And had a heart-to-heart with Yefim Naumovich. Khasya wasn't home either, for a respectable reason. But my son was."

"And where did Fima go after that? Did he go to Ostyor?"

"I don't know. Ask Motya."

"He didn't tell you?"

"What's to tell? Fima'd been drinking. Drinking a lot. He didn't add more at our place, that's true. We don't have vodka at our house for anything."

Lazar's ammunition had run out as far as statements went and he was taking his usual place as the henpecked husband. And here I, the pedagogue, took the gentle approach.

"Uncle, you're my only relative here. And you, despite everything, are messing with my head. You're sticking your hands into womanly gossip. I know Motya. He told you everything. Letter for letter. Tell me."

Lazar lowered his gaze. He's a good person and honest, it's just a bitchy woman landed in his life and completely broke him.

"Mayka, I would've told you. But Motya's keeping quiet as a murder victim. I myself don't understand what's up, why Motya's keeping secrets with the drunk. Why're you all nerved up? Fima's a stranger to you on all sides. So, he came over, so, he left."

I understood I wouldn't get any further and there was no need to discredit myself. I needed to catch Motya.

I warmheartedly said:

"Thank you, Uncle Lazar. I've always loved you, despite Aunt Khasya. And you have a good son. Deep down, he takes after you. So is he still working at 'Arsenal'?"

I inconspicuously cast a glance at my little watch—it was 12:30.

"*A yak zhe*. He's at 'Arsenal'. He's a metal worker. As they say, one who works with metal, and bread and salted pork fat, too. I love you, too, Mayka. You're empty-headed. Unlike your own mother. But you're my blood. Am I right or what?"

"Of course. We need to stick closer together, Uncle Lazar. You're right. Is Motya working the first shift today?"

"First shift. He's knocking off work at three. You going?"

"I'm going."

"You try. But I don't recommend it. Matters like this, you have to leave them halfway. Without clearing them up. It'll be worse. Honestly, I stopped looking to clear up what's behind Khasya's behavior long ago. I just live. Otherwise, who knows what'll come creeping out."

Lazar waved a hand.

"Arsenal" isn't Lazar's invalid workers' cooperative, you can't get further than the guard desk. I ran home to prepare food for Mishenka and Miroslav. But I was standing in place at exactly three.

Motya showed up in good time. He didn't even express surprise about our meeting. He looked me over from head to toe and nodded approvingly. He's a man, after all, even if he's a relative.

"Motya, Fima came to see you. I know. What did he tell you?"

"Nothing in particular. What can a drunk man say? He was actually in kind of a bad way. Showed up with an empty torte box, white with a chestnut on top. Not tied up, nothing. He was holding it under his arm. It kept falling, it was dirty, even *gidko*. He was dirty and smeared himself. Probably from the torte. His hands were sticky. He patted me on the head and I combed out crumbs later. They scattered off his sleeves, like in the circus. And that's all."

"Tell me, Motya. Did he say he was going to Ostyor?"

"He said he was going somewhere, but didn't talk about Ostyor. Just he was going. Sat for five minutes. Asked for some food to put in his box. I put some in. Cutlets, bread. He asked for something sweet, too. We only had preserves. I gave him a half-liter jar. Cherry. With pits. Mama's always cooking it up, you know that. He crammed it in his pocket. Of his jacket. It barely fit. And I tied up the box with a gauze bandage. Couldn't find any string. Fima redid it his own way. The tall part of the box ended up like a saucepot and the other part, where the cake sat before, ended up like a lid. Meaning it was backwards. He was glad it was good and roomy. He was mostly quiet. Just 'going' and 'going.' He was drunk, what can you expect?"

Motya told me this quickly. It was obviously unpleasant for him. For some reason I asked: "Did he smell strongly of vodka?"

"He didn't smell. Didn't smell at all. Just reeked of cake. A sweet sort of smell. Probably it overpowered the vodka. But, *sho*, I can't tell sober from drunk? The gait's all over the place and there's stupidity on the tongue. He was definitely drunk."

"Motechka, did he have a little suitcase with him? Brown, fiber, small?"

"No, he came empty-handed. If you don't count the box. And he had a penknife. It was dirty, too. The blade didn't open and close well, the grooves were filled with something white. Probably torte. I noticed when Fima cut the bandage."

"And did he show you his passport?"

"Why? Normal people don't stick their passport under other people's noses."

"That's normal people, Motechka."

Motya looked at me intently. He wasn't the brightest person, but he took my hint.

"You think Fima's not all there?"

"Not all there, Motechka. Very much not all there. Or here, either. And he wasn't drunk. That's why he reeked of torte a kilometer away, but not of vodka. He's not all there and he has a knife, too. It's horrible, Motechka."

I covered my face with my hands. But only for a short instant. My maternal instinct pushed me—I had to get to the kindergarten quickly. To Mishenka.

Motya shouted after me:

"He was singing a song, too, 'The enemy burned my family home.'" And he made me sing along. And I can't stand that."

Everything was calm at the kindergarten. Misha was in a good mood. I talked with the kindergarten teacher, with prophylactic goals. Hows and whats, and the boy's progress.

She fervently praised Mishenka: he was a sharer and friendly with children of both genders. And it was true that Mishenka was always surrounded by schoolmates because he instigated games. Not a trace remained of the short-lived withdrawnness resulting from the move to Kiev. In this case, though, I wanted to clarify if anything out of the ordinary had happened in recent days, meaning connected with Fima. The boy himself might not have made much of it, but an adult is always on guard.

"Why are you worrying? Our institution is in high standing, nobody hurts our children. Outsiders don't climb through the fences. We only let them go home with their parents and close relatives."

"I don't doubt that. It's just that my neighbor—her child isn't at your kindergarten—told me her former husband showed up and took her little girl without her consent. She searched and searched for her after."

"That's an obvious failure. We should always know the family's situation for certain. Who to release the child to and who not to. Former husbands are capable of a lot. But your husband is nice and, you know, Mishenka appreciates him very much. One time I asked the children who they love more, Papa or Mama. And your Misha declared: I love Mama very much, but Papa very, very much. Interesting, isn't it?"

I didn't hold back and made a pedagogical reprimand:

"A typical childish reaction. Just so you know, though, questions of that sort undermine a child's psychological stability."

There was nothing else to talk about so I called Mishenka to come with me.

As a direct person, I myself never drop any hints and don't welcome it when others drop them in my direction.

That teacher had long been unsympathetic to me—out of envy. Which was natural at her age, just before retirement.

Her tactless remark threw me off my stride. But it also brought me back to life. Fima was his own man. He'd changed his place of residence voluntarily and the police station chief was a witness. What Surkis would do later was none of my business. He could show up or not show up, he could scare people on the street, put ideas in Motka and Lazar and Khasya's heads, die under someone else's fence, or even be recruited somewhere—but what did it matter? He was incidental to my fate. A stage of my life had ended. Once and for all.

This picture arose so clearly before my mind's eye that I sensed a nearly total feeling of infinite freedom.

I pressed Mishenka to my chest and kissed him, as the person most important to me.

Miroslav announced some news that evening. He'd been appointed director of the shoe factory. Plus, there was a high salary and a personal car, a Pobeda. To mark that event, the whole family was going to his mother's tomorrow, Sunday. Nothing supports an ill person like the common joy of those near and dear.

Olga Nikolaevna turned out to be in a very weak state. Completely thin. She was glad to meet Mishenka: after all, this was only the first time she was seeing him. She asked him to sit by her on the bed and she looked and looked at him.

"A handsome *khlopchik*. Aren't you, Mykhailyk? Mykhailyk, oy, Mykhailyk, what a handsome little thing," and she patted him on the head.

Mishenka felt uncomfortable and had to lean in her direction, but he understood correctly and tried to tactfully hold his head a little lower.

Miroslav told Olga Nikolaevna about his successes, about the new job, and about the car.

"Now I'll never see you at all. *Ne pobachu zh?*"

Miroslav assured his mother that nothing would change since, on the contrary, with a car at his disposal now, he could call on her more frequently.

I opened the vent window a little under the pretense that there was wonderful spring air outside. Naturally, there was a bad smell in the room.

When we were leaving, I reprimanded Zoya Ivanovna in the hallway about airing out.

She waved a hand:

"I air it out and air it out, but it's useless. I got used to the smell, but you don't want to stand it for a minute. Such a delicate *zhinochka*."

It's a good thing Miroslav didn't hear, or he would have been upset by her rudeness. But I was fine. Just so everything's calm.

That evening we sat for a long time, the whole family, in the large room. I laid out a white embroidered tablecloth—my grandmother's—from Ostyor. There's one spot that just doesn't wash out. I covered it with a dish of cookies and watched that nobody moved the dish. And Mishenka kept pulling at its tall stem, until I specifically pointed that out.

Miroslav told Mishenka about the production process, about the conveyor belt. Clearly and accessibly, as always. Mishenka listened attentively. Then he asked to take out the train set, but I said there was no need today—it was better to talk. Miroslav assembled the train set anyway, and Mishenka got down to playing. We delighted in our son and glanced at each other approvingly.

I was curious about why the appointment for the job at the factory happened so abruptly. It turned out there was no abruptness. The question had been under discussion for a long time, the former director retired, and they'd proposed Miroslav's candidacy right away. But he didn't get ahead of events during all the bureaucratic red tape. Things could have gone either way.

"Your composure, Mayechka, is more valuable than anything on earth."

And then Mishenka spoke up:

"Mamochka, will Uncle Fima come back? He and I are going to play *shashkes*. Papa hasn't played with me in a long time."

I even leapt up.

"In the first place, it's not *shashkes*, it's checkers. Repeat that. Check-ers. Check-ers."

Mishenka repeated without raising his head or looking away from the train set.

"And in the second place, Uncle Fima's gone far, far away."

Miroslav looked at me with condemnation. But I did get nervous. He didn't care, though, because he wasn't aware of things.

"Shall we play Chapaev now, Mishka?" Miroslav moved the cups and plates aside to free up a place for checkers. He carelessly knocked the dish with the cookies. It fell on the floor and the cookies crumbled into little pieces. It's a shortbread dough, very fragile. They might have been from the store, but the dough was excellent. Tears gushed from my eyes.

Miroslav didn't notice. He took out the board and the little bag with the playing pieces, set them out, and calmly proposed: "Sit down, Mishka. You'll be Chapaev and I'll be Furmanov."

Misha was excited. They were loud and made various joking threats as they flicked at the checkers, which flew off far to the sides. I collected them and arranged them in little columns at the other end of the table, at the place where the tablecloth was spotted, as it happened. The spirit of the lady of the house prevailed.

Misha was victorious.

As encouragement, Miroslav said: "Good job, sonny."

And inside me there resounded: *Chapaev, Chapaev.* The White Army's psychological attack. And Lyonka was behind the Whites and behind Lyonka was Fimka with a little knife and who the hell knows who was behind Fimka: Mama and Gilya and Tarasenko and Motka with his mamas and papas and the Kiev torte. And Olga Nikolaevna. And her closed vent window.

It became clear here that I was not in a completely free condition at all. Fima had left me spinning on a merry-go-round that I couldn't stop. That's what had come out of his troubled head. And nobody cared. Nobody.

But that's not my point.

My mother arrived on Monday evening. And she wasn't alone. There was some biddy with her.

Mama introduced her right at the threshold: Blyuma Tsivkina, Fima's fiancée.

I will not describe this so-called fiancée. Big eyes as black as coal, a fat stomach, legs like pillars. Only every other tooth. Short, black, thin hair wound like wire. But what's the difference in this case?

Mama was supporting her by the elbow, as if she were injured.

Blyuma's question rang out before they'd even entered the room: "Where's Fimochka?"

"Accept the bitter truth," I said. "If Fima hasn't come back to you yet, that means he's a missing person."

Mama plopped on a chair. Blyuma plopped on Mama's knees out of inertia. It's a wonder the chair didn't fall apart!

I dragged Blyuma to the bed and sat her down.

Mama was running around the room, wringing her hands: "What does that mean, missing person? There's no war now. He has documents with him. Have you checked the hospitals? Made a statement for the police? Let them declare a search."

"Mama, sit still. Do you know Fima well?"

Mama sat at the table and lay her arms on it like a first-grader.

"I know him very well, thank you. He's responsible. He doesn't drink. He had firmly, very firmly, planned to return no later than yesterday. He asked for time off from work with extra: for three days. He didn't arrive today and he's absolutely not at work."

"Well then, my dear Mama and Blyuma. You don't know him. Whether he drinks or doesn't drink, that's not all there is for a person. He's lost his mind. And searching for an insane person is a nasty business. You understand that yourself. The person can't have a definite direction. Today it's one thing, the next minute it's another. I did what I could. I was at the police, had a preliminary discussion about this with the chief, and he doesn't have the authority to move the paperwork until a week's gone by."

Blyuma burst out sobbing. Very unattractively, too. She wasn't holding up well at all and her mood was transmitted to Mama.

My mother held out her hands to me through her tears:

"Something needs to be done, daughter. What does Miroslav say?"

Luckily, Miroslav and Mishenka were at Olga Nikolaevna's. The automobile did present strong advantages. Back in the morning, Miroslav offered Mishenka a ride to Olga Nikolaevna's in the Pobeda and naturally the boy was glad. They'd be back any minute.

"Miroslav doesn't know anything about the disappearance. And, to be honest, I'm requesting that you not bring it to his attention. His mother is extremely ill, he has a job with a lot of responsibility, and he was just appointed director, so there's no need to mix him up in this. He can't help, and he'd start to worry. We'll decide ourselves what further route to take."

Blyuma quietly blew her nose. Mama was silent and looked me in the eyes with a direct gaze.

I took the initiative.

"You'll stay and spend the night with us. Not a word about what happened. Talk about unrelated things. About Gilya, about Mishenka, go ahead. But if there's even one sound uttered about Fima, I'll find the opportunity to cut you off with no mercy whatsoever. As for later! We're waiting until Wednesday. Everybody in their own places. You in Ostyor and me here. First thing on Wednesday morning I'll go to the police and write a statement about a missing person."

"And the hospital?" Blyuma spoke up.

"I called the information line on casualties. There's nothing anywhere."

Strictly speaking, of course, I could have called every day. But I was firmly convinced that Fima could have landed in only one kind of hospital: psychiatric. And if he was in the nuthouse, there was no need at all to drag him out of there, that would even be criminal for those around him.

"And then?" Blyuma hadn't calmed down.

She'd knocked the coverlet off the bed onto the floor with her big rear end. And one of the pillows had fallen, too.

"Blyuma, stand up," I sternly asked her. Blyuma stood and I set to tidying the coverlet and pillows. "Sit on a chair. We'll eat supper now. How's Gilya feeling?"

Since I'd already gone to the kitchen, Mama answered unintelligibly.

Individual words and exclamations in Yiddish floated to me, but I didn't understand any of the meaning.

As I was setting the table, my mother asked:

"How could Fima have lost his mind in one day if he'd been completely normal the whole time in Ostyor, right in front of us? He worked at the bank, handled valuables of various kinds, and hadn't been reprimanded."

"The possibilities of the human character are boundless," I answered. "And believe me, dear Mama, he's not some meshuggana numbskull, but an absolutely insane person."

"And what was he up to that made you come to that conclusion?" Blyuma wanted to back me into a corner.

"Blyuma, unlike you, I lived side by side with Fima, and he and I ran a common household. And I know him well. Both from working together in one collective and in general. And about his insanity, that's not my personal opinion. Go ask Uncle Lazar's son. Matvei will confirm it. As for his antics, that's not important. We'll let that stay with me. You're not a doctor to discuss it, but after all, I'm a pedagogue."

Blyuma sensed the difference in our education and bit her tongue.

We summed things up: wait and hope.

The meeting with Miroslav and Mishenka went cordially. In order to avert undesired circumstances, I loudly said, right away:

"Miroslav. Mama and Blyumochka bring you greetings from Fima. Everything's fine with him."

At first I was afraid of what Blyuma would say, but I quickly sent her on her way to the kitchen to rest.

Mishenka gabbed nonstop with Mama, who seemed to have forgotten about Fima. Mishenka demonstrated the train set and Mama steadfastly didn't react when he pointed out it was a gift from Fima.

I was glad about the manner of their conversation, too. Not a word in Jewish. Although I'd made up my mind in advance not to remark if Mishenka and Mama included Jewish words. This wasn't the situation for that.

Blyuma was sniffling in the kitchen. She didn't sleep until almost morning. Mama slept in the room with us on the fold-up cot. The three of us were on the bed.

Late into the night, Mama whispered: "Gilya's so worried, so worried. Daughter, do you hear?"

What could I say?

I got up before everyone else. I rapidly woke the guests and sent them off to the port, instructing them to send off a telegram if any news took shape in Ostyor.

I fixed breakfast and started waking Miroslav. He pretended for a long time that he wasn't stirring. He finally opened his eyes and glanced at the alarm clock. We hadn't wound it since evening; we hadn't had it in us.

"I still have forty minutes. I timed the trip in the car, I can get up later now."

He was speaking very, very quietly, so as not to disturb Mishenka. Miroslav got up carefully and took Mishenka in his arms. Mishenka didn't stir. Miroslav carried Mishenka to the little daybed.

"Let's lie here for a bit."

I lay down. We lay, embracing.

Miroslav said: "Can you imagine, they're going to install a telephone for us soon. I have another dream, too."

I knew.

"Give birth to a girl. We have a boy. Let there be a girl."

I was in solidarity with him, with all my soul. I was overflowing, brimming, with happiness.

A telegram arrived that afternoon from Ostyor. Saying something on the order of: "No news." I wanted to respond that I didn't have any news, either, but decided not to pester my people in Ostyor with little things. If there was something crucial, I'd announce it.

It felt like I had second sight. I could see, though not all the way.

I went to meet with Tarasenko at the police station on Wednesday at 8:30. It turned out to be a day he wasn't taking visitors. I spoke with the officer on duty. He sympathized and offered lots of examples of people turning up on their own in inapt places. Even in storage rooms not far from their primary places of residence.

I took off from the police station at a run, for the basement of my own building. The door of our storage space was locked. With a hook on the inside.

"Fima, Fima are you here? I know you're here. Open up. It's Maya."

I pounded at the door and it was moving from side to side—there wasn't a sound in there.

I sat down by the door and was thinking: run to the housing committee for help, call for a locksmith, or maybe break it. Of course it was Fima inside. It couldn't be anyone else. Disgrace and the neighbors' insulting conversations, discussion, and all the rest. No, I'd pound at it myself.

I pounded again. With my heel. No reaction.

I took a fat stick lying around nearby and pounded with all my strength.

The hook didn't hold. The door opened.

Nothing was visible in the darkness. There'd never been a light bulb; we'd come here with a candle.

I called out gently, in a whisper: "Fima, it's me, Maya. Where are you in here?"

And Fima spoke up after all.

"You alone?"

"Alone."

"Nobody followed you?"

"Nobody."

"I was sleeping. Sleeping well. Will you feed me? My food ran out a long time ago. There's *polizai* all around. I'm afraid to come out."

"Don't be afraid, Fima. I'll bring you out. The *polizai* went to another place."

"Are they shooting?"

"Oh yes, they're shooting. They're shooting a lot. You'll sit it out with me until our people come."

"I'll take the children, too. You won't send them away? They're your own children. You won't send your own people away to their death. Right?"

And here a mass moved toward me. It was as if it was Fima but not Fima. He walked right up to me. Sweat, every kind of dirt, all mixed up. He'd been eating, sleeping, and everything in the storage space. And he was a mass because he'd bundled all that junk on himself. On his torso, on his head, on his arms, and on his legs. He wasn't human. I examined him as much as I could: a light bulb was just barely flickering in the passageway.

"Let's go slowly, Fimochka. There aren't any children here, Fima, they already left on their own. Went far away. All of them."

I took him by his tatters and led him behind me. Outside, in the light, it was enough to make me want to scream. Such fear.

He said:

"You go first, they won't touch you, you don't look like a Jewess. Who do I look like? Have a look. And you'll call for me. Signal with just your hand."

And that's what I did.

Fima even calmed down in the apartment. He himself went into the kitchen, started poking around in the pots and pans on the burners, grabbed something from there with his hands, and dropped it on the floor. He didn't get anything into his mouth that way.

"I ate. I'm stuffed."

I poured water from the boiler into the washtub where I bathed Mishenka and said:

"Fimochka, *ingele*, get in the washtub. I'm going to soap you up with soap. It smells good, like wild strawberries."

Fima uncoiled himself, took off everything he was wearing, then stood, naked, in the tub. Stood and covered his eyes like a little boy so the soap wouldn't get in them.

"Hurry up, *mamele*. Do you have enough soap?"

"There's enough."

And I washed him. As if he were Mishenka.

"You'll be so nice and white, a magpie will carry you off." That's what Mama used to say and that's what I said to Fima.

Well, I washed him. Spotless. I moved his feet out of the washtub onto the floor. I brought fresh clothes—Miroslav's—pants, undershirt, and a shirt. Large, not his size. Well, fine.

I dried him off with a towel.

I said:

"Don't be afraid of anything, Fimochka, little one, *mamele* won't give you away to anyone. *Mamele* has a cannon. And a tank. And a whole railroad. We'll leave. We'll leave."

Fima started whimpering:

"I don't want to go, *mamele*, I want to be here. I don't want to go."

I gently started in:

"Shall we go see Fanechka and Gilechka in Ostyor? Huh, Fimochka, shall we go? On a little boat on the nice water, on the nice clean water, shall we go? Go by water?"

"We'll go by water, *mamele*, we'll go by water. Together. Only together."

"Well of course. Only so it's all of us. Fimochka, my little one, my heart."

I saw Fima had calmed and wasn't shaking. He was attempting to put some things on by himself. I helped him. Fima was now like Mishenka was as a little boy.

I dressed him and sat him on the bed.

I started searching for his passport in the pile of junk. Not there. I needed to go to the basement.

"Fimochka, *mamele*'s going to run out for a second, to check that there's nobody that doesn't belong, then come back. And she'll buy tickets for the little boat. And Fimochka's going to lie on the little bed like a good boy and wait for *mamele*. Right, Fimochka?"

Fima lay down like an obedient toy. His legs stayed bent, just like when he'd been sitting.

I used a mop to push the rags into a tighter pile and transferred it onto an old sheet. I laid it on the floor and tightly tied the corners together crosswise.

Then I rushed off to the basement. I ransacked the storage space by candlelight. The passport was lying around in the muck. I tore off the leather passport cover with its rendering of the Kremlin and Red Square. Only a little bit had seeped to the inside. Despite my new crepe georgette dress, I pressed the document to my heart, and leapt off.

Fima was still lying the same way; he hadn't unbent his legs.

I wiped the outside of the passport with eau de cologne, neatly riffled through the dirty pages, wrapped it in several layers of newspaper, and placed it in its own small bag. The material was linen. Genuine homespun canvas.

Then I grabbed money from the cabinet and shoved it in my purse. I got Fima up and handed him the bundle, having in mind to throw it out along the way.

There was obviously no question of taking any mode of transport but an automobile. They all had their schedules and I needed to go immediately.

At the taxi stand, I bargained with a driver to go to Ostyor. Round trip.

We arrived quickly, at top speed. Fima sat with his eyes closed the whole way and an expression as if teeth were being pulled out with live nerves. But fine.

Mama was at home.

I handed Fima over to her, saying only this: "Here, Mama. I did everything I could. Call Blyuma."

I gave her the little bag with the passport. And ran back out to the car and off for Kiev.

We drove right up to the kindergarten. Only when I picked up Mishenka did I catch my breath. I wasn't reflecting on freedom. I understood there would be no more freedom.

But that's not my point.

The situation intensified because of Miroslav's new position. He'd hoped to have more time, but it worked out to less. The scope of his work had broadened significantly and he was no longer managing to devote attention to Olga Nikolaevna. Other than Sundays. And so I didn't see him in the full sense of the word.

He'd come home and exchange a few words with Mishenka about the past day. And then he'd look at me with a smile and say: "Oy, Mayechka, figuring things out and figuring things out! Let's have something to eat."

And off to sleep.

Immense proportions always await at a new job.

I, as Miroslav's wife, delicately sensed his mood and handled domestic chores on my own. Moreover, I'd made it a rule to go see Olga Nikolaevna in the middle of the week. In essence, my help boiled down to conversations. No small thing. In particular, I suggested inviting a medical nurse on a visiting basis, for additional payments. To take blood pressure and who knows what else. Miroslav and I could afford that now. True, Olga Nikolaevna objected that medical care wouldn't help her, that this was her fate. But an elderly woman couldn't have a different view.

I came to an agreement with Svetlana Denisenko, a young but experienced nurse from the regional clinic: she took it on with enthusiasm. And so the worry on that point receded.

The situation in Ostyor remained alarming. Mama sent frequent letters with detailed descriptions of Fima's behavior. And the accounts were like this: nervous breakdown but not for the hospital, resting quietly at home, loss of sleep, good appetite. Blyuma was offering help and watching his every step, so she'd moved in with Mama and Gilya. They'd allotted the small room that had previously been used for household needs to Blyuma and Fima; now there were two beds in there, right up against each other.

They'd registered Fima, though he hadn't gone in personally, so as not to attract attention. Gilya had a wide range of acquaintances so he'd assisted. Fima quit his job on his own accord. Also with Gilya's help.

Time passed quickly, though also tensely. Mishenka turned seven in September. Strictly by the rules, he shouldn't have started school until the next year, but then he would have been practically eight. Miroslav and I wanted him enrolled early and we had to come to a special agreement for that.

As far as me, personally, taking a job, Miroslav said:

"You have the household and practically my mother and our son and our future children on your shoulders. Your education will always stay with you. You can basically consider yourself a domestic pedagogue capable of handling everything."

In order to wrap things up on a good note, I went to the evening school where I'd intended to take a job and had already spoken with those in charge. I explained that I couldn't join the staff for the new school year because of family reasons. They assured me, with regret, that they'd always be waiting right there.

I had always considered—and continue to consider—that one must part with people in a respectful manner.

But that's not my point.

I'd prepared Mishenka well for school: his uniform, satchel, pencil case, textbooks, notebooks, and so forth, were in complete order. The distance to the educational institution was fine: fifteen minutes on foot and cross the street once, in a quiet spot at that.

The adoption process went through without complications. Mishenka was registered in the class grade book with Shulyak as his surname, Miroslavovich as his patronymic, and Ukrainian as his nationality. I liked Lyudmila Petrovna, his homeroom teacher, for her modesty and good-naturedness.

Complications had come up with Miroslav, though Svetlana Denisenko—whom I'd found through my own efforts and invited into Olga Nikolaevna's home—hit me with an unexpected low blow.

Of course there could be no talk about love here. This was the usual male impermanence. Romance based on a fresh outward appearance and a young woman's affected good-naturedness.

A chance event with treacherous consequences brought me to Olga Nikolaevna's with a gift. I'd managed to find some wonderful Chinese-made terry cloth towels at a haberdashery, while standing in line, by the way. The quality was delicately soft, the background had a tranquil light color, and the pattern was botanical and vivid. I took this as a hint that I needed to make my mother-in-law happy. Particularly since she always needed towels, sheets, and other items for hygiene because of the type of her illness. I headed off, intending to make it home by the end of Mishenka's school day.

I saw the full complement of them at Olga Nikolaevna's: Miroslav and Svetlana were sitting at the table, drinking tea. Olga Nikolaevna was snacking on something, too—a cup and plate stood on a stool by her bed. Zoya Ivanovna was sitting on the bed by Olga Nikolaevna, wearing a clean apron and watching for what else to serve or clear away.

Yes. A pleasant picture. If I'd been there instead of Svetlana. But I was standing by the door and nobody here was expecting me.

A woman doesn't need much for her heart to hint that something's amiss.

I showed surprise, nevertheless, as if nothing had happened:

"Miroslav, how good you're here! And Svetlanochka! How's Olga Nikolaevna's blood pressure? Olga Nikolaevna, how are you feeling?"

I headed toward the bed. You had to give Zoya Ivanovna credit: she tactfully stood and quickly left the room.

Based on the silence hanging in the air, it became clear to me that I was a hindrance in this case.

Miroslav cleared his throat and Svetlana pounded her little fist on his back, laughing:

"Miroslav Antonovich, what is this, frightened of your wife? Maya Abramovna, we were just talking about you. Miroslav was saying you know how to set a beautiful table. But forget to water the plants. And he always waters them instead of you."

Miroslav joined in:

"What plants are you talking about, Svetochka, it's one century plant, basically you don't have to water it for a hundred years."

I reacted quickly:

"We need to bring it here, by the way. You can make medicine from it. Both grind the leaves with honey and use the juice as nose drops. I've been planning on that for a long time. Maybe we should go get it right now, Miroslav? I didn't seem to notice the car by the building."

Miroslav answered with a slight delay:

"I let the chauffeur go. I'd been planning to stay a little while longer, then go home. As it happens, I was just about to. And now you're here."

"Home in the middle of the work day?" I expressed my surprise. "What, did you get sick? Or something else?"

"No, don't worry. Svetochka took my blood pressure. And listened to my heart. It's fine."

"Interesting. So that's the kind of medical nurses we have, they know how to listen to the heart?" I said. "Just like doctors.

Svetochka, is that really so, that you're allowed to listen to hearts? You need special medical preparation."

Svetlana was flustered, but answered with defiance:

"Of course I'm not a doctor, but I'm always alongside doctors and I learn various methods from them. I know how to recognize wheezing in the heart. My phonendoscope may be old, but it's good. One doctor gave it to me as a gift, in consideration of my achievements at work."

I quickly deciphered in my head what I'd heard and seen, and came to the conclusion that Miroslav and Svetlana had been intending to go somewhere together, but I'd interfered. And Olga Nikolaevna knew. And Zoya Ivanovna, too. It was completely humiliating that I'd shown up with towels.

I unwrapped the parcel nevertheless. I smoothly placed a towel on Olga Nikolaevna's chest—it was the largest, almost for the bathhouse.

"Here's a nice new towel for you, my dear Olga Nikolaevna. But I need to run. Mishenka will be back from school in no time at all. Goodbye. You, Miroslav, sit with your mother a while. Sit and talk for a while. As it is, neither I nor Mishenka nor your mother ever sees you. So at least let some one of us have the joy. Svetochka, are you leaving? Let's go together, I want to get some advice about Mishenka along the way."

This was against Svetlana's wishes, but she got up from the table and grabbed her purse, with her phonendoscope peering out: "Uh-huh, I still need to dash all around the district."

And only then did I grasp what had put me on my guard from the very beginning: Svetochka wasn't wearing a lab coat or a kerchief. She had on a narrow knee-length skirt and a thin little blouse with three-quarter-length sleeves and something lacy. Moreover, this was late autumn. People don't go to work around the district looking like that every day.

Miroslav was still sitting as he had been; he didn't even see us to the door. Only Zoya Ivanovna peered out of the kitchen, then immediately hid.

Yes, people give themselves away. If, of course, they still have a conscience left.

I struck up an insignificant conversation with Sveta.

To the question of how often she visited Olga Nikolaevna, she answered:

"Every day but Sunday, just as you and I agreed, Maya Abramovna. But I almost always come on Sundays, too."

"Well, that's unnecessary. Miroslav Antonovich comes on Sundays. I don't pay you for Sundays."

"And that's fine. I don't need the pay. Miroslav Antonovich, though, specifically considers Sunday the most important."

So that's how far it had gone. Instead of being with Mishenka—not to mention me—on Sundays, Miroslav was philandering the whole entire day with the medical nurse in plain sight of his ailing mother.

Miroslav came home literally five minutes after I returned. I'd even had a sneaking suspicion he was walking behind us. The strategy I'd chosen was: tell him my impression in no uncertain terms and let him dispel it however he wanted. And if he didn't want to, he could do as he wanted.

"Svetlana's been going to see Olga Nikolaevna for five months," I calmly began. "It seems to me that she appeals to you too much. I'm not taking exception. She's an appealing, pleasant girl. An ordinary, simple girl, as they say, that men like. They listen with their mouths wide open, ready to do anything for the sake of male attention. My question is different. How long ago did you decide to strike up a close relationship with her?"

Miroslav kept silent.

"Why are you silent? It's a simple, natural question. Mishenka and I haven't been seeing you at home for several months. You only eat and sleep here. Your whole inner life is taking place somewhere else. And now I understand where."

Miroslav kept silent.

"Our son will come home from school any minute and I intend to hear an answer from you before his arrival."

Miroslav said:

"You won't understand anything I can explain. Not because you're stupid. You're smart. Even very smart. It's not because I don't love you. I love you very much. But you won't understand my relationship with Svetlana. I immediately sensed she's kin to me. Like a sister. And my mother has come to love her like a daughter. This is a matter of feelings of kinship. I don't see her as a woman. I see her as a sister. She spoon-feeds Mama. She takes out her chamber pot. Even though we don't pay her money for that. She's as simple as the truth. That's not my thought, I picked it up from a book. You're mistakenly suspecting infidelity in Sveta's and my relationship. Love only lives independently, not accounting for circumstances. But I'm completely surrounded by circumstances. I can't not pay attention to that."

I listened, not believing him. Miroslav usually preferred to keep silent. Each word was clear on its own. But taken together, I didn't understand.

"Tell me in one word: do you and I have a family?"

"We do."

"Is Mishenka your son?"

"Mine."

"Should I bear you a daughter?"

"Yes."

I nodded as a sign of affirmation and started fixing lunch.

"She's kin. And I'm from another planet," I thought. At the time, I didn't formulate that thought properly in words, but many years later, after mankind's flight into outer space, I fully realized what my husband wanted to say.

We never returned to the question of Svetlana Denisenko. I stopped going to see Olga Nikolaevna. I gave money for Svetlana's work to Miroslav in an envelope with the sum written large. I purposely underscored the figures twice in bold lines. There it was, the price of phantom happiness. Along with that, I keenly enquired after Olga Nikolaevna's health like before, asking each time at length.

A heartening event took place shortly thereafter: our telephone was installed. Though I had nobody to call, I often picked it up and said whatever came into my head, paying no attention to the piercing dial tone inside the receiver. I could dial any incomplete number and speak into the quietness. But I liked that I wasn't pretending to actually speak. Because I never embellish reality.

But that's not my point.

I headed up the parents' committee. I had a large role in the life of Mishenka's school and his class in particular. I went to see the families of children who were behind in their work, gave explanations and reprimands, analyzed the circumstances, and advised on how to handle homework with children so they'd excel better. Especially since boys and girls were now going to school together.

Lyudmila Petrovna praised Mishenka, who was always first in everything: both for schoolwork and social activities.

There were unpleasant moments, too. One time Misha came home from school and asked me directly: "Mama, are you a Yid woman?"

"In the first place, I'm not a Yid woman but a Jewish woman. In the second place, stand up straight and don't slump when you're speaking. In the third place, who told you foolishness like that, that means absolutely nothing to normal intelligent people?"

"Sashka Sidlyarevsky told me you're a Yid woman because you stick your long nose all over the place. You came to his house and made a scene with his mother. And it wasn't her fault. And you tortured her with your Yid lecturing. And you're Abramovna. Sashka told me you're going to deny being a Yid woman. That I'm supposed to say Abramovna to you in the Jew way, so I don't say the 'r' right and you wouldn't be able to prove anything to me."

"Well, let's sort through this."

There was no hiding the truth, I'd been waiting for this kind of conversation. And now it had begun.

I calmly uttered what had matured in my heart long ago:

"Yes, Mishenka, I'm a Jewish woman. Some people consider that shameful. But I don't. They can call me a Yid woman to offend me. But I don't care at all about that word. Do. Not. Care. And I don't stick my nose just anywhere, but where people need help. And so Sasha Sidlyarevsky's repeating what his mother said; he's still little. It's just offensive to her that my son's a top student and hers is below average. That's the reason. Beyond that, my nose isn't long. You tell me: Is my nose long?"

Mishenka lowered his head and didn't look at my nose or anything else.

"And furthermore. If you're going to pay attention to bad words directed at Jews, you'll have a hard time living. Since you're my son, you're a Jew, too, even if only half."

"Which half?" Mishenka asked.

"Either. The right or the left. It doesn't matter. Choose for yourself. For clarity."

Misha kept quiet. He was thinking.

"Let's decide that your left side is the Jewish one. Where's your left hand? Correct. So that whole, whole side is Jewish."

"And what's there, in that half?"

"It's the very same blood as in your whole body. And the very same organs. Because they're in pairs. And they're sy-met-ri-cal. You'll study geometry later. And botany. And biology."

"Is everything in pairs?"

"We'll talk about that next time."

I could see from my son's face that the pedagogical method had worked. Beyond that, various subjects from the world of knowledge were used, as opposed to the dark feelings that bearers of age-old prejudices had proposed to my son in exchange for a broad horizon.

Here Misha mumbled: "Well and the second, you know, half, it's not, well . . ."

"Your second half is Ukrainian. Your father is Miroslav Antonovich Shulyak and you know that perfectly well. It's an absolutely Ukrainian surname."

"But in kindergarten my surname was Surkis. What kind of name is that?"

"Nothing. Remember that. No-thing."

As a question is posed, so it is answered.

I had repealed Fima. I wasn't planning to repeal myself.

After doing his homework, Mishenka was absorbed in playing himself at checkers. Then he abruptly announced he was running outside for a minute, to bring a book to his schoolmate in the next building.

He was gone for a long time, so long I started worrying. I went out to the yard: I knew a secret place where the little boys hid and played their foolish games.

Misha was sitting under a tree, right on the ground—February
had already come, with snow—and he was looking at his little
left hand. He was holding a large nail in his right. Rusty and dirty.
He kept bringing the nail toward his hand, then drawing it away.
As if he were trying to resolve himself to do something.

I took the nail from him.

Yes, every person travels a path toward self-awareness. But why
attempt to mutilate yourself with a rusty nail? Or whatever it was
Mishenka wanted to do.

That evening I thrashed my son with a belt for the first time in my
life. Mishenka screamed loudly.

Luckily, Miroslav came home from work late and didn't witness
that disgraceful picture.

Mishenka never again returned to the conversation on the
Jewish topic.

I noticed he was gravitating more and more toward Miroslav.
When the three of us took walks together, Misha would take
Miroslav by the hand, address him more often, and try to pay him
other forms of attention. That stung me each time, though not too
badly. I drove off unpleasant thoughts. The boy was maturing and
reaching for his strong father, not his fragile mother.

Unfortunately, 1963 was still a long way off, so cosmonaut number
five, Bykovsky, had yet to take flight. And, of course, this would
have been a life-affirming example since cosmonaut Bykovsky is
half Jewish. His mother, as it happens, is Jewish. This was broadly
discussed in Jewish circles as a change for the better.

Meanwhile, Mishenka continued making me happy with his
success at checkers. A famous national-level checkers grandmaster
came to Kiev—Veniamin Borisovich Gorodetsky, the USSR
champion—and spoke at the Pioneer Palace where Mishenka played.

Of all the members of the checkers club, Gorodetsky particularly accentuated Mishenka as showing great promise. These weren't unfounded assertions, either. When Mishenka personally played against Gorodetsky, it ended in a tie.

I was present and saw how the master got carried away when playing against the boy; there could be no question of yielding. Gorodetsky advised me not to abandon my efforts and to do everything so my son continued his active engagement in the sport of checkers.

Now, with regard to the possible second child.

The second child turned out to be impossible. I won't go into details. I'll say only that, of course, I was not to blame. Everything was in complete order in my body but the pregnancies didn't hold and terminated on their own, at the very start. The doctors tossed up their hands. Miroslav was upset each time and didn't want to resign himself to it. He made no verbal reproaches. But I sensed the reproaches everywhere: either the food didn't taste good or a shirt wasn't ironed or Mishenka had scattered checkers and textbooks all over and I hadn't picked them up.

The child, by the way, needed to do his schoolwork and I needed something, too. And Miroslav had abandoned the home. We never did install the bathtub.

And there was this.

An important job puts major obligations on a person. Sometimes the obligations become overwhelming. Miroslav's character was mild and accommodating. He hadn't noticed that some Prikhodko had schemed against him—all I knew from what my husband said about Prikhodko was that he loved speaking during meetings and making unfounded criticisms.

This Prikhodko criticized enough that, according to the party line, Miroslav was requested to resign because he was being transferred to another job. But we were in the queue for an apartment. Meaning Miroslav was in the queue for it as someone registered in a room of a communal apartment with his invalid mother. He was supposed to receive a two-room apartment any day now, and I'd planned for Miroslav and me to move into that apartment along with Mishenka, and bring his mother here, to Bessarabka.

I wasn't clinging to that director's chair, but the unjustified firing was a strong blow for Miroslav. He was named chief engineer of a third-rate enterprise that produced furniture. Not in his field, not anything.

He remained in that apartment queue but stepped aside for an indefinite period, for obvious reasons. Beyond that, his mother's health was in a fluid state and worsening. She was already absolutely weak. And if she died we might not live to see a two-room apartment.

Svetlana Denisenko—rather than Zoya Ivanovna—had already been living with her for a long time, though. And I wasn't certain, but maybe Svetlana was registered there on some sort of false premise. Under a guardianship or something. As before, I was allocating the money for looking after Olga Nikolaevna and, as before, I underlined the sum with bold lines.

But that's not my point.

The firing occurred in 1960, right at the end of May, as it happens. Miroslav had already managed to enroll Mishenka for his camp trip, for all three sessions, as usual.

I'd been whirling around at home all those years, rushing from Miroslav to Mishenka, accommodating them both. And what had come of that? My husband had been entirely consumed by his job: from the first instant in that new place, he'd taken to mastering its unfamiliar specifics. Our son had everything provided at camp.

I'll admit I'd been quietly saving money because I'd econo-mized rationally in running the household. As a mother and a wife, I constantly thought about the hard times that slyly lay in wait.

Authoritative rumors about monetary reform urged me to spend the savings. I bought four gold rings and earrings. Very expensive, though not especially pretty. Naturally, it wasn't possible to show them to Miroslav, so I hid them away safely.

Yes. Hard times had come. And they'd come for me, personally. Though they weren't tied to monetary resources.

The atmosphere in the house was latently white-hot. Despite all my futile efforts. During all the years of our life together, Miroslav and I had never once traveled anywhere together. He preferred spending his vacations in Kiev so he could visit his mother every day. When Mishenka was in kindergarten, that issue didn't particu-larly anger me. But now Misha was in school and would spend the whole summer at a Pioneer camp in Sednev. It wasn't that far from the city, but wasn't close, either. It was much closer to Ostyor.

When Mishenka started making summer trips to camp, Miroslav and I went to visit the child all the time, every Saturday. As one should. True, I didn't drop in on Mama despite Ostyor's close proximity to the camp.

This time, I made an original decision: to go and vacation on my own. And not foist my will on anyone.

First and foremost, I was thinking about my husband. It was best for him to be alone for a period of mental realignment. With his own thoughts and aspirations. To share his thinking with his mother. Sing folk songs with Svetlana at supper. He himself told me how well Svetochka sang.

I announced to Miroslav that I needed to go to Ostyor to see Mama and Gilya. So my husband wouldn't get the wrong idea about that, I invented details about an alleged letter from Mama, who was

sending my letters to the post office, for pickup of course, as was
her long-time habit: Mama wasn't feeling good, we hadn't seen each
other in many years, she needed my help around the house, and the
like. The main thing, though, was that I accentuated my attention on
the location of the children's camp and that I could visit Mishenka
nearly every other day. And that way I'd be of help in two important
directions.

Miroslav treated what I said with understanding and even a sort
of gladness.

"You're right, you go. I'd dreamt of going to the sea with you
and Mishenka. Like regular people do. Svetochka's doing everything necessary, but Mama can't get by for long without someone
near and dear. You and I will still make it to the sea. Later. But this
way Mishenka will be supervised and all your relatives, too, in one
fell swoop."

I didn't respond to "Mama" or "later" or "Svetochka."

I wanted to go to the sea. To see a resort, take part in the southern
holiday life. Had I really not earned that at thirty years old? But I
had no right to provide fodder for Miroslav to worry. And going
to see my own mother was something he understood without
questioning.

I was not, in fact, planning to stay with Mama and Gilya. It was
much better to rent a little room by the Desna, right on the riverside.
To go see Mishenka and delight in nature. Spend time, as long as
I could stand, but best until fall.

By that time, Ostyor had become an enviable vacation spot.
Dachafolk from Moscow and Leningrad—not to mention Kiev—
rented houses or rooms and vacationed all summer, along with their
children. Beyond that, rest homes for the officer corps from various
branches of the armed forces had been located near Ostyor since
pre-war times. They organized dances and entertainment and there

was a bazaar that evoked amazement because of its abundance and inexpensive prices. So life was humming along.

Naturally, Mama was happy about my arrival. She was surprised I wasn't staying with her and Gilya, but agreed it would be best for me to be completely free of everyone surrounding me. And let people talk if that fact was interesting for them to discuss.

Fima and Blyuma greeted me nicely. Fima recognized my face, but couldn't remember my name and addressed me as "woman" or "young lady." Blyuma displayed all sorts of obligingness that I didn't need from anyone.

She and Fima earned money by gluing cardboard boxes. Working at home. It was relaxed and didn't require responsibility, but brought in some money for foodstuffs. Depending on their mood, sometimes Gilya and Mama joined in during the evenings.

Mama assured me Fima wasn't deadweight to carry around, though he'd become something akin to a small child for all three of them—Mama, Gilya, and Blyuma. Hope remained, too, that Fima would come to his senses, but I thought the local doctor's opinion wasn't worth serious attention. Fima was no more. In his place was another person who held no interest at all for me. I even told Mama that. She sighed, understanding but disapproving.

"Fima gave his life to you, Mayechka. It's very bad if you don't understand that."

"Don't assign grades, Mama."

I didn't squeeze anything out of myself beyond those words. I had nothing left inside.

Convinced that everything was fine with Mama, I shifted my attention elsewhere. There was a lot around me to be interested in.

And my soul had gradually begun begging for a holiday filled with new sensations.

I met a man on the beach, completely by chance. He noticed me first. Only one thought managed to flash in my head: he's so interesting. Then I was no longer thinking.

Yes, destiny had taken place.

His name was Mark Mikhailovich Faiman. Muscovite. I liked a lot about him and I'm not speaking of his face. His face was astonishingly handsome. Although also not well-proportioned. Large nose, deep-set eyes, broad mouth. All that taken together, though, was a charming picture.

A Jew by nationality, he said about himself: "The nation doesn't interest me. Enough's been said about that."

A correct formulation. Especially since everybody took him for a Georgian or, if nothing else, an Armenian.

I sometimes caught an accent of unknown origin in his speech. I asked what it was. He told me he was born in Lithuania, which later became Poland and then Belorussia right before the war, and that he knew three languages, not including Russian and Yiddish, so all sorts of things slipped in. Out of curiosity, I asked him to speak a little with me in the languages he'd mentioned, but Marik wouldn't do it. He said, seriously, that it was unpleasant for him to recall the pronunciation.

Marik would wait for me somewhere nearby when I went to visit Mishenka, meaning the meetings with my son didn't drag on much. Though I asked in detail about his friends, his own behavior, and everything happening at camp. I talked several times with his group's counselor.

Misha was growing up before my eyes. I didn't tell him right away that I was vacationing in Ostyor. So as not to dampen his enthusiasm. I warned Miroslav by telephone, from the post office, that he not go to visit his son yet, that he rest and not expend his energy. Miroslav, by the way, didn't argue.

Marik was spending his vacation in Ostyor with distant relatives. The unavoidable happened: we were seen together. Our eyes and movements gave us away. In Ostyor, where everybody knows each other and follows local changes, the rumors quickly reached Mama's ears.

She herself showed up at the house where I was staying and—right in front of Marik—asked for all to hear: "Maya, have you no shame?"

"No, Mama. I've fallen in love with Mark and we're going to marry. And if you can comprehend this: twenty days is very, very serious."

And so Mama became the first person to find out about our plan for a future life together.

The plan had the following sequence: I divorce Miroslav, take Mishenka, and move to Marik's. At the same time, I exchange the apartment for Moscow. Marik had two rooms in a communal apartment at his disposal. By adding my living space to it, it would work out to a very decent two-room apartment in an unassuming area, not in the center.

Marik's profession was a moneymaker: he was a clock- and watchmaker of the highest qualification. He worked primarily with ancient timepieces. Marik sensed the mechanism not with his brains but with his gut, as he put it. Formally, he worked at a workshop, but in practice he saw, at home, a broad client base from all over Moscow and even other cities. People from museums often turned to Marik for consultations.

Of course I asked if he'd had dealings with the clock in the Spasskaya Tower. A wonderful radio show, "The Kremlin Clocks," had stuck in my mind. Marik responded with regret that he'd dreamed of rooting around in there, but had not yet had the occasion.

To make a long story short, Marik could make an additional payment during an exchange, if need be, since he had the means at his disposal.

There was bother again. But love justifies everything, even love in and of itself. And passion all the more so.

I left for Kiev without delay. Marik headed for Moscow. We agreed to keep each other informed. To call every day, morning and evening.

And here, my husband Miroslav stood tall before me.

He answered in a raised tone after my brief announcement regarding the fact that I'd met another man and was going to marry him:

"You're mistaken if you think you surprised me. You married yourself off to me with a deception about pregnancy. Fine. I loved you then and forgave you. You hung your son on me. It's good I came to love him, too. But what if I hadn't? Had you thought about that?"

I was petrified with my whole heart. All the lying and deception. From his side.

He went on mercilessly:

"I saved myself at Mama's and you built far-reaching plans at the same time. Fine. Do what you want. I'm not interested. I'm only interested in how Misha will react."

He'd struck the dearest, most painful point.

Yes. One can never see into another person's soul.

Miroslav left to spend the night at his mother's. And from that moment on, he only showed up at Bessarabka to pick up his things. He spoke to me through his teeth, only out of necessity.

We wrote a petition for divorce by mutual consent. By law, Miroslav was compelled to pay alimony for Misha. Of course not based on a director's income. But the law is the law.

One evening, Miroslav caught me during a telephone conversation with Marik. I wrapped up the conversation quickly. But Miroslav guessed who I was talking with.

"Maya, I recognize your voice, the one that cooed at me at one time. I'm in great pain. I'll let you think a little more. I do love you. Don't ruin our son's life. Think."

I answered firmly: No and no.

With all the new troubles, we were neglecting Mishenka. They called us from the Pioneer camp, wondering, at our son's request, what had happened, why we hadn't been coming. Why? We were sick, but we'd visit Mishenka in the near future.

I went alone. I didn't inform Miroslav.

I immediately set to explaining the situation.

"Mishenka, you're already grown-up, you'll be eleven soon. You tied at checkers with Gorodetsky himself. I need to tell you straight that I met a new man and fell in love with him. Miroslav Antonovich and I are getting a divorce. You and I are going to live in Moscow now. The capital of our Motherland, as you know. Kiev is the capital of the Ukrainian Soviet Socialist Republic, but what is Moscow the capital of?"

Misha kept silent.

"Moscow is the capital of our whole Motherland, the Soviet Union. Do you want to live in Moscow, where the Kremlin is?"

Misha kept silent.

"It's very important for me to hear out your thoughts. I'm your mother and you're the person dearest to me. But that doesn't mean I should take only your opinion into consideration. Each person has his own opinion. It needs to be heard out in order to try to come to a mutual opinion later. Do you understand?"

Misha nodded and asked: "When?"

"If it's according to plan, by September. So you can start school without a delay. In the new place."

My son and I parted warmly. I warned him that I was very busy and wouldn't be showing up in the near future. Misha didn't ask about Miroslav. And I paid no attention to that. I would have constructed the discussion differently had I known Miroslav had gone to see Misha several days earlier. And had set something forth himself. But I hadn't known. And it was useless by the time I found out.

As the senior camp counselor told it, Misha ran off to the river without permission, went far out into the deep water, then stood for a long time in one place; fishermen saw him. They shouted to him to come ashore, but the boy didn't answer or move from his spot. They used force to drag him out. Misha cried and screamed for them to let him go into the deep water alone. They barely restrained him.

That strange display put the camp counselor on his guard. He called Kiev so as not to take responsibility upon himself. I came immediately. Picked up Misha. Brute strength had to be applied since he was kicking and didn't want to go.

I was only able to make out one thing coherently:

"Papa's going to pick me up, he said so. He came to see me before you. He's picking me up."

Those are the conditions I ended up in at the very moment I needed to throw all my strength into the divorce and apartment exchange. I was afraid to leave Misha alone in the apartment or let him go into the yard by himself. Particularly since Miroslav's influence could manifest itself at any second.

And then there came a liberating thought: send Mishenka to Ostyor to Mama and Gilya's. A change of scenery, within a circle of loving people, always has a beneficial effect. Of course my mother's quarrel with me personally had no bearing on her grandson.

I sent Mama a telegram summoning her for a telephone conversation and said I'd bring Mishenka for the remainder of the summer—nearly two months. I didn't go on and on with the conversation because it was hard to hear.

Misha was glad for the announcement about the trip to his grandmother's. I thought he'd forgotten Ostyor. It turned out he remembered.

In order to reinforce what I'd achieved, I asked if he missed his father.

Misha looked me straight in the eye and answered: "No."

I had no other choice but to believe him.

Marik found an apartment exchange, moreover it was a very good exchange.

In any event, only toward December did I move to Moscow.

Mishenka had to go to school in Ostyor. It hadn't seemed possible to combine the apartment exchange process and Mishenka's schoolwork in Kiev. I understood that certain losses on the level of knowledge would occur, but then again, I was calm about my son's health. Under Mama and Gilya's supervision, he had an even disposition and regarded the necessity of the delay in Ostyor with an understanding uncharacteristic of a boy his age. He'd made friends among his peers in Ostyor during the summer and expressed no regrets whatsoever about parting with his Kiev friends and classmates.

Mishenka and I communicated by telephone: I used telegrams to summon Mama to the public telephone booths at the post office, where she would show up with Mishenka.

My heart sank when I recalled this picture.

I'd come to Ostyor at the end of August with documents for registering Mishenka at the local school and a huge bundle of his fall and winter things. I also brought significant material help for supporting Mishenka. My divorce from Miroslav had already been formalized, but the alimony had not yet come through. I had to sell one of the rings. I also grabbed the railroad set Fima had once given as a gift. I couldn't bring myself to throw away a good item.

But that's not my point.

In Ostyor, I found only Mama at home. Gilya was at work. I wondered where Mishenka was spending his time. It turned out Misha, Fima, and Blyuma went fishing on the Desna. I focused my attention on the fact that Mishenka shouldn't be near water: he and deep water did not get along well. Beyond that, he was in the company of one not particularly smart woman and one crazy man. To which my mother responded that Blyuma was actually quite smart, despite her appearance. And beyond not being dangerous, Fima had made significant progress with respect to returning to normalcy. On the whole, his health had strengthened. And Mama particularly noted that Blyuma hoped to become pregnant.

The main thing, though, was that this fishing had become a salvation for everybody. In the first place, it was good food: the fishermen brought home huge catfish, breams, and pikes. In the second place, there was the joy of cleaning the fish together, right in the yard, then fixing it in the summer kitchen with stories and reminiscing.

I asked what the reminiscing was about. Mama answered that the reminiscing had a most general character. Gilya made a survey of his numerous trips throughout the region, in the distant and recent past, and told about the war and about ancient life in Ostyor. Blyuma talked about Chernigov and the books she read in great quantities. They'd been subscribing to the literary digest *Roman-gazeta* since last year.

Mishenka mostly listened. And actively asked questions. Fima always kept quiet. And often smiled.

I figured there was no danger. There were positive characteristics present in the boy's communications with Fima. He was developing skills for patience and indulging another person, particularly someone who looked adult. All the more so since Fima was not disposed toward Mishenka as a son. Either that sliver in his brain was locked shut or I didn't understand something. It didn't matter.

Mama also told me Miroslav had come calling several times. And taken long outings with Mishenka. Misha was upset after the meetings and ran outside in the morning and tore around with the boys. He ate well.

I didn't recognize Mishenka when all the members of the household returned that evening. He was as tanned as an Ethiopian. His eyes were huge and he was all skin and bones.

I rushed to embrace and kiss him, but he pushed me aside with a hand and looked at his grandmother. Maybe for her to defend him.

Misha had recalled all his Jewish words in Ostyor and picked up new ones.

I reprimanded Mama:

"Why are you giving him unnecessary information? You keep giving it. And you're probably recalling everything about Ostyor's Jewish purpose."

Mama answered with a challenge:

"It was Jewish. And we're talking about 'was.' I don't specially give him anything. It's that kind of place. Wherever you poke it, it's Jewish and Jewish."

"And where else is there a place that Mishenka will apply all that now? They'll hound him. It would be better for him to go to a checkers club."

"We don't have one for checkers. Only for chess. He and Fima play fierce matches of Chapaev checkers. And if he's serious about wanting to play, he sets up the checkers and plays against himself."

We organized a festive luncheon before I left. Gilya, Mama, Mishenka, Blyuma, and Fima gathered at the table.

Fima sat for a brief minute and then left for his tiny room, to glue boxes.

We talked about various topics. Then, after Gilya drank a shot, he abruptly proposed the following toast: the Jewish l'chaim.

And he illustrated that toast with a story:

"During my time as a partisan in the Great Patriotic War, I was a participant in a sort of incident. I've never told this for all to hear, but I want to now. Mishenka knows. He's up on things. Right, Mishka?" Gilya winked at him. "In the winter of 1943 on one of our battle operations, we blew up a bridge near the city of Rovno. It injured one of our boys. And how: it tore off his arms and legs, and his eyes were gone, too. His name was Semyon, I remember that as if it were today and will never forget. I personally was next to him at that moment. It barely hit me. He was conscious. I asked him if maybe I should shoot him, as a comrade, since he was armless, legless, and blind. Straight from the heart, I thought there wouldn't be much of a life for him. But he said there was no need. My comrades and I carried him to our camp on a sheepskin jacket and the jacket got all wet from Semyon's blood. We sent our battle comrade to the mainland. I don't know his further fate. I often reflect on why he didn't accept death from a dear friend and preferred—at that moment—life in such a shattered condition. What tortures me most is this: What if Semyon didn't believe me when I said he no longer had legs or arms or eyes?"

We drank.

I was watching Mishenka, not Gilya. The boy was shining with an inner light. And I felt uneasy. Not even as a mother, but as a person. Here they were cramming this and similar kinds of tales into Misha. As if that's what a child's consciousness needed.

Yes. Those moments cost me sorrowful wrinkles and several years of life.

There's not very much space inside a person's psyche, though. And I found myself completely caught up in Marik. He'd been waiting long years to meet a woman like me. And I'd fallen genuinely in love for the first time.

I painstakingly furnished and equipped a new three-room apartment in a building on Bolshaya Yakimanka Street, number 24. Set right in a yard lined with lilacs. The apartment was very small in terms of total area. But three rooms is three rooms.

Marik helped with everything. After all, I knew nothing in Moscow. I had to learn to speak differently. With different intonations. Despite the fact that I'd always watched my own Russian speech, the influence of the Ukrainian, plus the Yiddish I'd mastered slightly from hearing it, beginning in early childhood, made themselves known every second and more than once served as the root of joking remarks.

It worked out that no official meeting took place between Marik and my relatives. He introduced me to his Moscow loved ones right away, though. They took a liking to me.

Marik was an orphan as a result of the war. He ended up in Moscow in the care of a distant aunt and uncle, the Galperins. Their three sons had perished at the front with varying fates. The last to leave this life was the auntie's husband, who was arrested in 1949 because of the Zionist question. He'd worked

at the Second Clock Factory, moreover since 1924. He'd come
to the factory as a craftsman, when the enterprise was formed.
One time during a work gathering, he said, in a positive sense,
that clocks run identically everywhere. Meaning that all peoples
around the world look at clocks and see the same thing. What did
they see? Correct: communism. And he added a Jewish saying:
"The house is burning but the clock still keeps time." But that's
neither here nor there.

They reminded him of that when his time came. He was taken.
They decided he'd been talking about some kind of Jewish clocks
he was allegedly dreaming of inventing so they'd show the time
properly to Jews. But not to other Soviet people. And this was
allegedly how a planned plot would come to victory.

Marik worked at the factory during that time, too, as an
apprentice to his uncle. A regular criminal gang. But for some
reason they didn't touch Marik.

Their famous relative, Natan Yakovlevich Beinfest—who in his
youth knew Grigory Kotovsky himself because Kotovsky lived
near Belaya Tserkov during the Civil War—was a military attorney
by line of work. He fought his way to a meeting with Prosecutor
General Rudenko and declared:

"You looked straight into the eyes of the damned fascist ring-
leaders and their hirelings of all stripes in their conquered den
at the Nuremburg trial. Look into the eyes of my relative, Isaak
Shmulevich Galperin, born in 1890, who was criminally arrested.
You'll immediately discern that he is guilty of nothing. Especially
because Galperin and the best masters from the factory labored
together in the city of Chistopol during the years of the war with
Hitler, for the good of the Motherland and the military industry,
and he was awarded a medal for that. Otherwise, he would have
personally gone to the front. But the motherland said, Don't go. So
he didn't go. But his children all went and fell as heroes. And now

my Party membership card and all my military awards guarantee what I'm saying."

Marik particularly dwelled on Chistopol because he'd written a note by hand that his aunt dictated, so Beinfest wouldn't forget. Marik wrote it instead of his aunt because his aunt was crying and couldn't see anything on the paper. Marik misspelled "Chistopol." Beinfest read it and made a scene, that Marik had bungled such a crucial matter as a person's life.

Marik cried a lot, but his aunt didn't console him. It should be noted that Marik was twenty-one years old then.

And so. Galperin was released with an acquittal in 1956; it wasn't a personal release, but for many people at once.

The aunt died back in 1951 from fear and grief. Beyond that, she suffered tremendously from ever-present tension: she was awaiting the arrival of authorized persons from the housing committee.

The housing was transferred, in full, to Marik after Galperin's death. It was clear that, in all fairness, one room would need to be given to someone else. What was a lone person going to do with two rooms? But a certain influential relative used connections and fought for the housing.

Marik still had numerous family members with varying degrees of closeness: second cousins, step-relatives, and the like. Permanent relationships had been maintained. They took turns gathering for holidays at someone's house. They hurried us about Mishenka's move so the whole family could assemble.

Marik and I reasoned that it wasn't worth tearing Mishenka away in the middle of the school year. We postponed his move until summer. Especially since I was expecting a child.

A little girl was born. Ellochka.

But that's not my point.

And so, in June of 1961, Misha joined ranks with the rest of us: Ellochka, Marik, Mishenka, and I. Ellochka was two months old and Mishenka was almost twelve.

Marik went to Ostyor to get Mishenka. He delivered him in good shape.

A friendship sprang up between them. Though without excess words. Mishenka didn't call Marik "Papa" and he avoided titles as such. As a last resort, he called him by his first name and used the formal "you." I was so caught up in Ellochka that no time at all could be found for establishing connections between Marik and Misha.

Misha attended a nearby school. He was in good standing. He'd resumed his pursuit of checkers at the Pioneer Palace on Polyanka Street.

Of course he was teased at school and in the yard because of his Ukrainian-Russian-Jewish speech. Misha was able to turn this into something fun and amusing, though, and purposely mangled words even more. That's how he quickly became a favorite among his schoolmates.

Miroslav conscientiously sent alimony. I didn't raise the question of Misha's adoption with Marik. I didn't see the point.

One time, though, he said:

"What would you think if I were to adopt Mishka? You're Faiman, Ellochka's Faiman, I'm Faiman, but Mishka's Shulyak. It's silly. Not family-like. Let's wrap up this question. Do you agree?"

I joked it off, saying there's no such thing as two fathers and there was no use fussing with paperwork. Deep down, though, I reasoned this way: Miroslav had done some very good things for Misha. Let Misha's patronymic be Miroslavovich. And let Misha be recorded in his passport as a Ukrainian. Because who knew how life would turn.

So I told Marik:

"Listen to this idea instead. A surname is nothing, zip. Nonsense. I don't feel like pestering Mishenka about it."

"Then you should refuse the alimony from Shulyak. That's probably the right thing to do. Misha's now living with us on a full-fledged basis. That means I should provide for him the same as for Ellochka. We're one family. Miroslav Antonovich is another. Don't you agree?"

I expressed my fervent approval.

Even when we were finalizing our divorce, Miroslav requested that I write to him at the main Kiev post office if anything came up. I'd left the same kind of address for him, but in Moscow.

I wrote about the alimony.

I received a letter in response:

"Hello, Maya!

"Three years have passed since we separated. I haven't seen Mishenka for two of those years. He's been living in Moscow that whole damned time. I miss him a lot. What is he like now? Send a photograph.

"Regarding the alimony, I'm prepared to say the following: so you know, I'll be demoted at my job in the near future. So the alimony doesn't come as a surprise, my salary will be cut significantly. I'll send money to Misha personally. If you don't need it in your new life, open a bank account, and save it for his adulthood. I'd save it myself here in Kiev. But I know you through and through. I'm not sure I'd be able to find Misha at the right time to give him the funds.

"I thought for a long time about how to proceed so it's most useful for Misha. There's this, too. Keep in mind that I save all the stubs of the receipts for sending money. And I'll send money in the future. And inquire about it with you. Don't worry and don't doubt.

"Hello to Misha and your husband Mark."

For what? Why? It was unknown.

I told Mark I'd renounced the alimony and I wrote Miroslav a letter with several statements:

"Dear Miroslav!

"I'll do as you wish. I'll start a bankbook for when Mishenka becomes an adult. I can give you an accounting at any second.

"With gratitude for our good years together. Maya.

"I'm not sending along greetings from Misha since it's exam time at school now and I can't disturb him with worries about the past.

"I'm sending a photograph of our whole family: Marik, Ellochka, Mishenka, and I. Send the money to this address: Moscow, Main Post Office, Hold for Maya Abramovna Faiman."

I very clearly wrote "Handle with care, photo!" on the envelope in various places. Then, after I'd sealed the envelope, I realized I should have put the date on the back of the snapshot and written something, as one should for a keepsake. But it couldn't be unstuck.

Yes. He'd written his way. And I'd written mine.

Every summer, Misha asked to go to his grandmother's in Ostyor. Mark and Ellochka and I went to the sea for at least a month each summer without fail. We wanted, of course, to bring Misha with us, too. But he wouldn't go for anything. Only to his grandmother's. Well, fine.

What really surprised me was Mishenka's character. He only went to the Palace of Pioneers and Schoolchildren for a very short time, about a half year. He quit without explanation. They called from there, asking that—in light of his excellent abilities and because it's bad to bury talent—I influence my son since he could become a candidate for master and all that before long, and travel the whole world for competitions.

Marik and I held a joint discussion with Mishenka on the subject. He listened well, thoughtfully.

In explaining his conduct, Mishenka stated: "It's not interesting."

And no matter how we tried, Mishenka never went back to lessons.

Mishenka was either calm or thoroughly high-strung. Especially his eyes. He tried not to look at me.

Marik fussed with watches and clocks from morning until night. And I with Ellochka. Misha would surround himself with textbooks in the kitchen, but only for appearances: he'd be reading unrelated books. Or playing himself at checkers.

Marik went into the kitchen—not at mealtime, but to drink some tea—and asked: "So, who's winning?"

Misha answered seriously: "Today I'm playing against some (he gave the surname of a classmate or someone else). And he's winning. There's nothing I can do."

Marik told him: "How's that? He's within your power. However you make a move for him is how it'll be."

Condescendingly, and even insultingly, Misha said: "I have no power over him. He is who he is. He has his own manner and his own mind. I can't adjust his brain."

And then Marik said: "How's that if you're playing for him?"

Misha: "Well, I can but I don't want to. It's not interesting. And a game's a game."

In all seriousness.

Marik was drinking his tea. He was looking at the board (by this time an expensive wooden board, a gift from Marik, instead of cardboard, like when Mishenka was a child) and not understanding anything. He shook his head.

Misha was moving the pieces. He finished the game, scooped the checkers into a bunch, placed his hand on top, fingers splayed as if he wanted to collect all the checkers in his hand and throw them like a grenade.

"Marik, I've nominated you to play against me tomorrow."

Mishenka was thirteen years old then.

Marik told me about that and wondered what I thought. I explained that the boy was at an awkward age. And that for his own entertainment he imagined he was playing against someone specific, not against himself. And each person had his own character, so Misha maintained a line for each, befitting the person's character. As a smart child, Mishenka stuck strictly to that line of each character. And moved his checkers accordingly. Nothing complicated, if you think about it. That kind of behavior testified to the boy's exceptional development.

The next day, Marik looked at the board and asked: "Are you playing against me?"

"Yes. You're trying. But nothing's working out for you. I have you surrounded. It's also interesting: you made the mistake you always make. Take a look . . ."

And he began explaining to Marik how Marik had allegedly made an incorrect move right from the start and brought defeat upon himself.

Misha's eyes were flashing, his ears were red. He poked his finger at the board:

"Well, take a look, take a look, right from the beginning, the first move. When will you start thinking?"

Marik put him in his place gently, in a fatherly way:

"Misha, stop with the show. You're playing against yourself. You won against yourself. I have nothing to do with it."

And he turned to leave the kitchen.

Misha threw the board at his back, with the checkers on it. It didn't reach.

Marik wasn't offended. He said:

"I had a situation once, too. I flung a watchcase with the parts into the face of a customer who taught me how to handle his watch and where to place which wheel. And there was a lot there that was sharp and prickly. Fine. It happens. You're a good boy. A hothead."

Mishenka received his passport at sixteen. Nationality: Ukrainian. After his father. He hadn't discussed it with me. What was there to discuss, anyway? Mishenka showed me the document when I asked. I leafed through all the little pages respectfully.

"Congratulations, Mishenka. You're an adult now."

He nodded and plainly said:

"Don't think anything of it, but I registered as Ukrainian so as not to deal with fools. Don't be offended, Mama, I didn't have you in mind."

I hadn't even thought that. But it turned out Mishenka had very much been pondering it.

Other than that, it was "Yes, Mama" and "No, Mama." And not a word more. Mishenka performed his obligations around the house exemplarily. He took out the trash and went to the store.

Ellochka stayed at home until kindergarten age. We signed her up for kindergarten at four. Mishenka, as it happens, was in eighth grade.

Mama and I rarely exchanged letters.

But then horrible news arrived in 1967, as it happens, right before New Year's and 1968. Gilya had taken severely ill.

I'd been sending money all the time as a form of material assistance, but Mama requested something else this time. It would be good if Misha came, if only for a couple days. Gilya was crazy about his grandson and begged for Mishenka to appear before him, if only for a second.

The doctors had made a terminal diagnosis. Agony and slow decline awaited Gilya. His hands didn't respond at all and he could barely walk: he couldn't even make it to the toilet in the yard. Mostly, he went under himself. Mama was suffering and suffering over it, but at a certain point she realized nothing good was in store. Goodbyes needed to be said while he was relatively conscious.

Mama didn't invite me. She'd summoned Misha. As a mother, though, I had no right to let the young man go alone. Seeing a severely ill person is too serious an ordeal.

Misha and I went together. We managed to leave on a Friday evening train so as to return on Tuesday. I didn't reveal the entire disheartening situation to him, but hinted that it was a hopeless matter.

We went by train as far as Kiev. Then we took a taxi to Ostyor.

We showed up in the late evening.

Mama greeted us with tears.

The situation was the following: Gilya was in very bad shape. Fima's head felt the same, but he was practically healthy otherwise. Mama took care of him and Gilya. Blyuma had found a good job as a cleaning lady at a cafeteria and was able to run home and help in the middle of the day.

We discussed this in the large room where two beds stood, just as before. One was for Mama and Gilya—a large bed with knobs on the headboard—and the other was Mishenka's little daybed.

Mama somehow slept on the daybed now. Only Gilya slept on the large bed.

Mama spoke in his presence without feeling shy. That showed me the whole depth of her sorrowful despair.

I wondered how Mishenka could possibly fit on the daybed during his summer visits. He probably put a stool next to it.

The winter was chilly. It was warm in the house. Blyuma stoked the stove—she scurried around right there like a housekeeper, though silently. I also immediately suspected a certain purposefulness in her behavior. The door to her small room with Fima was open so the warmth circulated; Fima's snoring could be heard from there. Blyuma went several times to turn him on his side so he wouldn't snore, but was unsuccessful.

Medicines, powders wrapped in white waxed paper, liquid mixtures, and the like—what's customary in cases like this—were on a chair by Gilya.

Mama waved an arm:

"So. We're spending so much money. Uselessly. What am I saying about money. *Vey iz mir*. They should let him into the great beyond. He himself asks. Asks and asks. Asks and asks. *Vey iz mir*.

Mama cried and didn't look in Gilya's direction. He sometimes opened his eyes, peering and peering. And at a certain moment, he seemed to recognize Misha and started mumbling.

Mama complained that Gilya had been expecting Mishenka very much and had asked that if he were to lose the ability to speak before Misha's arrival, then she was to repeat one parting word to Misha and he would understand.

I asked what the word was. Mama said: l'chaim. Though Gilya had asked that it be repeated personally, face to face, and not before witnesses. Meaning like a password. I thought then that Gilechka hadn't wanted to part with his glorious partisan past at all.

Misha lowered his head down and tears poured from his eyes.

Then he approached Gilya closely.

Gilya nodded his head as much as he could, just barely.

Misha squeezed his hand and immediately stepped back.

Mama rushed to the bed and started calming Gilya so he wouldn't be upset that the sheet needed to be changed. She and Blyuma changed the sheet and washed Gilya. He seemed to go to sleep.

Misha and I lay down on the floor for bed.

Mama and I went to the bazaar early in the morning to get a considerable supply of groceries. I'd brought money and wanted to choose quality foodstuffs myself for the patient and everyone else. We took Gilya's children's sled: it was very, very old, from back before the war.

Misha and Fima were asleep. Blyuma left the house with us, to go to work.

Mama and I were out—for the trip, plus the bazaar—two hours. And the snow kept falling and falling.

Gilya was already dead when we came home. A frozen smile played on his face.

I noticed immediately that the pillows under his head were lying differently from before. Completely differently. And he himself was lying as if his neck had been forcefully turned to the side, like it had been turned with force. And one little pillow, a throw pillow, was even under the bed. Tossed off. But Gilya hadn't moved at all for many days; he lay like a log.

My mother and I exchanged wordless glances.

Blyuma came in right after us. Fima was still sleeping, from the effects of his tranquilizing medications.

Misha was fully dressed and washed up, paler than Gilya. His eyes were sunken in black circles. Mishenka was sitting at the table and playing travel checkers on a small magnetized board. Each checker was difficult to tear off but easy to stick to a new spot.

We were all silent and kept shifting our gaze from Gilya to Misha.

Misha was the first to break the silence.

"Gilya Melnik died."

Only later did the feminine weeping begin. Fima recognized something scary and began crying, too, half-asleep. I sobbed out of pity, confusion, and an uncertainty that had covered me from head to toe.

Misha finished his game, neatly gathered up the checkers, and slammed the box shut.

We sent a telegram to Lazar. He arrived an hour before the funeral, along with Khasya. They pointedly didn't speak with me, though Khasya made an exception for a minute and held forth about what had been bugging her for the last ten years.

This meeting with them left me thinking the primary sentiment of their accusation was that I'd driven Fima crazy; abandoned my son to the whims of fate with my third husband; didn't work anywhere myself; and loved only myself, my figure, and my face.

But that's not what this is about now.

Misha behaved courageously. He consoled Mama and Blyuma. Took care of Fima.

We buried Gilya in the old Jewish cemetery. To my surprise, Misha recited a prayer. Mama, Blyuma, and Fima repeated after him. Misha solemnly rocked back and forth, as if he'd been ceaselessly reading the Kaddish his whole life. And nobody was surprised. Except me.

We were silent on the train. Misha looked out the window. He said only:

"I'll go to Kiev this summer. To my father's. Then to my grandmother's."

I didn't argue with him even though summer was supposed to be to prepare for institute entrance exams. Or so I'd thought and assumed.

I should also note that Misha hadn't asked me for the address where he'd need to go to see Miroslav in Kiev. I realized he knew without me. And maybe he'd been there during the summer without my knowing. A bus now ran from Ostyor and there were more than enough cars for hitching rides, too. Not to mention the hydrofoil.

We never returned to that question again.

I was running myself ragged at home. Ellochka would get sick at kindergarten, so sat at home with me more often than not. Once again, my dream of going to work in my field could not come true.

I subscribed to *Teacher's Newspaper*, *Literary Newspaper*, the journal *Soviet Screen*, and other publications important at that time. I was aware of issues in the country and the world. Not for one moment did I isolate myself within our close family circle. Marik liked that. He himself loved reading literature and watching television. Especially the *Club of Funny and Inventive People*. Despite his not having much of a sense of humor.

When possible, Marik, Ellochka, and I went for outings close by—so we could walk—in Neskuchny Garden. We strolled in the open air and sat on benches right by the water of the Moscow River.

After we'd returned from Ostyor, Mishenka took a keen interest in Marik's work. Marik was happy with this turn of events. He explained, showed, and entrusted several procedures to Mishenka just as soon as he'd expressed interest. Marik said Misha was very capable in the area of timepieces.

Mishenka would sit up all night with interesting situations. A workshop had taken shape in Marik's room the very first day we lived there; he always closed the door so Ellochka wouldn't get in and grab anything dangerous. And not one single unfortunate incident had taken place; that's basically a rarity when there's a small child in the house.

Misha dragged watches and clocks into the kitchen and worked on repairs there. Ellochka was horribly frivolous even at the age of six. Of course this was understandable. She never left my arms, I blew every little speck of dust off her, and I literally followed each of her tiny steps. Her maturation was progressing slowly and the notion of danger was obscured by the certainty that Mama would protect her, come what may.

Anyway, one day Misha didn't put the parts into a special little box when he went to school. Ellochka went into the kitchen alone for something. She grabbed a little notched wheel out of childish curiosity and started playing with it. It was shiny and pretty, so it attracted the little girl's attention and she was so delighted she had no idea what to do with it. Ellochka stuck the little wheel in her mouth like a hard candy.

I noticed something was amiss when Ellochka started choking. It's obvious that the sharp edges of the wheel scratched her throat, and blood came out her mouth. I don't know how, but my maternal instinct helped me save my little daughter's life. I extracted the wheel and then pressed it so firmly in my fist that I deeply injured my palm, too.

Misha came home from school and quickly ate. Then he sat down with the clocks and watches.

I came into the kitchen to see him and placed the little wheel right in front of him.

I purposely hadn't wiped off the blood, either mine or Ellochka's. "Here. Have a look at this. Your sister nearly died."

Misha took the little wheel, turned it on all sides, and examined the notches in the light. Maybe he was checking to see if it was bent or something. But he didn't react. He didn't even wipe off the blood in my presence.

I told Marik what happened, mimicking. He was upset about Misha's behavior but refused to investigate.

"All kinds of things happen. I think Misha will pick up his things after this. Even better, I'll ask him to only work with timepieces in my room. I'll make a strict request. The main thing is it wasn't on purpose."

Yes. Marik also correctly emphasized the main thing: "wasn't on purpose."

The school year was nearing its end. There was no discussion on Misha's part about continuing his education. He'd spoken earlier about his plans with great murkiness, too, but now he'd completely retreated into himself and was sitting for hours at a time with clocks and watches instead of his studies. He often said he didn't feel well and skipped school, and he'd lost his appetite.

I decided the time must have arrived for him to experience the first joyous feeling of being in love. I was waiting for that to somehow manifest itself in his home life. But no. Mishenka was obviously not going on dates, wasn't calling girls on the telephone, and wasn't dressing neatly. In terms of his studies, Mishenka had slipped to just average grades, which particularly affected me, in a negative sense.

Mishenka's future remained a mystery to me. At this rate, only the military lay ahead. His health and outward appearance gave no hope for rejection, so there was no doubt they'd take him.

One time I hinted to Misha about intensifying preparations for higher education. Maybe a good tutor—or several—would help him along. Misha told me not to waste my energy or nerves. He was convinced higher education wasn't the most important thing. He'd chosen a specialty, literally thanks to Marik. Timepieces, that was his interest and inclination. And his primary tutor here was Marik.

I resigned myself to that. If only Mishenka had shown an extended interest in something earlier in life, a thirst for knowledge, or diligence. But no, that hadn't happened. He'd grow up and choose, for himself, a specialty to his liking. That was my sacred conviction, based on observations of my son's character.

After our conversation, I felt like a great load had been taken off my mind. I'd done everything I could. I'd warned him and explained the significance of education. Misha was an adult person and if he didn't realize something now, he'd realize it later. That's a law. Coercion never leads to anything positive.

He passed his final examinations with average and good grades. His innate intelligence helped. He left home the day after receiving his high school diploma. As he said: first Kiev, then Ostyor for the whole summer.

Misha hadn't yet turned eighteen by that time, but I handed him the bankbook for Miroslav's alimony.

I said:

"Show your father, he promised to demand precise explanations from me about where and how I'd spent his money all these years. Let him see that nothing's been taken out since the account was opened. You familiarize yourself with it, too. If you want, we'll withdraw the whole sum now and you can handle it. Whatever you prefer. I don't think we need to be too formal about this."

Misha thought for a brief second and asked to withdraw all the money so he could bring it with him. Yes. A fair amount had accumulated over six years.

I entrusted a certain additional and considerable sum to Misha, on Marik's behalf, as material help for Mama.

The time was coming for Ellochka to start first grade. She knew how to read and count a little. I'd worked with her as a home-based teacher.

That summer, Ellochka, Marik, and I went to the sea, to Feodosia. We'd been renting the same place at some old woman's for many years now. Without facilities, but then there was a view out the window of a wonderful rosebush that glowed scarlet and greeted us every clear Crimean morning. It was five minutes to the beach and ten to the bazaar.

We usually spent a month at the sea. That year, though, was an exception, since Marik insisted that Ellochka and I stay on until the middle of August. The little girl needed to improve her health as much as possible before school.

Marik was with us for twenty days, then left for Moscow. We stayed, in female company.

It's no secret that rest makes you younger. I'd turned thirty-seven then. Women who've been through that age remember it's a woman's blossoming. I ran tirelessly through the mountains during tours, and traveling companions took Ellochka and me for sisters. There was also innocent wooing, to which I, of course, responded with only a slight smile.

And then, suddenly, one time on the beach when I was observing from the shore as Ellochka splashed around in a kiddie pool, whipping shallow water into a stormy froth under her childish little arms and legs, it felt to me that I had only one child—Ellochka—but not Mishenka, now or ever. That all my previous life, filled with its ordeals and adversity, had never existed. And if that's how it was, I should provide a happy life for Ellochka, come what may. Be alongside her always and everywhere.

The oppressive thought of Misha—who was either with Miroslav or with Mama, Blyuma, and Fima, many kilometers away from me and my maternal heart—was such a burdensome addition. And my heart felt nothing regarding my dear son.

But that's not my point.

I decided to get a job at the same school where we'd enrolled Ellochka. Ellochka and I immediately cut our vacation short and returned to Moscow.

My high school and specialized post-secondary education was no longer welcomed at her ten-grade school because of my lack of practical work experience. Fortunately, there was a primary school institution for mentally retarded children in the same location (though on the second floor) and there weren't enough teachers. They apprehensively offered me a spot there, certain I'd turn it down. I agreed, though, if only to be alongside Ellochka the whole day.

There was some time left until classes so I went to the library to read research and methodological literature.

A telegram arrived from Mishenka a week before September 1.

"Report receipt draft notice. Misha."

Marik and I deciphered this statement as follows: Misha wasn't planning to continue his studies anywhere, but was planning on draft service. He'd turn eighteen on September 20, and if there wasn't a draft notice before then, that meant he'd report for the spring call-up.

Yes. And he couldn't call his mother and let his dear voice be heard. And then there was his frivolity—he might not make it in time for the enlistment meeting.

The idea flashed for me to go to Ostyor for several days and figure out what was happening there and how. But events like teachers' meetings and distributing textbooks were starting at school, before the beginning of the academic year. I didn't want to begin life in the collective as an absentee. Not to mention Ellochka.

No draft notice for the autumn call-up arrived for Misha.

I threw all my energy into Ellochka's studies and my work. I'm an idealist and I also wanted what was best. At that time, we didn't yet know the law about how when you want what's best, things work out the same as always. And that's not meant to be a clever-sounding line.

Instead of being glad about my closeness for the duration of the school day, Ellochka was embarrassed around me at school. She answered my questions reluctantly when I went down from the upper floor—out from behind the bars that fenced off the department for mentally retarded children—to see her during breaks between classes. Kisses and hugs were out of the question. She even avoided calling me Mama around her little friends.

Yes. I'd used my very own hands to construct a huge divide between myself and my daughter. To her and her schoolmates, I was a teacher for sick idiots and was thus partially an idiot myself, too. And, by the way, the so-called normal children spat just as well as the retarded ones—they expressed reciprocity at very high levels.

Yes, you never know what kind of cruelty to expect from children.

As for the excruciating time I worked at the school: It gave me a lot. I especially attempted to take what was good, outside the mental aspect: little hats fashioned so they had to be tied under the chin, mittens on a piece of elastic so they didn't get lost, a knapsack instead of a satchel with a handle since it's harder to forget it in an inappropriate place. Though with that you had to immediately and firmly train the child to put it on the back instead of dragging it on the ground. Wherever at all possible, you had to sew things up rather than depending on buttons and zippers. There are lots more little things that parents of normal children scorn because they look funny. I came to the conclusion back then that there's no such thing as looking funny if there's a serious reason behind it.

Marik consoled me that I should continue working. He saw my aptitude for pedagogy. For the sake of our daughter, though, I left teaching after the second quarter, right after the 1968 New Year's holiday. With a scene and reproaches of irresponsibility, too: I left the students in the middle of the academic year, but I didn't have the opportunity to wait until the end of the year.

But that's already getting a little ahead of myself.

Meanwhile, Ellochka was making no progress at all. Penmanship, yes, that was her strong suit. With letters and numerals both. Beyond that, though, she was going nowhere. There were hysterics regarding average and below-average grades she thought she didn't deserve.

I went to see the teacher every other day (not including general parents' meetings) informing her about the little girl's nervous condition and vulnerability. Basically, we spoke as two professionals. With no results whatsoever. In the end, the teacher asked that I either stop interfering with the learning process or enroll my daughter at another school.

Ellochka conveyed to me that there were loud whispers in her class that her mommy was arranging for Ella to go to a school for imbeciles so she'd be a top student. Moreover, it wasn't the school on the second floor, but a special one, for people with connections.

Ellochka was upset but didn't cry. A strength of spirit as strong as her frivolity had been manifesting itself since early childhood. That is actually a big rarity.

Ella went to a new school for second grade.

And so.

Misha went into the military in the spring. Owing to his good health, they sent him for four years of navy service.

The short meeting that took place between us before his departure brought no joy. Sparse bits of information about Mama, Blyuma, and Fima spoke of everything being in perfect order with them, and Miroslav sent greetings from his new Kiev apartment in Svyatoshino, where he'd recently moved. I was curious regarding Miroslav's family. Misha evasively answered that he'd buried Olga Nikolaevna several years ago. No wife was foreseen.

I asked in passing: "Was there one?"

Misha vaguely shook a head that had been shorn down to nothing at the military recruitment office.

But that's not my point.

Misha looked sadly and indifferently at his sister.

Ellochka told me in secret:

"Misha should leave as soon as possible. He's untidy. It's not nice when he eats. His pants are too short. Is it true he's my brother?"

I know that thoughts and questions like that don't come out of thin air. In this particular case, though, I couldn't imagine ground under them, either. Ellochka had sensed that Misha was now a stranger in our amicable family.

Misha's physical appearance attested to excruciating thoughts about his own life. As a mother, I felt sorry for him, but had nothing to offer.

Mama called not long after Mishenka was drafted. She pled for Marik and me to take in Motya, his wife, and children for a few days. She didn't state the reason for their trip, but hinted that wasn't a conversation for the telephone. Naturally, I didn't refuse.

Of course Motya showed up in Moscow on his own personal family matter, with a crushed Kiev torte box. One way or another, he wanted to buy a couple of rugs plus a television, if that could work out. I'd never heard that Khasya had acquaintances here involved in those sorts of things, but they'd arranged the purchases. And there was something else I don't want to know and didn't know then, but found out later. Yes, and to go to Lenin's Mausoleum with the children. Fine. Good. You have to do that, too.

Motya showed up with his wife, Lilia, and two daughters, one fifteen, the other eight, Mila and Asya. The younger one was apparently named in honor of Khasya, but in a contemporary way.

Motya had never distinguished himself through intellect and smarts, and he started talking about everything there was to know about my past life and about today's situation for all the relatives and acquaintances, one after another, as soon as he'd walked through the door. Despite Lilia's undisguised discontent, I snapped at him to be quiet. She's quite the personage herself, too. I'm asserting that without malice, I simply want to give her credit. She had a patchy dye job and her plain stockings were constantly bagging at the ankles.

Motya and Lilia ran around all over for days at a time, so I had to have the girls with me. Motya attempted to shove an outing to the mausoleum for all the children on me, but Ellochka and I had already been there so standing in line for a second time . . . well, excuse me. It was the end of Ellochka's school year.

Ellochka looked at the girls warily and worried a lot that they'd stay a long time, so she and I wouldn't be able to leave for Fedosia in June as usual.

An ordeal ensued for me every evening. It was a combined family supper.

On one of those evenings, Motya announced:

"Your Mishka should have gone to a military school. His head is like a whole military general staff. In Kiev, he was running to the libraries, studying geographical maps, sketching diagrams, drawing comparisons, and calculating. I'm talking about the Israeli war. You know, six Stalin blows in six days. His conclusions, whoa! He didn't talk about that? No? Surprising. Misha was sorry Gilya wasn't there, his partisan experience would have come in handy. Instead, it was all that Misha'd do everything all himself, with his own brains, no prompting from anyone seasoned. He came with Miroslav, my apologies, for Mama's little blintzes with poppy seeds."

As he said that, Motya was looking at me and Marik as if all we did in our family was discuss the Six-Day War.

In the first place, we hadn't uttered a single word about it at home. In the second place, Misha was taking his final exams and the rest of the family was already vacationing at the sea with Ellochka when it was actually going on. And it's unclear what Misha was doing at home in our absence: watching the news, reading *Crocodile* magazine or *Overseas* newspaper, or brushing up on his geography. In the third place, why debate it? An aggressor is an aggressor. And if Misha wanted to study the question independently—using television or newspapers—nobody was holding him back. That was up to him.

I expressed that point of view to Motya. And if Motya was so keenly interested in that question, then he had to understand what he was talking about and what he was pushing the children toward. You're buying the rugs here, but you're all carried away about what's there. If only rugs and Czech crystal were all they really had on their minds.

Motya didn't question my tactful reprimand. An understanding had kicked in that he was in my home and had to respect my rules, especially without support from Khasya.

At the end of tea, though, Motya didn't hold back:

"Yes, dear cousin, you're correct. And your mother, Fima, and I thank you for that. And Misha, too. You released the boy from yourself in quite a state. It was obvious a kilometer away that he'd been crushed. Soundly crushed."

"And what crushed him?" I wasn't interested in Motya's thought, but it was clear his words were echoing Khasya and Lazar and Mama's opinion.

"You crushed him. You think you're dragging your living space from place to place throughout the Soviet Union? You're dragging your own entrails. And your son's entrails. Only it's not painful for you. But it's painful for him. You're basically always confusing the difference between vileness and unvileness."

It's a good thing the girls were playing in the other room.

I won't say anything else.

He came, took care of his business, didn't ask advice, and didn't say thank you. I'm not certain his Kiev torte turned up without special meaning. Lilia ruined one of my terry-cloth towels by using henna on her hair and wiping off her shaggy wet hennaed locks; it was as if the rusty remains had stuck to the material. And his daughters drove my Ellochka to hysterics with their behavior: give them a doll to play with, give it. Motya spotted the box with the train set on the shelf: he saw the picture with a train carriage. Mishenka's old one. Misha always handled that train set very carefully. Always laid everything in the box himself. Took care of the box so it wouldn't be crushed or torn. Motya told his children, ask, he said, play, we'll be making our way back on a train soon, too, to distant places. The girls pestered my Ellochka: Take the train set off the shelf, take it. Then: put it together, yes, put it together.

But take/put together/pick up was to me. Instead of devoting my shaken attention to Marik.

Yes. Marik endured it all. Without remarking. Without hesitating. And helped shove their boxes and packages into the train carriage.

But that's not my point.

I thought and thought, then got a ticket to Kiev in order to go farther, to Ostyor. Ellochka had finished second grade—not too badly—and had gone with Marik to Feodosia and I'd promised to join them soon, taking a direct train from Kiev.

I took the idle time allotted for myself so I could disprove Motya's false accusations with my own eyes and my own ears. They had wounded me so much, to mortal pain.

The set goal: disprove and put the fibs in their place. Once and for all.

I arrived without any particular warning. This wasn't the situation for a warning.

Of course my heart stood still when nearing my homeland. Both at the train station in Kiev and at the bus station in Ostyor, not far from the bazaar.

But what was my heart if my soul felt ill at ease?

A general picture of poverty and neglect caught me unawares at the house. Without Gilya, nobody was keeping up with the house's outside condition and it had quickly become rundown. The fence was crooked; boards had been dislodged. The kitchen garden was completely abandoned. Apparently, nobody had planted a single seedling on time. Mama's age was making itself known, particularly in the absence of the sound male shoulder Gilya had been.

We asked questions back and forth about health and talked about buying provisions. Mama turned the conversation to Mishenka and his military service. She was distressed that he'd gone into the navy for so long, particularly since he didn't know how to swim. I assured her that in any case they'd teach him how to swim in four years and said that wasn't the main thing. The main thing was for him to come to his senses and stop making a fool of himself and getting on people's nerves.

I showed studio photographs of Ellochka, both with Marik and separately: Ellochka in her school uniform and outside in a new little coat, a green herringbone pattern. We'd taken it in the winter. A knitted penguin hat, dark brown like her eyes. No photos were color at the time so I described it in words.

Blyuma participated in the conversation as much as she was able. Fima was in his own room and hadn't come out when he heard my voice. Blyuma explained that they were prescribing good medicines for him and he didn't react much to anything.

I suggested to Mama that we go to the market together right away to stock up on groceries and buy her some clothes if there was a need. I inquired regarding their material situation.

Blyuma butted in:

"We have plenty of money. We have enough. Thank you, Mayechka. Misha brought us money the last time he came."

Mama added to what Blyuma said, both with her eyes and her distinct voice:

"You, Blyuma, don't interfere in somebody else's business. Just don't be offended," and then in my direction she said, "Blyumochka's gotten so touchy, it's just horrible. It's true about the money. Misha gave us money. We only spend it on necessities. Of course, we economize. Thanks to you personally and to Marik, too. Misha gave us your envelope. I'm always certain you won't leave us in poverty. And now Misha's involved, too. He won't leave us behind, either. It's such a joy, such a joy."

I didn't begin to clarify how much Misha had given them. It was money from the alimony, obviously a large sum. I wasn't talking about Marik's and my money. What was done was done. But making some sort of paltry gift to your own mother? No.

With that, my mother had immediately put me in my place. That's what she thought.

The market was small; there were hardly any sellers. The fact that it wasn't a market day was making itself known. Back then, there was only a large selection on Sundays.

We bought good groceries: chicken, scallions, parsley, dill, butter, milk, farmer's cheese, eggs, new potatoes, and homemade sunflower oil from roasted seeds. And all sorts of candy from the trading co-op.

On the way back, we sat down in the park for a rest.

My mother had retired and could treat herself by not hurrying. Or so she said.

Away from Blyuma and Fima, I got down to serious clarification.

"Mama, you know Motya and his family stayed with us at your request. He told me a lot about things I hadn't suspected. Did he describe anything about his Moscow visit to you?"

Mama was silent, she just waved a hand.

"Fine. It's not worth paying any mind to what Motya said. I realize that none of you consider me a person. You consider me a monster. Tell me what you're thinking."

Mama looked off to the side and straightened a heavy basket on her end of the bench so it wouldn't fall off.

"At my age, Mayechka, my daughter, you have to look the truth in the eye instead of thinking. But I don't want to look: I love you recklessly, however you are. Let's not dredge up what Motya said, what Khasya said, what Lazar said. People say what they want. So let them."

I hadn't expected that sort of twist from my mother. It seemed to me she needed to speak out to me about something. So many years had passed since the moment we'd started living apart and here she couldn't find expressive sentences for her daughter and was getting by with empty phrases.

"No, Mama. That won't do. Misha was raised in your surroundings. You practically raised him to be what he became. Motya voiced your common opinion. He flung mud at me from head to toe in front of my husband. It's possible Ella heard, too. And now you're dodging. Mark asked me—tactfully, of course—what Motya had in mind and it should be noted, too, that Marik looked at me with the suspicion of something bad. But that's something I'd like to know, too. I stand before you in plain view."

Mama kept silent. I'd given her a difficult assignment, but it's possible to have a talk once every eighteen years. That's if you count from when Mishenka was born. You could, after all, dig earlier, since my marriage to Fima. Or even earlier. I wasn't born yesterday. And they were taking my whole life to task, my whole character. It's well-known to me, as a pedagogue, that it's parents who build a child's character. So who should answer my sincere question if not my mother?

"Mama, of course I understand you're not a well-educated person. Speak in simple terms. I'll help you with leading questions. Talk, Mama. I'll understand."

And Mama said:

"Mishenka thinks Fima's his real father, he's known that a long time. He saw Fima's passport and read the surname. He told me straight that Fima was his father before Miroslav, because his surname was Surkis before there was Miroslav. Gilya confirmed it for him because what else could he do. Gilya couldn't lie.

Then Misha asked that we not tell you he'd come to the conclusion about Fima himself because you'd be very upset. He approached Fima often to talk about the topic and if Fima remembered him as a child. He tried to force recollections out of Fima by mentioning various circumstances from his early childhood. But Fima didn't react. He patted him on the head and that was that. We were very worried. Gilya had conversations with Mishenka more than once, about how he had two fathers, one dear as a blood relative, the other by documents and circumstances but also dear. Misha didn't cry, but his huge grief was noticeable."

"And then what? How did Miroslav behave? Did he come here often when Misha was here?"

"Miroslav came often. Went for walks with Misha. Misha was glad. Papa this, Papa that, he'd say."

"What did he call Fima?"

"He called Fima Fima."

"Mama, please answer in detail. With examples." I had to behave like a schoolteacher, there was no way around it.

"What kind of examples? I don't remember. Basically, the whole burden was on Gilya. Misha was very drawn to him."

"Did Misha talk about me?"

"No."

"Did he say he loved his mother?"

"No. I don't remember. Still, he probably said it. Don't torment me, Mayechka. I have so much torment in my head that you'll only make things worse for yourself. I could say things we'll both regret later."

"No, Mama. Tell me."

Mama tore the top off a scallion and started rubbing it in her hand, between her fingers.

"Misha was always in tears when he left for Moscow. He didn't want to go. One time, to distract him, Gilya promised we'd take him in with us forever. And at his own risk, Gilya came up with the idea that there'd been a conversation with you and you were thinking about it for now. And as soon as you hit on a definite answer, everything would be resolved immediately. Gilya thought the boy wasn't grown-up enough, but that everything would pass on its own when he got a little older. The same thing repeated every year. We thought it was easier for Misha to think that with time he'd live with us instead of you. He even joked about that later. Gilya seconded his joking. Even if it was groundless, the boy had to find some sort of escape in hope. At first Gilya was always waiting for a letter or telegram from you to arrive, or a summons to the public telephone, where there'd be a scene about us filling the boy's head with ideas. But Misha never said a word to you, he never asked? That means he didn't believe it from the very start. He pretended he believed it, though. There's an example for you. I don't have more examples."

"Now the main thing. I know you know this, too, but I need verbal confirmation from you. About Gilya, how he died."

Mama clenched her fist. Firmly. Even I could feel her badly trimmed, not completely clean, fingernails digging into her skin.

I looked at the ragged green part of the scallion in Mama's fist. The onion smell hit my nose, making my eyes tear up. Mama didn't feel it, though; she had a weak sense of smell. But it was unpleasant for me; I scolded her to throw away the scallion and wipe her hands. Mama tossed it and leaned to the side to wipe her hand on the grass. Then she collapsed and slowly sank to the ground with her eyes open.

I wanted to ask a lot more, but Mama had died.

A funeral again. Lazar, Khasya, Motya and his wife, their children, and Blyuma and Fima again. At the new civil cemetery, without prayers. Gilya had been buried by his distant relatives in the old Jewish cemetery, but now it had been closed forever. Even then we'd had to give a bribe, but they wouldn't take Mama, even with a bribe, though I wore myself out running around and making offers.

She was buried, incidentally, with funds I'd brought. Blyuma hinted at being willing to present me with Misha's money, but I furiously refused. What fools they are anyway.

I didn't want to stay in Ostyor another minute. I hadn't found anything out, I'd only grasped yet again that they're all alien to me and I couldn't expect anything good from them, either in the past or in the future.

As far as Misha went, I'd realized something fundamental: Mama and Gilya had handicapped the boy. Instead of bringing him down to earth, they'd crammed him full of tall tales from various walks of life. And this was the result. The boy considered crazy Fima his father and Miroslav, too. And maybe Mama also told him about Kutsenko. And what might be going on in his unformed head after that? Who would answer for all that? She and Gilya had died, so I'd have to answer for it.

But that's not my point.

It turned out I hadn't imagined the result in all its depth.

Legally, it worked out that the house went to me, as the only relative. Even though Fima and Blyuma were registered there, they had no genuine rights to anything. A registration meant a lot, though; I couldn't put them out on the street. The law gave one possibility: for them to live in the house until they died or officially changed their place of residence. But they had nowhere to go and, incidentally, I'm not a beast, so I let them live there.

I didn't tell Misha anything. He was out there with all that complex technology in the middle of the seas or even oceans and it wasn't worth distracting him. You can't fix anything.

Of course I told Marik. He felt sorry for me and didn't question me.

He said only:

"Mayechka, you're an orphan now. I went through that a long time ago. I understand you. You can't imagine how I understand you."

But no, he did not understand me. I'd become worse than an orphan. I had a son I knew nothing about and now—without Gilya and without Mama—I'd never find out. He himself would never give anything away because I wouldn't ask him personally. My life was dear to me; my young daughter was still growing.

My face most likely expressed that sort of thought clearly, so Marik added:

"Children are our salvation. We have to think about the children. Misha's a grown-up. Think about Ellochka. And I'll think exclusively about her."

I agreed—after all, I'm a mother. And a mother is more than a wife, no matter how you look at it.

My unintentional estrangement from Marik began that day. He displayed heightened attention to me, but I was irritated and gravitated toward Ellochka. My daughter seemed like my life perserver.

And then I found a letter from Misha in the mailbox. Blyuma had informed him of his grandmother's death. I'd thought in vain that I could get away with my independent decision to not notify my son. Misha wrote several lines, speaking in them of his grief. He addressed us using "Hello!" and there was neither the word "Mama" nor any other personal form of address. As a result, Misha expressed his dissatisfaction that we hadn't sent a telegram and that he hadn't paid his respects to the deceased.

I didn't write any response. Misha's page felt closed for me at that regrettable moment. Three and a half years of his military service remained ahead and I could be calm during those. The army's the army, the navy even more so, you couldn't run away. People weren't yet running from their service at that time.

My state manifested itself adversely on my relationship with Marik, though I showed concern for him in various ways. He loved good clothing and footwear. And I would stand in lines for hours to buy him a decent imported sweater or shoes. I remember a wonderful Czech overcoat with a plaid flannel lining and buttons shaped like little soccer balls matching the color of the fabric. I never made mistakes with sizes. It was more difficult with Ellochka, thanks to her body build, though she mostly went around like a little doll thanks to cuffs, little bows, and shoes.

Materially we were completely content. But my mental distance from Marik was consistently deepening. He began working more on-site at his workshop on the Arbat. Clients rarely came to the apartment now. Marik no longer locked the door of his clock room because there was nothing there to take. Beyond that, Ellochka had grown up a little, and shiny little wheels and weights with chains from old clocks didn't interest her.

One time, Marik hinted that I could enroll at the correspondence department of the pedagogical institute and receive a higher education degree that would open the way for me as a pedagogue in any secondary general-education institution. Whether it was a regular school, an academy, or a vocational school. After all, I'd just recently turned thirty-nine, and he trusted in me in all matters.

I was burning to do that, but quickly flamed out. I had the desire, but was wary that the study would take energy and I wouldn't be able to devote appropriate attention to my family.

My lack of initiative caused an unexpected storm. Marik shouted that I was demoralizing Ellochka with my behavior because this way she'd start thinking she wouldn't need to work and it was still unknown how her fate would turn out or if she'd find the sort of husband I had found.

I didn't understand the cause for that scene. Marik was always glad that I was at home, the family was well cared for, and there weren't any misunderstandings in the household and everyday life. He was proud of me. And his relatives, by the way, were all delighted with how I carried myself.

Yes. This was likely a midlife crisis manifesting itself. That apt term had not yet reached the public at the time. When reading specialized literature later, though, I compared and concluded that the issue wasn't with me. Nature had taken its course.

Ellochka and Marik's relationship had also worked out to be very complicated rather than simple. He saw only good things in her and considered her positive traits to have come from him. Traits like thoroughness, seriousness, and the habit of sticking to a routine. He attributed her other traits to my side: "Ellochka's restless, exactly like you," "Ellochka says one thing one day, something else the next, like you do," "Ellochka changes her ribbons twice a day like her mama." He said it with a smile, but it was hurtful.

One time I answered:

"Ellochka, by the way, is a future woman and not some master process estimator. And even if she changes her ribbon during the day that's precisely because there's a lot of femininity in her. She wants to bring joy into everydayness. You, Marik, have dealings with expensive, ancient things, but all you see in them is a precise mechanism. That's where your big mistake is."

I don't have the habit (and never have) of insisting on my own correctness, though. I simply had a candid talk with Ellochka, as

a mother with her daughter and as a woman with a future woman.
There's a well-known pedagogical method for this.

"Ellochka, your papa loves you very much. Even more than he
loves me and his own life. You shouldn't upset him for anything. Do
everything as he says. Help him with everything. But always know
that the person closest to you is your mama, meaning me. You can
entrust all the secrets you have now and in the future to me. We'll
certainly find flawless solutions together. Men often make mistakes
in their relationships with women. I'll explain some of the details to
you later. But a woman is obligated to understand a woman as she
understands herself, although a man doesn't have that obligation.
For now, remember all this and don't question it."

Ella treated my words very seriously, but I received a most
unplanned reaction.

She retold our conversation to Marik. In his reverse telling, it
worked out that I was forcing Ella to pretend she loved her papa,
but she truly did love him and so refused to pretend.

Marik particularly caught on the "pretend" and tried to find out
why I'd approached the child with such a treacherous suggestion.

What could I respond? Ellochka had twisted what I said. This
was childish provocation, something described repeatedly in methodological literature. The misunderstanding seemed to pass after an
explanation, but I literally tossed up my hands as a result.

Lack of understanding: that's the sort of situation I found myself
in. In my very own home, which had come to me with such difficulty.

But that's not my point.

And then a fortunate meeting unexpectedly took place. I stopped
by Vanda, a new store selling Polish goods on Polyanka Street, not
far from my home and also across from the Palace of Pioneers and
Schoolchildren, where Misha had worked on his checkers game at one
time. That fact surfaced in my memory out of nowhere and reminded

me again of unpleasantries. I was searching desperately for something to raise my dejected mood on the threshold of the New Year, 1969.

And there it was: they sold the Polish perfume, "Perhaps." It had a light, grassy scent.

That was how I made the acquaintance of a most interesting person: Alexander Vladimirovich Repkov.

Alexander Vladimirovich wanted to purchase a gift for his sister's birthday. I got in line behind him and asked him to warn the next person joining the line that my place was saved. When I returned, some woman was standing right up close behind Alexander Vladimirovich and refused to let me in. He insisted I'd been in line and that he'd warned the woman earlier. She would have none of that. I nearly cried. After all, the tail end of the line that had formed behind her was about three meters long. Should I go to the end?! Alexander Vladimirovich whispered that I not argue since it was useless and he'd buy two vials: one for himself and one as my share. So as not to irritate the line, we agreed to meet a half-hour later outside the entrance to the store.

For some reason I believed him immediately, stood in the wind, and waited, all aflutter.

Yes. At an age when there are no longer secrets in the relationships between men and women, it seemed that a ray of mysterious light had begun burning in my fate.

Alexander Vladimirovich refused to take money from me. I vividly remember it was two rubles, fifty kopeks, though this wasn't about the money.

"What good fortune to make a gift to a lovely lady! You're not a woman, you're a lovely stranger. I'm seeing such beauty with my own eyes for the first time."

I thanked him reservedly. He walked me to my house. I told him honestly that I was married and had a daughter. He responded that he was married and had children, too, and he asked permission to call me at sorrowful moments, to recover his strength. I didn't give him my telephone number. He wrote down his own—his work number—on a slip of paper and presented it to me. He kissed my hand through my glove in parting. I was bewildered, but Alexander Vladimirovich said it can be done that way, too.

I wasn't planning to call. And called about a week later.

I'll be honest: there was no thought of this being love. I had the need for a true friend. I couldn't talk with Marik at home about abstract subjects. He didn't listen, just smiled and reduced everything to the material: Ellochka's health and progress. Her health was good, but not her progress. And each of our conversations left an unpleasant taste for both of us.

It was different with Alexander Vladimirovich. Since he worked in the production department at the Ministry of the Oil and Gas Industry, he had to travel a lot around our vast country. He'd amassed many impressions, some not even related to work, but simply from encounters with people and the varied outdoors. He admired beauty in everything.

We managed to meet near his work four times, on the Maurice Thorez Embankment, which he called the Sofia Embankment for old time's sake. When I corrected him about Maurice Thorez, he asked:

"You're not a muscovite? I did understand that right away by your speech, though. You're from the Ukraine. Right?"

His remark wounded me. I looked after my language carefully and what was the difference if I was a muscovite or not a muscovite?

"Is that important to you?" I asked.

"Of course. Don't be offended. It's even good. I love various kinds of people."

"I'm various?"

"Exactly."

We would meet during his lunch break. That was convenient for me and for him, too. "I need to show up at home on time after work," Alexander Vladimirovich immediately warned me, adding his characteristic soft smile, "How fortuitous that you live nearby."

I listened to his stories and set my own reflections aside for later. I wanted to get to know this person better and not bare my soul to him immediately.

We would stand over the Moscow River; December was as chilly as January. We'd observe the ice, guessing its strength and thickness.

One time during a date on the embankment, roughly four meters from shore, the fishermen below had apparently hacked a hole in the ice with an ax in our presence; it was immediately clear that they were drunk. They just picked at the ice and left it.

"Drillers! They should come to me. I'd teach them!" Alexander Vladimirovich burst out laughing.

The men, who were wearing heavy sheepskin coats, felt boots, and soldiers' fur hats with flaps, settled in on little benches to drink vodka. One accidentally moved to the smashed-up part. The ice was probably very, very thin there to begin with and the fisherman fell through. His drinking buddies ran around screaming, not helping at all. I covered my eyes with my hands from horror.

Alexander Vladimirovich said:

"Let's get out of here right away. If he drowns now, the police will come. And my lunch break's ending."

He kissed my hand in parting.

Yes, if you can't help, go about your business, be a decent person.

For some reason, at that moment I thought about Mishenka and his difficult navy service. And the black hole on the white ice was a black checker in my imagination. In short, it worked out that an image of Mishenka had popped into my head. But it's unclear what kind of image.

I'd already bought a ticket to Kiev so I could make an appearance in Ostyor to handle the documentation for my inheritance. I told Alexander Vladimirovich about my departure. I answered the unspoken question—Will we see each other or not?—with silence.

I'd already decided for myself that this was fate and that the future depended only on me. Independent of the question of assessing the feeling of closeness that had sprung up.

Blyuma was in a good mood when she greeted me. First off, she showed me letters from Misha. I learned lots of new things. It turned out Misha was serving on a submarine. Scary pictures from the movie *The Volunteers* appeared in my mind's eye. He hadn't written anything to me about a submarine. Basically, he hadn't written anything at all to me beyond reproaches about Mama's funeral.

About twenty letters had piled up with Blyuma. She was aiming to read them all, one after another, and said directly:

"I know Misha doesn't write to you. He stated that intention pretty much in the first letter. Your mother and I thought—and now I think—that Misha's in the wrong as a son. Here," Blyuma tapped a fat finger on the stack of envelopes, "is his entire military life. About his comrades, about the ocean, about his dreams. Read them, go ahead, his handwriting's gotten pretty illegible. But I make it out well; it's a habit, understand? A habit means a lot."

I refused to read the letters. Of course everything in them was untrue. If Misha had some sort of truth he wouldn't have been writing it to them here. Basically, he wouldn't have written to anyone anywhere. That's what my heart told me.

I wondered if Misha'd sent a photograph. Blyuma ran into her little room, the one she and Fima had occupied from the start, and brought a photo. Misha in a sailor's uniform and a hat that said "Pacific Fleet" on its black band. Eyes sad, desperate. But his mouth smiling. A tiny, tiny bit, but visibly.

"Handsome, isn't he?" Blyuma pressed the photograph to her heart, like she was talking about a movie star.

"Yes, Blyuma, he's handsome."

"He's handsome, Mayechka, but not with your beauty. Your mother used to say, too, that he doesn't look like you."

I grew wary: "Whose is it? Fima's beauty or something?"

"What does Fima have to do with it, anyway?" Blyuma pouted and buttoned her lip. "Fine, that's none of my business. What're your plans for the summer? Maybe you'll come see us? It's fun here in the summer, at the movies in the park, out in the air, and there's dances, and the bazaar's big. It's just expensive. Lots of dachafolk. Less people from Ostyor, more dachafolk. Misha used to laugh, say they'd start displaying local Jews in the regional history museum soon. It's true. He loves Jews. He'd just say it, directly: I love Jews. A good boy, we put that in him."

I was tired from the travel and didn't feel like getting into it. I asked where Fima was. Fima was on a trip to the store, he'd gone for bread.

It was darkening outside, though the clock showed four in the afternoon, Moscow time. It was all the same then, Moscow time and Ostyor time. Identical.

I lay down on the big bed in Mama and Gilya's room.

Fima came back soon after. In a sheepskin jacket and a quilted insulated hat with the earflaps down and tied under his chin, large insulated mittens, and insulated pants tucked into felt boots.

He could barely move and was pressing a large round loaf of brown bread to his stomach; the thick crust had been plucked at. And there were crumbs in the stubble on his chin.

He saw me and smiled with his mouth open. His only remaining teeth were in the front: three above and two below. I hadn't seen that in the summer.

Blyuma noticed how I was looking at Fima and blocked him with her body. She pressed in close, like a wall.

"Fimochka's back. My little one's back! We'll take off the warm clothes now. Mayechka's here, our dear, beloved Mayechka's here to see us! Right, Fimochka?"

Fima looked at me and smiled. Recognized or didn't recognize. It was unclear; he hadn't recognized me on previous visits.

Blyuma continued her performance:

"Mayechka's here, we read all Mishenka's letters carefully from beginning to end, kissed the little snapshot on the lips and on the eyes and on the forehead and on his handsome sailor hat and on his hair under the sailor hat! Right, Fimochka? Where's our Mishenka? Where's our beloved little son?"

It was as if Fima had heard something familiar. He smiled even broader. Out of habit, Blyuma wiped the saliva off his chin with her hand and then grabbed Misha's photograph from the table with that same hand. She started sticking it in front of Fima's eyes.

"There's our Mishenka, look, Fimochka, there's our dear little son. He'll come see us soon."

I ran out on the cold veranda barefoot, right in the thin wool dress I was wearing. I wanted to go farther—into the yard—but the door started knocking against the piled-up snow.

I stood for a second and went back as if nothing had happened. Without saying a word, I made the bed for myself and lay down. I swore I wouldn't eat a bite in that house.

Of course I lay there not sleeping.

It was clear Blyuma knew about Kutsenko. Mama told her. What else had she told her? What had been simmering in Blyuma's unsound head for all those years, what had she instilled in Mishenka together with Gilya, what words, what notions were fermenting in my son? What brew was in his head? It was beyond me.

And, of course, Miroslav came here. And they'd all sat together at the table and eaten. And talked and discussed the Israeli war and who the hell knows what else they discussed with my dear son. Some people had nothing to do and were at war, then others had to clean up the mess after them. Others set a son against his mother. And still others died unnatural deaths. And some collapsed like they were dead, for no good reason. And everything was on me. On me. They'd put that in him. Well, what could they put in that was good? What did they understand? And to think: declaring that Misha loved Jews. It would have been better if he loved himself for what he was. Disregarding nationality.

I was lying on the same feather bed where Gilya lay dead just a year ago. And the pillows were the same, too. And they were suffocating me all by themselves. And now Blyuma had the nerve to invite me to my own house for the summer.

I woke up during the night. Screeching, moans, squishy sounds, and something else carried from Blyuma and Fima's room. I turned toward the sound. The bed started squeaking. It was obvious what was happening there. You have to close the door, though!

The light went on in their room at nearly that same minute. Blyuma appeared, like a ghost, in a wide night shirt with her long hair down. A disheveled, fat old woman.

"Apologies, Mayechka. We woke you up. Apologies. Sleep, sleep. Rest. I'll wake you in the morning. I'll be going to work and I'll wake you up. Fima's so glad you're here. So, so glad."

I lay there until morning with my eyes open. I prayed to God that everything could be completed in one day so I wouldn't be delayed here for even a minute.

And that's how it worked out. Cordial, good-natured office workers greeted me everywhere in the system. Small bribes were needed, but what could you do. The documents were finalized by evening.

Blyuma behaved as if she were in charge of the situation. She behaved herself at the level her brains allowed. I took her down a peg, politely but decisively.

Blyuma, though, smiled guiltily and drawled out:

"Mayechka. Apologies. You didn't understand me correctly. You probably think I don't know how to hold my tongue. No, you're very mistaken. I'm as silent as the grave."

So as not to make a scene, I didn't clarify what she had in mind. I'd grasped one thing: Blyuma was a swine.

I wore an elegant little watch on a gold band, a gift from Marik that had come to him by chance from some officer or other who'd served in Germany.

Misha had noted my new acquisition immediately, though he usually accepted everything indifferently. I told him it was a trophy watch, from Berlin.

He asked to have a look. Turned it, stroked the band, and said:

"Mama, you probably know the Germans made items from Jews' dental crowns. And maybe this, too."

Then he went along to the kitchen to play checkers. He was about fifteen then.

Where did he get the knowledge about dental crowns? They didn't talk about that in school. Now it was clear whose influence that was.

And I'd put on that ill-fated watch to go to Blyuma's in Ostyor. Without thinking. Gold is gold.

Blyuma was looking at my watch and talking, looking and talking. Then, after everything she'd already said, practically without stopping:

"What a nice little watch. Is it gold?"

"It's gold. Do you want it as a gift, Blyuma?"

"For what?" Blyuma played out surprise.

"For watching over the house, looking after Fima. Want it?"

I took the watch off my arm and put it on the table. Right on Misha's letters—they'd been lying there since evening. Blyuma probably hoped I'd read the letters at night.

Blyuma stuffed the watch in her apron pocket as if she weren't looking and assured me:

"Silent as the grave. Keep that in mind. Just like the grave."

Yes. I was returning to my own life from the other side.

On the train, I put my thoughts into the order of things. I was attempting to grasp the nature of my fear.

Well, let's say Misha knows Kutsenko is his father. So what? And if he doesn't know Kutsenko's his father and thinks crazy Fima's his father? So what?

Misha'd grown up. Let him sort through his fathers and his heredity, all the way to Miroslav. I wouldn't say a word to him in that regard. If he asked.

And if he didn't ask, but told Marik on his own? About both Kutsenko and Fima? And not just about his own observations, but about Mama's thoughts, Gilya's, and worst of all, Blyuma's, too? So what?

This was what! Then what kind of mother would I work out to be for Ellochka in Marik's eyes? That was in the first place. And in the second, what kind of wife?

Thus, it wasn't Misha who need sheltering, but Marik and Ellochka. And they needed to be sheltered from Misha.

Yes. My secret weapon against Misha was Gilya and his l'chaim. In any case, though, Blyuma remained. Maybe she was aware of that. And through her own dimness, she could speak out against Misha and against me and against everybody. Because she was only for Fima and nobody else.

And how would Blyuma squeeze her fat hand into my little watchband? And how had I not thought of that? It worked out to be nothing more than a bribe. No practical meaning whatsoever.

With that idle thought, I fell asleep to the clacking of the wheels somewhere beyond Kaluga.

I dreamed of Misha, that he couldn't swim and was afraid.

At home, I scrutinized my face in the mirror and saw I'd aged. Just like that: two days ago I hadn't aged yet, but now I had.

But that's not my point.

Marik was at work. Ella was at school, for the after-school program. There was a new experiment: as a student making poor progress, Ella went to do her homework with qualified supervision after classes. Her homeroom teacher'd recommended it. I didn't want to explain that I, too, had certain qualifications. So be it. She usually came home at around four o'clock.

Disorder had reigned in the apartment during my brief absence. I needed to tidy up, wash things, and do laundry. I couldn't bring myself to do it.

So I lay down on the sofa. But rest didn't come. I called Alexander Vladimirovich. He was glad, but said his lunch break was already over, that it would be better to meet tomorrow. I don't know why, but I suggested he come to my house right away. He was silent for a bit, then said he'd be over very soon.

Yes. Our first tryst took place in the middle of an untidy apartment. It was brief but substantial. I understood there was a lot of womanliness in me and it required external confirmation. And Repkov had turned out to be the necessary external.

I'd banished the images of Blyuma and Fima, but they persistently let themselves be known. It was precisely to stifle them that I needed Alexander. He, Sasha, knew absolutely nothing and had no idea what I'd gone through during that short night in Ostyor or about the content of my inner fate.

If someone were to say unfaithfulness had come to pass, I wouldn't agree. And wouldn't explain.

And so my meetings with Repkov had taken on a close nature and I impulsively gave him my telephone number. But regretted it right away. Marik or Ellochka could pick up the telephone. That served as yet another addition to my lingering alarm.

Our meetings at home had begun. Almost every day. I was beside myself. I came to my senses approximately two weeks later. And it was on account of this.

New Year's was approaching. Marik asked what gift I'd like to receive and what best to put under the tree for Ellochka. I asked him to give me the opportunity to buy a mouton fur coat. If that seemed too expensive to him, then another coat, maybe just Persian lamb. I'd seen fur coats in the fur store one time when I was strolling down Petrovka Street and crossed to Stoleshnikov Lane.

I expected Marik to object to the price, so purposely looked for something so I'd end up being offended. But he agreed. We decided to buy Ellochka the two-wheel bicycle she'd been dreaming about since several little girls from our courtyard already had similar ones. Beyond everything else, this would be useful for her in working off extra weight. I said just that: she'll lose weight and maybe her head and brains will clear.

Marik greeted my remark with despair:

"Ellochka's in a sorry state. She gets neither attention nor sympathy from you. She eats a lot because it gives her pleasure. No other pleasures are available to her. And that's in a home where the mother doesn't work and could be devoting all her time to her daughter. You don't sign her homework journal, she brings it to me. Do you know her grades? Average and below average, those are her grades. She's fat and ugly. That's why she doesn't interest you. There was a time when you went for walks with her and sought out nice clothes for her. But now her coat sleeves are too short."

I kept silent. It had been impossible to buy anything for Ellochka as of late. She didn't fit children's sizes so I'd abandoned my searches for good things—industry, neither ours nor imported, didn't make them—though not because I didn't want to look.

I answered out loud:

"You know, Marik, I don't need a fur coat. I don't need anything. You wouldn't be saying silly things if you knew how I'm suffering."

Marik probably attributed my complaints to Ellochka. That I was suffering because of her appearance and condition, from powerlessness on that issue.

"Mayechka, let's start all over again. Let's devote ourselves, full strength, to Ellochka. First and foremost you, as her mother and as a woman. And I'll get involved at any stage."

I left him to his delusion. Where would I get full strength if I didn't have either strength or a place to take it from? In any case, a showdown would be taking place, too, owing to the fact that Ellochka was Jewish. Time was short because of her age.

I immediately shifted the conversation to that sore point. I advised Marik, as the father, to be prepared so he wouldn't be caught unawares.

He looked at me with strange eyes:

"Whatever gave you that idea? What, will this definitely happen?"

"Definitely. This happens in the life of every person of the Jewish nationality. It did for Misha. And will for Ellochka. And some people do very stupid things to themselves later, owing to this fact. And to others, too."

"What about you?" Marik asked this defiantly.

"I lived in Ostyor. It was only Jews all around. And that was considered good. And then I became an adult and figured things out on my own. What about you?" I purposely stressed the question by gazing right into Marik's eyes.

"I went through things you wouldn't wish on anybody. But there was also a war. I didn't ask questions. When I wanted to ask, there was nobody to ask. My father and mother were burned in a synagogue when the Germans arrived. And my grandmother and grandfather were there, too, and about another two hundred people with children. I ran off into the forest. I specifically didn't tell you about it, so as not to rub salt in the wound. Recollections like that don't lead to anything good. Everybody knows that. You didn't exactly discover America for me here. Understand? There was nobody for me to ask."

"But Ellochka does. Have someone to hold to account. She'll hold us to account. Keep that in mind."

No. I hadn't known anything about Marik, either.

Bits and pieces. Bits and pieces.

Basically, the fur coat had receded far into the background. The agenda for the time before the New Year's holiday had become completely different. I hadn't aimed to ruin Marik's mood. But how long could I carry the responsibility inside myself? Particularly since he was the first to start shifting everything on me: Ellochka's weight and clothes and achievement at school.

And it was only at that moment that I realized I was leading my life on several fronts: Ostyor, the Pacific, and two in Moscow, one with Marik and Ellochka, the other with Repkov. Four fronts and even more.

We somehow celebrated the New Year in our family circle. Ellochka was glad about the bicycle, but the tires deflated under her weight when she sat on it. I took note of that fact. She was in tears. Marik waved me off, immediately grabbed the pump, and inflated the tires.

I gave Marik a nice notebook and a Chinese ballpoint pen with a gold tip. He was eternally jotting down client contact information on scraps of paper and losing them.

I was left without a gift, though, even without something small. Nevertheless, I purposely displayed cheerfulness and ease. When *The Thirteen Chairs Tavern* came on TV, I sang along loudly, paying no attention to Marik and Ellochka's opinions.

No. I don't have a voice. And I don't have an ear. I don't have anything.

But that's not my point.

About a week after New Year's, I discovered a greeting card from Blyuma in the mailbox. Nothing bad. New happiness, good health. And signed: "Your dear Blyuma, Fima, Fanya, and Gilya." The way the card was signed didn't surprise me. Blyuma is Blyuma.

Under the pretense of changing the lock on the mailbox, I took away Marik's key and resolved for myself that only I would handle correspondence. The box no longer existed for Marik.

I needed a sober view. Even a masculine one. Nobody but Repkov could sort out the situation.

I'd come up with a plan: tell Repkov the situation in general terms. Scrutinize his reaction, that of an uninvolved figure. And take further action at my own discretion.

Yes. In the end, a person needs not the truth, but to see how everything stands in reality. If only for one's personal accounting.

I held out for about ten days, not making my presence known to Sasha, so he'd be the first to call.

I grabbed the telephone whenever it rang, risking tremendously. But I got my way. He missed me and asked to meet. He called in the morning when Marik was at work and said he could come over right then. I refused without making anything up. I refused. Period.

I said: "I'm tired of being secondary for you. Maybe somehow you'll arrange it so you and I can be together a whole day?"

"Well, what can I do if I have a family and you have a burden, too? We could go to my dacha during the weekend. I sometimes go by myself, nobody'd be surprised. But you can't go for a long time, especially on Sunday."

"I can."

I decided in my head right then what to tell Marik: someone had recommended an excellent seamstress, a master of foreign fashion magazine styles, and she only took clients on Sundays because she also worked at her primary place, a theater. I'd first apparently go to stores to look for material, then to see her. The day was at my disposal. And Marik, by the way, let him spend a day alone with Ellochka. And he could report back later on how to hold a conversation with her and listen to her whims about everything.

It had worked out that I hadn't made my own friends and personal acquaintances in Moscow. They were all through Marik. He was surprised someone had suggested a seamstress. I explained it away easily, that a girlfriend from the school where I'd taught had called.

He remarked through his teeth:

"Yes, of course. Ellochka and I will go on a tour at the planetarium, then to the zoo. She's been asking for a long time. I'd counted on the three of us. Without you, now there'll be two."

"If you'd warned me earlier, I would have gone. But now I can't back out on the seamstress. People are on a list for the next six months."

Marik knocked his fist lightly on the table. Not to make a scene, simply as a gesture.

"It's good it's six months ahead. Because sometimes it happens that it's six months back."

And he looked me in the eye.

I quickly calculated what happened six months ago. Nothing noteworthy other than Mama's death. Even now I don't understand what he had in mind.

Pure white snow lay on the entire visible area around the dacha. I was equally glad for the beauty and the quiet. Sasha was in an elated, festive mood. This was our first genuine meeting in independent circumstances.

I chose an opportune moment and said:

"So you and I have already been together for more than a month. You don't know anything about me, though. Does that interest you?"

"Does what interest me?"

"Finding out about me, about my life. What do you think about me?"

Sasha pondered. Then he affectionately said:

"I don't want to think. I look at you and admire. And that's all. Why think? We're not twenty years old so we're not going to remake our lives. If you start telling me things, it'll work out I have to help you with something. Of course, that's fine materially. But what could I do beyond money?"

Sasha was speaking calmly and precisely, as always. There was nothing to object to.

Even so, I answered as I'd planned in advance:

"I need some advice. Just advice, it won't add any troubles for you at all."

Sasha burst out laughing:

"For me, no. But it might add some for you. And just think: there's no need to say anything right now. We're having a happy day. Our only care in the world is to not miss our train home."

"Fine. Don't answer in detail. Just yes or no."

I saw that Sasha was interested. I steered the conversation further.

"A person consists of facts and reflections regarding those thoughts. Yes?"

"Yes."

"The facts are these: I have a husband, daughter, and son. My daughter's in school, my son's in the military. My husband works. Yes?"

"Yes."

"I'm afraid of my son. My daughter's a stranger to me. I no longer love my husband. I didn't do anything in particular for things to work out that way. A combination of circumstances and nothing more. But there's life left, ahead of me, and I need to lead it in a worthy fashion. I'm thirty-eight years old. Almost thirty-nine. You're older than me. But you're a man and age is no obstacle for you. It's an obstacle for me, though. I'm aging by the minute. Is my life over? Tell me in one word."

Sasha kept silent. I'd specially steered this so it wouldn't work in one word.

"You haven't revealed the most important things to me. Why you're afraid of your son, why your daughter's a stranger to you, and why you don't love your husband. But I'm not going to pry into that. Don't even hope for it. You said it so you said it. That's a fact. Particularly since I know as a result of my own life that the result is what's important. Period. Since you've virtually resolved within yourself to consider that fact, that 'period,' it means your life is over."

Sasha was looking me in the eye and smiling.

I asked again:

"Over?"

"Yes."

I started dressing, quickly and haphazardly: underwear, stockings, skirt. I forgot my slip and only pulled on my sweater by the door.

Sasha lay silent. I heard his calm voice as I was forcing my head through the sweater's narrow neck:

"I told you what you wanted to hear."

I started crying. The collar squeezed my neck. I pulled it in every direction. But the yarn was strong and the knit specially didn't stretch: double cable.

"Calm down. You're an actress at heart. There aren't enough effects for you so you think them up yourself. I'm saying that for certain. You think them up. Right?"

I answered the same way I'd set the conditions, in one word:

"Right."

My far-reaching mistake consisted of the fact that I'd only partially retold the problems troubling me and thus received one more question as a result: Is life worth living?

Sasha had given me a thought, though: reassess the part I'd concluded at the period. In any case, I'd come away from the conversation with a positive outcome. And I'd carried it off on my shoulders. As for living or not living, you can always think about that when you reach a definitive conclusion.

A lull set in.

Marik proposed organizing a grand celebration for his birthday. Particularly since it was his fortieth. I agreed since I thought events of that sort strengthened common ties.

I enthusiastically bought groceries and pondered what to cook and how to divide up the workload in the kitchen so as not to pile everything on one day.

I involved Ella. I talked with her about a gift. Ella offered to draw a picture. They'd showed them at school how to use watercolor paints and the girl was enamored with it. She had everything she needed.

For my part, I wanted to buy something unusual but related to Marik's profession.

A thought came to me unexpectedly after one glance in an antique shop on Kirov Street: an ancient clock. Not too expensive since it didn't run—it had some sort of hidden defect—and shabby on the outside, too. The salesman convinced me I wouldn't find a better gift in that category. A true master would be pleased. It offered restoration and a mechanism and searches for needed solutions. A pursuit for long months or even years, if handled with love. I bought the clock and securely hid it away.

And so the day arrived. It happened to fall on a Sunday. Counting the three of us, fourteen people gathered. Even people we hadn't seen in about ten years. Meaning since I'd moved.

Ella wanted to present her gift—the picture—to Papa in the morning. But I convinced her she had to wait until three in the afternoon, when the guests would gather, then present it in front of everybody; at the same time, I asked her permission to have a look. Ella wouldn't let me, but she didn't sulk as usual.

I laid out an outstanding table. All with my own hands: I'd boiled and diced and cut and stuffed.

Our dear main guest was Beinfest. He hadn't made an appearance at our house since Ellochka's first birthday.

Beinfest came early and talked with Marik for a long time. I didn't hear: I had to cook so didn't need to.

Ella was impatient so she brought her picture to the table and loudly called out:

"Papaaa! Come out, I have a present for you!"

The picture depicted a wavy ocean, watery and gray-blue, with two figures over the waves, one apparently wearing pants and the other in a dress, and two figures below the waves, too, one in very wide bell-bottom pants, the other small and round, dressed in something incomprehensible. All along the edges, like a frame, was the inscription "happy birthday, happy birthday". It was all somehow dirty and slovenly, too. The sheet of paper was also warped and uneven all over.

Ella was literally sparkling from the joy of anticipating praise.

Marik and Beinfest came out to her summons.

Ella loudly said:

"Dear Papa! Happy birthday! I drew it myself and nobody helped me."

Marik regarded the painting in passing. It didn't matter to him— what mattered to him was that his daughter had remembered and tried.

Beinfest looked, too. As a lawyer, he peered at it intently and sternly asked:

"Ellochka, it's Mama and Papa above. That's obvious. But below, in the sea. I don't understand, who's that?"

"Misha and me. He's serving on a submarine."

"So, Marik, Misha's in the navy? As a submariner? Are you aware that drafted submariners are definitely entitled to vacation? How long has he already served?"

Marik answered without hesitation: "Eight months."

"Well then, be patient a little longer and he'll roll in for vacation. So, Ellochka, what are you doing under the sea?"

"I'm helping Misha. I'll be a Young Pioneer soon. I'm a Little Octobrist now, they won't let me on the submarine, there's military secrets, and I'm under the water. Misha came out of the submarine to see me and ask me to say hello to Papa."

Beinfest started laughing loudly. And Marik smiled, too.

Yes. They'd talked and talked. Marik and Beinfest had talked for an hour in Marik's workshop, just the two of them. And not a word about Misha.

And Ellochka's quite something. Hello to Papa. What about Mama?

Beinfest, too. "Are you aware, Marik?" And what, I can't be aware of anything at all?

I brought out my gift, simply from annoyance: I'd wanted to do it when everybody sat down at the table. This sort of thing demands an audience, it's art after all. Well, fine.

Marik regarded the clock for a long time, walked in circles, touched it lightly, looked through the loupe, and all the rest.

Beinfest ardently approved and contributed his bit:

"Izya gave me a chess clock right before the war. It was fashionable then, chess. All those kinds of things. They'd only just gotten the production on track for the clocks. My wife stuck it somewhere. I'll find it. It can also be considered an antique, by the way. That was twenty-eight years ago."

"Twenty-eight isn't an antique," I said, entering the conversation. "It's bric-a-brac. You're looking at different things with the exact same eyes, but you have to reorient yourself, sense it."

Those words escaped against my will. I don't tolerate stupidity. Beinfest answered conciliatorily:

"Of course. Twenty-eight years isn't a long stretch. I was expressing myself figuratively. As a lawyer, of late I've grown accustomed to speaking figuratively. I had in mind, Mayechka, that it's a historical item. Historical from all angles. Particularly as the years pass. It may be broken."

Marik put in his word:

"Give it to me, Natan Yakovlevich, if you don't mind. At the very least, I'll repair it if it's broken and give it back to you. It's very interesting for me. I'll think back to my youth. And my uncle, too. Repay my debt to memory, as they say."

Beinfest promised to bring it as a supplementary birthday gift.

Misha's name wasn't uttered that time around. But I did sense Marik had been thinking about the boy, just as I had. We hadn't bought Misha a clock like that. We'd planned and planned to, but hadn't found one for sale. And then he quit the Pioneer Palace and the idea was gone.

Marik's second cousin, Borya Simkin, and his wife, Raya, gave Marik a crystal vase. Small but pretty. German or Czechoslovakian. Not new, probably from a consignment store.

His pals from work—Fima Slutsker and Volodya Lozbichev— brought as a present a set of German instruments I didn't know the use for, though they were very rare.

Roza Ilinichna Belkina—an aunt, though I'm not sure which side of the family she's from—brought a porcelain figurine from her own house: a ballerina sitting and tying her pointe shoes. The skirt's made of fabric, dense frills, raised to her knees. Very pretty. Roza told us immediately that her oldest son brought the figurine from Germany as a trophy. I knew where these figurines came from without her saying. A couple of shelves in every antique store were crammed with them and nobody bought them.

One family all together—they were getting on in years but spry—Samuil Borisovich Shnitman and Rimma Izrailevna, plus their son Yuly, an engineer and subway builder who was already retired, and his wife, Marina Alexandrovna, presented a set of six teaspoons made from nice metal. Not silver, I realized right away, but pretty, with light blue enamel on the handles.

Natalya Ivanovna, the wife of Marik's other second cousin, Zhenya Khlyubarak, who'd died, brought tea bowls she'd bought in Samarkand, where she'd gone on a business trip. She was a chemist by profession, just like her deceased husband.

I'll tell later what Beinfest gave.

I'm telling about the gifts since a person is revealed through his gifts. His taste and his mood. I remember all gifts. Always.

My clock was standing in an honored, visible place and the guests admired it constantly.

Ellochka's picture went around the table and she received compliments for her talent and abilities.

Everything went well. But then Beinfest, in his capacity as master of ceremonies, proposed a toast:

"I'd like to drink to those who aren't with us today. As an elderly person, I'm calm knowing that life is the exception and death is the rule. There's no need to be sad. We need to live. And so, as they say: l'chaim!"

A lot of people loudly said, "L'chaim!"

It was explained in a whisper to those who didn't understand. Overall, though, people got by without interpretation.

Marik had had a lot to drink, since he wasn't in the habit, and spoke in response:

"Exactly, dear Natan Yakovlevich! L'chaim! I won't list everybody by name. But first and foremost, today I'd like to name my mother and father, Moishe-Yankel Ovseevich Faiman and Fira Markovna Faiman, as well as my aunt and uncle, Isaak Shmulevich Galperin and Roza Motlovna Galerpina, who raised me and gave me a start in life. L'chaim! I'm saying this to all of us, dear guests, and not to the dead, only because that's how it's supposed to be. Though it's to them at the same time. The dead are living, too, in the great beyond. And sometimes it's unclear who has things better. I ask you to eat well after you drink because we'll still raise many toasts to various occasions in life. And I also want to propose, using those same guidelines, that each of us stand and list, with first name and patronymic, parents or other relatives no longer living. Well, l'chaim to everybody, everybody! So, who'll go first?"

Yulik started laughing and even interrupted Marik at the very end:

"Name them according to their passport or what? You can tie your tongue in knots that way."

"According to the passport, Borechka, according to the passport. Like in prison," Beinfest chimed in.

Everybody began laughing.

Marik's face had gradually lost its color during the course of his speech and toward the end he'd turned completely white.

I led him away and put him to bed on the fold-out couch in the other room. I didn't unfold it or put on sheets because Marik wasn't standing on his own feet. He'd weakened suddenly from what he'd drunk and said. Basically, he'd worked himself up.

Nobody followed Marik's lead, particularly after his shameful departure. And rightly so. What kind of dead roll call can there be under conditions like those?

I had to bring the celebration to its final notes: sweets, tea, and farewells.

In parting, Beinfest, who'd had much more to drink than Marik but didn't allow his drunkenness to show, embraced me and smothered me with kisses.

"Mayechka," he said, "you're such a beauty! Take care of Marik and the children. Don't lose touch with me. I'm a widower. All I have is my work and I'm not a social person. I'm a private person. Call. I'm always a helper in all manner of things."

I took his words very much to heart.

Ella was finishing off the leftover pastries: she'd piled all five of them on her plate and was eating with a large spoon.

"Everybody's gone?" She asked this with her mouth full.

"Yes."

"Are they all Jews?" Ellochka was swallowing pieces without chewing. Looking me in the eye. Right inside me. Like some sort of magic trick.

"Not everybody. Why do you ask?" and I was thinking, there you have it. But Marik was sleeping as if nothing was happening.

"I was testing you. I can tell a Jew from other people myself. With the names. Jewish names: Abram, Izya, Zyama, Moishe," Ella was counting on fingers smeared with crème, "Girsh, Roza. I don't know more. Tomorrow I'll write down what I heard today. Jews always disguise themselves. Something always gives away a Jew. Either the nose or the name or the patronymic. Or that egg drink. Such a special Jewish food thing. And Jews definitely have gold, too. You have to know how to tell them apart."

Of course Ella was discussing this in an adult tone, repeating things she'd heard.

"What nonsense are you talking? Who told you that? Why do you have to tell them apart?"

Ella started shoving a new portion into herself and went on, already looking at the plate as she did. Probably out of greediness because the pastries were running out.

"A girl in class explained it to me. She's Russian. Her parents are Jewish, but she's Russian. She told me you and Papa are Jewish and I'm Russian, too, like her, and that's why you don't love me. Especially you."

I felt sick. This wasn't Misha. No. This was the kind of dopiness you just can't get through your head. Ella was disseminating contrivances about whether or not her parents loved her to her collective at school.

Exhaustion was taking its toll. I found strength and patted Ella on the head, though:

"Papa will have a talk with you tomorrow. And explain."

Ella answered calmly:

"Papa already talked with me. I understood. I'm not stupid. Like you think I am. He said that if they call me a Yid girl I should laugh instead of answering. It doesn't work for me to laugh. Because they don't just call me a Yid girl, they call me fat. And always both: a fat Yid girl. But I'm Russian. Well, and fat. But I'm Russian! Mama, say I am!"

There was fury in Ella's eyes. But no visible desperation.

I didn't answer at all, just advised her in a kind way:

"Eat less. Soon you won't fit into your school desk. Whether it's Russian or Jewish."

Ella burst into tears and ran off to Marik. She tugged and tugged at him, but didn't get the slightest response. She lay down alongside him in her party dress as much as she could—she was about to fall on the floor. I wasn't worried, though, since the sofa wasn't very high.

As a pedagogue, I know that sometimes you have to give a slap instead of reacting to hysterics. I gave Ella a box on the ears with my forced ambivalence.

It's unclear how much that cost me.

A letter with birthday greetings for Marik arrived from Misha. The usual wishes. A few words about himself: healthy, service going well.

Marik read it and sighed:

"Misha doesn't write with any details at all. But a person needs to tell the details to someone. I just hope he's made some friends. If he were doing his service on dry land, we'd visit him, bring him something delicious and home cooked. I hope they give him a vacation soon. Right, Mayechka?"

"Of course. But he didn't like delicious things very much even as a child." I answered emotionally since I thought about Misha constantly.

Marik went into a rage, though.

"And what did you give him that was delicious?"

Well, there's how you can turn everything to the stomach. And Ella was just like her Papa. That was now clear.

I kept calm and said:

"Mishenka's at such a depth now that you won't reach him. And we're only worsening his situation by arguing."

But that's not my point.

My meetings with Repkov brought joy. But not complete joy. An easy relationship based on mutual infatuation had come about between us. Fortunately, my attempt to let him in on my problems hadn't succeeded. We hadn't returned to that conversation. Only once, about a month later, did Sasha remind me of my doubts.

"Are you still fighting like a partisan?"

I was surprised not to understand what he meant.

He explained:

"You're at war with your own people. You're on their rear territory. But the thing is they're on your rear territory, too. And in the end, victory's forged on the front line."

As a former combat soldier and reserve officer, Sasha had hit an important note. With a laugh and a smile, but he'd portrayed the situation correctly.

That day particularly stayed with me because he told me about a long-term business trip to Tyumen and mentioned the Samotlorsky oil deposit—more precisely the Shaimsky fields—as the location for the duration of a two-month stay.

I asked him to repeat: "Khaimsky?"

Sasha started laughing.

"Well, I knew you were Jewish, Mayka, but not to such a degree! Khaimsky fields. Well said. I'll share that with the drillers. The foreman there is Jewish, from Baku. Avdil Efraimov. He produces two hundred tons a day. He and I'll have a laugh together."

Right that instant, a thought arose along some mysterious pathway:

"Sasha, there are great prospects in your manufacturing. Do you know anybody at the Institute of Oil and Gas? My son will come back from the navy. And he'll need to start a civilian life. Could you arrange a spot for him at the institute? Don't worry, it says in his passport that he's Ukrainian, by his birth father."

Sasha let my remark about nationality go in one ear and out the other. Though it even seemed to me that he'd blushed. Very, very slightly, but I noticed.

Sasha asked: "Is the oil institute his dream?"

"I don't know what his dreams are. But I think that's a profession for him. Travel, field trials."

"The future will tell. I do in fact know someone there. At a high level. I'll do it. There's still plenty of time."

The conversation brought me extraordinary relief. I'd glimpsed Mishenka's future in a good light. In any case, now he had a starting point: Sasha's firm promise. And I, his mother, had taken care of that.

After Sasha left, I sat down to write a letter to Misha. Based on Repkov's stories, I outlined the profession's appeal plus developments in the petroleum industry. I hinted that his time in the service shouldn't pass without a trace and that this was an opportunity to prepare for applying to a post-secondary institution. I very carefully hinted at possible help from specialists. There was, after all, military censorship. I wasn't sure of that, but just in case. I closed with wishes for health and a speedy return. I also asked if he was planning a vacation. To add something pleasant, I enclosed a photograph taken of the three of us: Ellochka, Marik, and me. It was a pretty photo, I'm in my favorite terracotta-colored jersey dress. That's not obvious in the black-and-white rendition, but all the same. Let him show the photo to his comrades and talk a little about home. It would bring us together in his thoughts.

Yes. A photograph is a big deal.

My impression of the world had been abruptly upended. Apprehensions that had tormented me for so many years had disappeared. I'd realized there were no grounds for them. There was nothing to be afraid of. Especially from Misha and Blyuma. With all manner of things from Ostyor trailing behind them. The past was gone.

I'd fought as hard as I could for the impression I made in Marik and Ella's eyes. But that would no longer trouble me, either. So Blyuma wasn't worth a kopeck. Or even Mishenka, if he were to say anything about the past.

I tried to shelter those supposedly near and dear from unpleasant knowledge. But I practically had no family now. Ellochka had a monster's instincts. Marik was a tongue-tied person, a nonentity. And I was supposed to reveal my whole life to them?

Mishenka remained. My Mishenka. Grown-up, independent, handsome, smart, kind no matter what. His anguish with his fathers, even Gilya's death—whether that was fiction or a fact he'd invented—it all belonged, undivided, to him alone. So let him figure it out himself.

I had no fear from this point on. Fear had been buried at an unspecified depth. Nothing was my fault.

Yes. Conclusions need to be reached gradually. And constantly, otherwise you could go too far.

I sealed the letter with joy and inspiration. I took it to the post office because I couldn't entrust it to the postbox at the entrance to my building.

But that's not my point.

I was aflutter waiting for a response. Misha wrote two weeks later. He thanked me and asked me to find out if there were study guides or programs to help applicants, if it was possible to get textbooks, and so on. Clear, distinct questions. A thought followed: the boy had grown up a lot. He wrote in almost printed letters, he'd obviously tried.

I vividly imagined the missive being composed during a moment of rest, in the sailors' crew quarters after an anxious watch shift. Perhaps hindered by strong rocking and a storm. But Misha had diligently drawn out each letter in order to bring his greeting and gratitude to his mother. I didn't know if there was rocking under water, but in any case, there weren't many conveniences.

It troubled me that Mishenka accepted my proposal from the first call. But he'd never had any particular interests other than checkers and, to some degree, timepieces, so he needed to study and work in a good, reliable place.

An everyday profession is an everyday profession. People go through life with those until the very end.

Misha also wrote that his MOS was acoustics and maybe that would come in handy at the institute. That was for me to clarify.

The comment about some sort of MOS angered me a tiny bit because of its irresponsibility: most likely, Misha had blabbed part of a military secret, but since the letter had arrived without anything crossed out, that meant everything was fine.

I proudly read the letter to Marik, though he wanted to look at it himself. I agreed, but initially read it anyway, with feeling, and invited Ella to listen.

Marik smiled when things got to the MOS:

"MOS is an acronym: military occupational specialty. My Uncle Izya loved repeating 'Is it the mos' you can do?' Yes. He knew nothing about the military occupational specialty."

Ella shot a glance at Marik and ran off to her room. Probably to write down new information about Jews.

The two of us were left with Misha's letter.

I tapped my finger on the envelope:

"I'll work on this in earnest right away. I'll go to the institute, clarify things, and get textbooks. Right?"

Marik responded: "Is it the mos' you can do?"

He took the letter to read on his own. I reminded him to return it later.

Yes. Repkov went away at a bad time. He would have advised me and sent me to the associates I needed for consultations and establishing connections. There was plenty of time ahead, too. And Sasha would be returning in a month and a half. I needed to do what could be done right this minute. I was brimming with a thirst for action.

Everything came to me easily. I wheedled study guides and obtained textbooks and detailed information for applicants. I threw together a package and sent it to its destination.

I didn't ask about acoustics, deciding to wait for Sasha instead and learn firsthand.

And then, just after I'd rushed forward, just after I'd calmed down. It happened.

They summoned me to the school personally, by telephone. Not for a parents' meeting, but for a one-on-one talk.

My little daughter's teacher told me the children in her class had picked up the habit of reading the class record book. Sometimes the teacher left it on her desk unattended. It wasn't just a document, there were grades and the like there, too. There was also a special section at the end with the first names and patronymics of parents, along with telephone numbers and nationalities.

And so for some reason the pupils focused on that very last page, with the first names, patronymics, and nationalities. And they laughed. It's well-known that everything seems interesting for children. Things they can tease somebody about. I'd gathered that from my pedagogical experience.

There were two Jewish girls and one Jewish boy in the class. Including, naturally, my Ella. Despite what she'd been imagining for herself.

And so they came to the first Jew. Anatoly Meirovich Kaplan, father of the little boy Yura Kaplan. "Jew," they loudly proclaimed. Then, as luck had it, alphabetically there came Lilia Tovievna Lifshitz, a Jewish woman. Mother of the little girl Sveta Lifshitz. Also at full strength: "Jewess." And then at the very end they came to my girl: Mark Moishe-Yankelevich Faiman, our Marik. Meaning our dear Papa. And, drawing it out:

"Now there's a Jew if ever there was one!"

Of course you can understand them. It's an unusual patronymic, even compared to the other Jewish ones.

Everybody was laughing. The Kaplan boy kept quiet but was pale as death. Sveta Lifshitz stared at her desk, it didn't matter that she'd egged on my Ella about them being Russian compared to their Jewish parents.

And my daughter walked up to the desk, took the record book, neatly closed it, and hit the head of that bandit boy who'd stayed back and had barely learned to tell his letters apart and had been reading out the nationalities for all to hear. And she flogged him so hard on the head that the little boy had blood coming out his nose and ears.

At this point, the teacher entered the room and took away the record book. It had been rendered almost worthless. Because my little girl had enough nasty energy to wear out anything at all, to say nothing of a paper record book.

The teacher immediately started investigating what had caused the incident and why they'd dared take the book at all.

Everybody kept quiet.

Only Ella said:

"Slavik Kutuzov took the record book without permission and read the nationalities out loud."

The teacher asked:

"And is that why you hit him?"

Ella answered:

"Yes. I'll say in front of everybody now that my classmates are stupid. And you, Marina Petrovna, are stupid. Because things like that shouldn't be written in the record book."

And my little daughter went to her place.

The teacher sent her out of the room without further conversation.

And now she'd called me in.

Ella hadn't informed me of anything. Marina Petrovna reconstructed the picture herself after detailed questioning of the second-graders and had now recounted it.

I found out Ella hadn't shown up for class during the three days since the incident. But today she'd come in as if nothing had happened.

In the first place, I assured Marina Petrovna I was completely unaware of the incident. Ella left the house every day at the routine hour and returned as usual after the after-school program.

The teacher looked at me sympathetically.

"You have a very difficult little girl."

I nodded, but objected:

"This isn't about her being difficult."

Marina Petrovna asked:

"Then what is it about?"

"You know yourself what it's about."

"Ah, of course you mean that. You've turned down the trodden road."

"Yes, I have. I respect you as a pedagogue. But you should have devoted a lesson to explaining that there are good Jews, too. And you changed the subject."

"I'm not against that, moreover, I happen to have a girlfriend who's Jewish. But your daughter called me stupid. In front of the whole class. And I'm retiring in three years. I still have three years left to work here. What kind of name will I have when I leave? They'll be retelling this story at lots of schools. Now, I call that an appalling fact. This is a problem of social significance. But nationality—what is that? I don't understand. Well, they said 'Jew.' Well, yes, even in front of everyone. Well, it's written in the record book. You can't throw the words out of the song, as they say. And good gracious, people raise their own children—I have you in mind—so they recoil and go into a rage just from the name of their own nationality!"

I used my last strength to keep quiet. But I asked a question as directly as possible:

"What do you want?"

Marina Petrovna answered plainly:

"Ella needs to apologize in front of everybody. To ask my forgiveness."

"Fine. She'll ask it."

Yes. One has to fight for one's child. Whether you tear him from the clutches of a grave illness, carry her from a fire, or what have you. But this was a different case. I hadn't formulated how different. Because that was impossible.

Studies in the after-school group were just finishing up. I found Ella in the empty classroom. She was packing up her satchel at the last desk, the biggest one.

I saw her from the door: alone in a huge room with tall windows. The walls were hung with portraits of eminent people of the past and present. Cosmonauts among them. They were looking reproachfully at my daughter. And some were smiling. Especially the cosmonauts. The thought flashed in my head that cosmonauts were always photographed smiling. For posters and even newspapers, wearing the medals and stars of Heroes of the Soviet Union. Members of the Politburo never smiled, though. Yes. They were of a different age group and knowledge.

And I quietly but audibly said:

"Ellochka, let's go home. We'll buy some pastries at the corner. Do you want some pastries?"

Ella looked at me in bewilderment for several seconds and answered:

"Yes, I do."

I wasn't planning on any hearings regarding apologies. A certainty had arisen in me that everything would blow over on its own.

We'll live till Monday, as they say. The film by that name, starring Tikhonov, had just come out then. Ella had seen it at the cinema with Marik and they'd breathlessly told me about it. She'd seen quite an eyeful.

Tikhonov is Tikhonov. Ella is Ella. And so on.

A week later, though, I discovered this. My gold rings and earrings I'd bought using pre-reform savings had disappeared. They'd lay calmly for so many years in the wardrobe, deep under the sheets, right by the back wall. Without boxes. In a knotted handkerchief, so they'd take up less space. The empty little velvet boxes were kept separately.

And so.

During that time, a couple of clients, respectable people, had come to see Marik. They hadn't had time to rummage around in the linens.

Marik didn't even know about the jewelry. That left Ella. She always displayed curiosity in various enterprises that had nothing to do with her. But it was simply impossible to suspect a child when valuables like these were concerned.

So I asked Marik first.

"Did you take anything from the wardrobe that wasn't yours?"

"What do you mean?" Marik was surprised.

I had no other option but to tell him about the rings and earrings. After all, we're one family living together. And he's my husband and should know about hidden resources, just in case.

"I'd wanted for a long time to let you in on those circumstances, but never had the time. And then the time came—after a thief appeared in our house. What do you say to that?" I was having difficulty holding back my rage since there was nobody in sight but Ella.

Marik agreed.

We called Ella in.

We made the mistake of not developing an advance plan for questioning her. We'd been thinking of other things.

I asked first: "Ella, is there anything you want to admit to Papa and me?"

Our daughter was silent and looked at us trustingly with her big blue eyes.

"Ellochka, it's better to admit it to us. After all, we'll always learn the truth. The truth always comes out. Even over time."

Marik was speaking affectionately and his entire appearance showed he believed, in advance, whatever Ella might say.

Ella kept quiet anyway. Then I opened the wardrobe door and demanded she demonstrate, clearly, how and when she found the jewelry and where she'd hidden it or, even worse, taken it out of the apartment to an undisclosed place.

The wardrobe door came off one of its hinges, most likely because I'd jerked it too hard in a fit of indignation. Now it hung crookedly and squeaked, too. The picture lost its tragedy because of that and Ella started laughing.

I cut her off:

"I'll tear that damn door off completely and break your head! Then you'll stop mocking us!"

And I really did tear the door off its remaining hinge. But it turned out to be too heavy and I fell. Marik rushed to me and freed me out from under the door.

I didn't lose my composure and went on:

"You talk right now! Or I'll put you in an orphanage. There's underage criminals there and when you reach adulthood you'll go to prison, where you belong!"

My strength ran out unexpectedly and I looked at Ella with different eyes. She read in my eyes that I already lacked energy so there was no reason to fear me.

"Papa," Ella said, "calm Mama down. Yes, I took three gold rings and one pair of earrings. Because I'd promised to show Sveta Lifshitz that she'd described signs of being a Jew to me correctly. You have gold lying in a secret place. You were hiding it. I found the secret place. Everything was right. You were hiding it. I found it."

"And then what?" I was sitting on the bed and Marik was supporting my shoulder with one hand and reaching the other out to Ella. He probably wanted to pat her on the head.

Ella moved aside and finished her thought:

"And then was that Sveta and I made our own secret place. You can torture me, but I won't tell you anything. Look for it. I looked. Now you look. But you won't get it just like that."

It was as if Marik's mouth had been glued shut. He wanted to object somehow, but couldn't. And I couldn't. I was numb all over—not only was my mouth locked shut, but my legs and arms had frozen along the entire perimeter of my being.

Marik squeezed my shoulder even stronger and uttered distinctly, but haltingly:

"Good. I myself will personally look. If I don't find it, the gold's yours. But you can be sure I'll find it. First I'll ask Sveta to come over. If she doesn't admit anything, I'll ask her parents over."

Ella answered:

"I'm not afraid. Ask Sveta over. She and I have an agreement, sealed in blood. We're against Jews. We need money to escape from you. She from her family, me from you. She won't betray me. Not for the life of her."

My little daughter turned around and left.

And this child was nine years old. With such iron calm.

Marik and I exchanged glances.

I asked: "Marik, do like you said. She's a stranger already anyway. It won't be worse."

Marik nodded: "Yes, Mayechka. This isn't about the gold. We have to save her. Isn't that right?"

I nodded fervently.

Sveta Lifshitz lived in the next building and we had her telephone number written down. But how could we call and ask the girl to come over? Especially to speak to her without her parents?

Marik proposed:

"Let's not rush. A child's mind can think up anything. And in a state of anxiety and stubbornness, undesired manifestations are possible. Let Ella feel triumphant for now. She can let Sveta in on this tomorrow. We'll see how events unravel."

But Ella did things her own way. It was she who called Sveta over to our house that evening. Fifteen minutes after our investigation, Sveta arrived under the pretext of doing homework. Which she announced in the hallway to Marik, who answered the door. Ella was standing there, smiling expressively.

"Sveta," she said to her little girlfriend, "get ready. They're going to torture us. They found out about the gold we hid. We'll show them we're not afraid of anything at their hands. Let's go into the big room, we'll sit down there and keep sitting. And let them chirp to the whole world."

Ella went first. Sveta was so scared she turned crimson, but trudged after Ella anyway. They both sat on the sofa and put their hands on their knees.

I observed from the bedroom. Marik froze in the doorway to the room where they were sitting.

Several minutes passed in silence.

Sveta Lifshitz whined:

"Let me go home. My parents will be looking for me. They'll tell the police."

Sveta started crying, but didn't take her hands off her knees. Tears flowed down her face, falling on her clenched little fists.

Livid, Ella looked at her and hissed:

"You have no shame! They're glad you're sniveling. They won't do anything to us. And if they do, they'll be put in jail. You said so yourself!"

Marik said in a loud but uncertain voice:

"Knock it off with the show. You're two little fools. Nobody's planning to touch you. Although we should. And hard. You go home now, Sveta. Or even better, I'll go with you and speak with your parents. I'll tell them you hate them because they're Jews. And you'll stand there and listen."

Marik wanted to continue along that line but Sveta started sobbing:

"Oy, you can stop! I love them very much! I love them so much I don't even know how much! We were just playing! It's a game! Tell them, Ella! We were just playing! We thought it up that we don't love you! And I'll show you where the rings and earrings are. We played a secret game and hid it under some glass in the yard. It's here, in the courtyard! Right here, next to the flowerbed! I'll show you! Just don't say anything to Mama and Papa!"

The straightforwardness confused Ella.

Not wanting to lose the initiative, Marik commanded: "To the courtyard now! Coats on!"

He took a flashlight and went outside with Sveta.

Ella refused to go.

She and I were left on our own. She moved over; her legs were wooden. She tilted her face upward so her eyes focused on the ceiling.

"So what. So what." She said this in the absolutely adult voice of a person who's already doomed.

And then it seemed to me that a hundred years had passed since the day she was born.

So, yes. Marik and I didn't discuss the situation that had come about. He'd promised Sveta not to tell her parents anything. I objected but agreed in the end: it wouldn't make anything any easier for anyone. A new scandal would only reflect on Ella since she was obviously the instigator and her depraved mind would keep moving rather than calming down. Where it would go was still the big question.

Despite my anxious expectation, the teacher didn't contact me regarding public apologies. All conversations with Ella about nonessential topics had ceased on their own. There was only what was necessary.

Sometimes I caught her empty gaze on me.

Marik tearfully asked when she'd become a stranger and why?

I think she was born a stranger, though. As a woman, I can sense things like that.

An unbearable atmosphere reigned in the apartment.

One thing kept me going: Mishenka's occasional letters, which were becoming ever more heartfelt. Of course I wrote to him every day.

About acoustics and its role in Mishenka's future.

Sasha Repkov had explained to me the approximate difference between the use of acoustics in the petroleum industry and in the navy. Of course the difference was huge. Then again, the principle's the same. It wouldn't hurt Misha.

Given that, though, Repkov clearly illustrated to me that it would be best for Mishenka to go for the specialty of "field geophysicist" or something of the sort. Stratification depth and so on. Explosions, sensors. Contaminants. It sounded very enticing. But the explosions put me on my guard.

After Repkov left, I rewrote the outline he'd presented while we talked and added my own thoughts on the dangerous topic of explosions. Let Mishenka think about that. Maybe it would be better to become a geophysicist.

I liked to imagine my son listening to the ocean's depths and all the interference around the submarine, then warning his comrades in the event of trouble.

Yes. Misha was located at such depths that nobody up above could reach him. Neither I nor Marik nor Blyuma and Fima.

Blyuma hadn't let me forget about her, though. She wrote letters with accounts of matters in Ostyor. All kinds of little things. At her level of mental development, she couldn't make any sort of generalizations, but she had enough of her wits about her each time to give a numerical count of Mishenka's letters to her. How many had arrived, how he'd addressed them ("Dear Blyumochka and Fimochka") and what promises there were for the future ("If they give me a vacation, I'll definitely come to Ostyor").

But then a different kind of letter arrived from Blyuma.

It was the end of the school year. Ella's lack of achievement had driven me to white-hot anger and I was in a very nervous state. Beyond that, it lay ahead to decide what to do for the summer. Neither I nor Marik wanted to go to the sea with our daughter.

We were also afraid to send her to camp. Anything could happen in a collective of children, particularly in relative freedom.

It was at that very moment that Blyuma wrote—without any external reason from my side—that she could no longer take it and wanted to warn me about using all my strength to pressure Mishenka's nerves. That he was tired of my bossing and planning out his future. That he had his own designs and the institute I'd suggested as matching his specialty didn't fit him: he had dreams of something completely different. And Blyuma had been counting on something entirely different when she'd implored him in her letters for an entire year to reconcile with me, saying that for the sake of appearances Misha shouldn't grouse with me about anything.

I've retold this so it's close to her text because it's impossible to reproduce literally: everything was thrown in one heap. It ended up, either logically or somehow else, that Misha had been writing to me that whole time out of charity, but was in no condition to take it any longer. And I was pressuring and pressuring him. Pressuring and pressuring. Just as I'd supposedly pressured Fimochka in my day—and look what happened with Fima, and then everything had fallen into Blyuma's hands and into her heart.

I sat up all night over Blyuma's letter. I read and reread it. Was she lying? Or not lying? It was impossible to understand. And impossible to move on. It would be stupid to write to Mishenka for explanations. And scary. Complex technology and his military comrades depended on him.

In the morning I got a ticket to Kiev and went to Ostyor. I'd counted on one day. But things turned out differently.

Blyuma greeted me in the middle of a flowering garden. She had a fright. Her arms were dirty with soil and it was with those arms that she dashed to embrace me and cry out:

"What happened, Mayechka, my dear, my sweet! You could have sent a telegram, I don't have anything tasty cooked up to treat you with!"

There was one genuine question in her eyes:

"What have I, Blyuma Tsivkina, done so wrong that you, Maya, turned up without an invitation to get on my nerves? You don't come to your homeland for nothing."

I, however, held on to the remnants of the composure I'd filled myself with during the train and bus rides. My visit basically already seemed excessive to me. In essence, decadent. Particularly when I saw Blyuma in photographic clarity. What could you expect from her? You couldn't expect anything from her about anything, especially regarding Misha's and my future fates.

And right there, in the garden, I asked:

"Blyuma, are you aware of what's in your letters? Do you understand you've handicapped my whole life? That you're interfering with the holy of holies—maternal love and care?"

Blyuma lifted her shovel and drove it into the ground with all her might.

"Aha, now I understand. You showed up to scold me. I gave Mishenka to you on a platter and set his brain straight, turning it in your direction. But you ruined it yourself and now you're telling me off."

Then I noticed that the watch on Blyuma's fat wrist—my watch—was now held by an elastic, not the watchband. Blyuma probably wore it like that and didn't take it off, day or night. The elastic was blackened and tattered, and ate into her yellow skin by at least a centimeter.

Blyuma caught my gaze. She wasn't even embarrassed, to the contrary.

"What's it you're looking at with those eyes? I'll give it back to you. I'll give it back now." She started tearing off the elastic and pulling it downward. The elastic tore from the pressure where it was attached. The little watch fell into the flowerbed.

Yes. Blyuma had planted my former watch. Planted it. And nothing would grow from it.

"I'll give you back the band, too. It broke. It broke right away. You wouldn't give me something good. You shoved the thing at me on its last gasp. But I'll give it back. I always give things back. I'm not you."

I picked up the watch, wiped off the dry earth, and shoved it in the pocket of Blyuma's apron.

"You're a fool, Blyuma. And you're not a fool because of your mind."

I wanted to continue developing my thought and move toward condemnation, but stopped short. Fima had risen up in front of me out of nowhere.

I didn't understand how he'd approached. He was smiling. With his gold teeth. At least the front ones were; whatever was in the depths there wasn't visible.

Blyuma grabbed him by the head and abruptly pressed it to her bust:

"There, Fima, pull out your teeth and give them back. Let her melt them down again and wear them on her pretty little arm. Take them, take them," she was poking a finger right into Fima's mouth. And Fima bared his teeth. By the tone, he understood there was nothing to smile at, he just couldn't close his mouth because Blyuma's hand was in the way.

Yes.

I went into the house. Into my own house, by the way. It didn't matter who was registered where.

Blyuma appeared behind me, holding hands with Fima.

Blyuma was red, Fima was gray. I was white.

And then I started crying. And I cried as much as I had over my wool dress that I left on the bed during evacuation twenty-eight years ago. And I cried a half hour, no less. And shouted and wailed. And whatever else is done in situations like that.

Blyuma didn't shed a tear. She just rubbed and rubbed her fat wrist where there was a crimson mark from the elastic. Rubbed and rubbed. And Fima looked at us in turn, blinking.

Then a conversation took place. With the facts.

Blyuma showed Mishenka's letters. Not all of them, of course. The ones where he'd complained about my pushiness. They'd already been tied up separately, with a cord. Yes, Blyuma's a fool, a fool, but she's smart. She'd been preparing for a meeting. Though she didn't know when it would be.

And so. And so, what Misha wrote: "I feel very sorry for Mama. She has an unhappy life. She piles her love on me because she doesn't have anywhere else to put it. She thought up the oil institute for me. I think she wants the oil institute both because the business trips are far away from home and the money's good. A lot of us want to go to Samotlor after service. As workers. At political information sessions that's all you hear, in a good sense: oil's black gold. Or things like that. Everybody wants some gold. Even the black kind. But it's hard for me to keep Mama's letters inside me. They settle on my heart like a rock. From understanding her loneliness. I imagine that when I go back I'll have to live under the same roof as her. And put up with it. I'll put up with it. I've grown up a lot. I have nowhere to put Mama's textbooks: there's not much space and there are more important items for everyday use. I throw them away as soon as I get them."

So what do we see? The primary thought is favors. Favors and favors again.

I'd bought textbooks, stood in line for them, tracked things in the newspapers and on television. I wrote about everything pertaining to the future profession.

Yes. My son had heard me through his acoustics. But my primary maternal wish—to be nearby and always with him—didn't reach him through those acoustics.

But he did love me after all. I came to that conclusion when I was with Blyuma. And what did it matter what he had to go through to love me, whether it was his own patience or my pushiness?

Yes. Everything has to be won. Love, too. And I'd won that.

Over all, Blyuma agreed with me.

"He loves you, Mayechka. He loves you very much and adores you. And he's always loved you. And he told Gilya he loves you. But Gilya, may he be resting in peace, taught Mishenka: love your mama, love your mama, love her even if she's a so-and-so. You're her son."

I smiled.

Blyuma reacted to my smile in her own way:

"Gilya always had a smile, too. The life he went through from end to end . . . and always with a smile. All of Ostyor came to him for advice. Only you, Mayechka, didn't ask him for advice. And he would have told you how to do things and how not to."

"Blyuma, people don't ask the living. Particularly relatives. You yourself understand that. Did you ask Gilya about much?"

"I did. They used to invite him to speak at the school. And at the construction vocational school. He went. And they asked there. And he loved to talk. And knew how. May he be resting in peace. And he used to read to Mishenka, when Mishenka was still little. Misha grew up and wanted to read himself. Gilya was against that, 'Listen with your ear, it'll get through faster.' "

"And what did he read?" I wasn't interested, but had to keep the conversation going.

"More often than not, for example, *The Story of a Real Man*." A pilot without legs. A real man. He knew it by heart. Hardly looked at the pages. Rattled it off from memory. Not in full, but most of it. Even now everybody in Ostyor has the same opinion: Gilya was a real man. And I'm personally confirming that. Only he had his legs."

I called Marik from the post office that evening. I didn't feel like going to Moscow. I asked how he was coping with Ella, how they'd been eating. I'd cooked extra food, but no quality and quantity was enough for Ella. Marik assured me all was well, Ella was drawing and doing her homework. Speaking calmly. I abruptly said I'd come home in a few days since circumstances had arisen in Ostyor. Marik didn't gripe. If I had to, I had to. He'd cope.

The thought of lingering for a couple days in Kiev had come to me on its own. Meet with a few people. Including relatives. The thought hadn't fully formed into a goal, but I couldn't sit still.

End of May. Darkness came late. I requested Miroslav's new address from Blyuma, for the sake of what was good. I was certain she knew where he was and all that.

Blyuma didn't let me down, she even gave me his telephone number, too.

She stood holding a scrap of lined paper with numbers jotted on it, waving the little sheet around in front of her face as if she couldn't get enough air.

"Very good. He used to be a close person, at any rate. And Mishenka loves him. And his life has been unsettled after you. All alone in the world. Gilya loved him and Fanechka, too, may they be resting in peace."

The way she looked was so touching it made me wince.

"Blyuma, they're resting. And resting in peace, don't worry. But I'm not resting, I can't sit. You just check with Fima about who loves and respects who and who's all alone in the world after who. Got it?"

Blyuma pursed her lips:

"Oy, Mayechka, you're unbearable. I was just saying that. No reason. I said it, so I said it. Go see Miroslav if you want. Don't go if you don't want. It's none of my business."

"No, it is, Blyuma. It is your business. Everything's your business: Miroslav and Mishenka and Fima and Mama and Gilya. All of Ostyor is yours. There's nothing here that's mine. And there never was. Whatever you think, give it to me straight. Don't hedge."

My patience had ended without ever beginning. Blyuma was putting on a show and I couldn't stand shows.

"Well, fine, Mayechka. I'll tell you. You're thinking I don't understand anything here. That's right. I don't have an education, nothing. But I understand you decided to untie all your little knots in one fell swoop. You think you've already untied Fima and me. Now you're going to Miroslav to untie that string. Go on, go on. You have enough knots for a hundred years. Your mother told me a lot about you. Is the name Kutsenko familiar to you? It's even very familiar to me. And his face is familiar to me. Just so you know."

Blyuma triumphantly plopped down on a stool. Laid her hands on the table. And didn't let the scrap of paper out of her fingers.

I noticed she'd pulled a new white rubber band into the pins of the watch. And the knots were secure. Strong. Blyuma caught my gaze and rolled her sweater sleeve higher.

"What, did he come here? When Misha was here?"

"No, it was without Misha. Misha'd already gone into the military. But I'm holding my tongue. I'm like the grave."

"So what did you tell Kutsenko, you grave?"

"Well. I said Misha was in the military."

"Good, Blyumochka. Good. Was he here long ago?"

"Misha'd just barely gone. More than a year ago. Last fall, as it happens. In November."

"And how did he find you?"

"He found me, so he found me. Didn't explain."

"And does Mishenka know about Kutsenko?"

"Know what?" Blyuma pretended she didn't understand.

"You know yourself 'know what.' Stop fooling around."

"I don't know anything about Kutsenko. I saw his face. And I'll tell you straight. I'm just telling you what I saw. You were planning to go to Kiev, good riddance. You won't get it out of me. I'm like the grave."

There was nothing you could do with her. Tell a smart person and they'd understand and answer. But she wouldn't answer and wouldn't understand.

But that's not my point.

Blyuma and I did not part on good terms. She apparently regretted having said too much. But I was only firmer about needing to go see Shulyak.

I headed to the post office again. With my things.

I called.

Miroslav picked up the phone himself.

I started speaking. He recognized me immediately. And after so many years! Too many to count quickly. Yes. Love is love.

"Something wrong with Misha?" Of course that scared him.

"No, Misha's fine. Can you take me in for a couple days? Just as an outsider? Or do you have a family?" I said that as if I weren't aware of the situation.

The phone operator had said I was calling from Ostyor when she connected the call, so I openly indicated I was a two-hour drive from Kiev so could come quickly by taxi. Funds permitted it.

Miroslav answered briefly and clearly: "I'll be expecting you."

And here's what came next. Next was that Miroslav had aged a lot. After all, he wasn't significantly older than me. His face was showing his diet of cold meals. I remarked with regret that he'd been handsome but had really gotten old in ten years. Miroslav brushed it off because he was delighted to concentrate on me.

Unfortunately, I hadn't dressed my best when I was getting ready to see Blyuma. The train's the train and so's a mood. But Miroslav wasn't paying attention to the clothes: he looked and looked at my face and figure.

"Maya, my mother was right when she used to say you're a witch." Of course he was laughing, but I was offended.

"And you believed that? So that's why you had something on the side with that little nurse? So she'd wean you off me with medical means?"

Yes. Out loud, we were both joking. But we weren't joking in our souls. Each of us had our own distress about the past. You can't fix anything. Especially when adding in the passage of time.

I surveyed the apartment. Nice, bright. Two connected rooms. Not bad in exchange for one small room in a communal apartment. Things were getting worse and worse for Miroslav at work and now he was in a low-paying job, almost a rank-and-file foreman. I didn't get into asking where and he didn't share that.

We almost immediately shifted to talking about Misha.

Misha wrote to Miroslav regularly. Miroslav brought letters in a shoebox to show me. It was a large box: he'd recently bought some good Czechoslovakian shoes and moved the letters into the box. They'd been lying all piled up in a kitchen table drawer before. Miroslav talked and was glad that a convenient and roomy place for Mishenka's letters had turned up before my arrival.

I was curious first off about what Misha'd been communicating. How his mood was.

"I won't read the letters, he didn't write to me so they're not for me to read. I'm not asking for a report, Miroslav, just a story based on the themes."

"His mood's good. Feisty. He's waiting for vacation. Promises to come."

Miroslav smoothed the papers, pulling out sheets and putting them back. Misha's handwriting turned out to be completely different here. Small and agile. Unlike the letters addressed to me. In block print. The writing in Blyuma's was different, too. It leaned to the left and the characters were like beetles, spread out. As if a left-handed person had written them. I'd just figured that out right then. But the same person had written them. It was immediately obvious he was imitating something for a reason.

Miroslav went on:

"He's not planning to go back to school after his service. He wants to have a look around, have a rest. And that's that."

"What does he write about me? About the family? His sister? Does he reminisce?" I posed the question directly and impartially on purpose.

Miroslav wasn't at a loss for words, though, and answered without hesitation:

"You know, don't be offended, but Mishka and I have never talked about you. It's not just that we haven't discussed you, God forbid, but we basically haven't even said half a word. And he doesn't write about you. He wrote once about his sister, wondering how she'll turn out. He doesn't write about your husband Marik, either. Well, that's understandable."

"What, did you come to an agreement about me or something? Not to reminisce?"

"What do you mean, an arrangement! We don't reminisce with each other, period. Leave the boo-boo alone. As my mother used to say. She suddenly stood up before her death. Yes. Imagine that, she stood up and walked for a couple weeks. Somehow or other, but she walked. And went to the bathroom and ate seated. She'd sit down at the table and eat. And then she died. Did Misha tell you?"

"No."

"Well, and that's the right thing. There's no need for you know. Don't worry about Mishka. He reminisces about Gilya often. Looks up to him. I'm all for that, completely. That's what I always write to him. Remember Gilya, remember Gilya. Judging from the letters, he's on the right track."

I no longer had any doubt.

As a last straw, I asked:

"Does the name Viktor Pavlovich Kutsenko mean anything to you?"

"No. I haven't heard of him."

Miroslav answered honestly. He'd never been able to lie. He said his mother hadn't taught him. And Mama hadn't taught me, either.

We went our separate ways to sleep.

I would have let him in if he'd come to me.

But he didn't come to me.

I had two spots left in my visiting plan: Lazar and Khasya, and Kutsenko.

Kutsenko was living at his old address. It turned out he wasn't at home. A neighbor woman opened the door and said he'd be back in the evening; the time depended on his class schedule. And his wife was definitely always home at five. I wasn't asking about his wife. I asked if there was a telephone in their apartment. It turned out there wasn't. I received confirmation to my question about whether Kutsenko worked at the technical college, as before. Yes. Viktor loved his work and was always wholly dedicated to it.

Despite the risk of not catching Kutsenko, I headed for the pedagogical technical college, the place my youthful years had passed. Agonizing recollections swarmed in my head and impeded my thinking. I wasn't even thinking.

I looked at the schedule. Viktor's lectures started in an hour. I sat down to wait on a bench outside, by the entrance.

He saw me first. He rushed over, arms wide-open for an embrace. He hadn't changed at all. And hadn't grayed. Unlike Shulyak.

I stood to greet him.

"Hello, Viktor Pavlovich!"

"Mayechka! You're in my dreams every night. I'm seeing you and not believing my eyes!"

"You'll have to believe it. I'm a fact."

"Yes, yes you are! Are you here on some sort of business?"

"I came to see you. Regarding Misha."

Viktor was immediately on his guard.

"What Misha?"

"Your son Misha. Did you go to Ostyor? Looking for Misha?"

"What do you mean Ostyor? I don't know any place called Ostyor. And I don't know Misha."

I'd applied the element of surprise and caught Kutsenko unawares.

"You still have twenty minutes until your lecture. Be nice and tell me everything. You know how I can be not nice." I looked Viktor in the eye, all the way in, to the very depths.

And he told me.

My mother, Faina Leibovna, hadn't been sitting around twiddling her overworked thumbs. As soon as she suspected I was seeing someone seriously, she set up independent monitoring either near the house or the technical college. And she'd noticed me arm in arm with Kutsenko. She came to her own conclusions and awaited her daughter's happiness. Later, though, things were heading toward marriage with Surkis. Mama knew Fima's character, based on what Lazar and Khasya had said. That he liked to have a drink and so on. And that his head was a little off at times, when he thought a lot about his missing family. So my mother went to see Kutsenko a few days before the wedding. And threw herself at his feet right at some back entrance to the technical college, so he'd take me for his own or at least give some hope. Anything so I didn't rush into marrying Fima. Under her reasoning, she knew I was pregnant, which is why she went.

Viktor Pavlovich cheered her and pinned things on me, that I was the one who didn't want to. And if I didn't want to, then let it be as I wanted. As far as a possible child went, it was unknown whose it was.

Yes. A good answer. Even now, nobody'd thought up anything else new to say. Let alone back then.

Mama couldn't bear it and spat hard in Viktor's face. He wiped it off. He left for his lecture and said nothing in conclusion.

The situation had apparently bruised Mama, too. About a year later, when Misha had already begun fully resembling a human being (and Kutsenko, too, by the way), Mama went out with the boy, ostensibly for a stroll, and showed the child to Kutsenko. She shoved Misha's face right at Kutsenko's.

By that time, Viktor had divorced Darina. But I'd already been given in marriage to another. Meaning, in fact, to Surkis.

Then Mama left for Ostyor. She'd done her job. Stood up for her daughter's good name. And at what price!

When I reappeared in Viktor's life, he'd already come to terms with my not being his. He might have intended to enter into a relationship with a married woman, but a nice, simple woman had been waiting in the wings. The slovenly one washing the floor in her bathrobe. Yes. He'd found someone for himself.

And so I graduated from the technical college and was fully absorbed in my not-so-simple family life. Then Mishenka was temporarily transferred to Ostyor—to Mama and Gilya—for health reasons. Then this, then that.

But Viktor always kept track of his son from afar. Not like in the movies. In simple ways. For example, he'd walk past the house. Or something like that.

And so he noticed when Misha disappeared. He made little inquiries with the neighbors. There was this one woman who told him I wasn't living with Fima, that I'd supposedly sent the child to my mother's in Ostyor. I'd made no secret of it. It was a good place. Not an orphanage. To his dear and loving grandmother and grandfather.

Well, in Ostyor you can find whoever you're looking for.

And Viktor Pavlovich went there whenever he felt a yearning. Not often. He'd have a look at Misha. That's how Mama spotted Viktor one time.

"Aha," she said, "have a look, have a look. A nice boy's grown up. He grew up in our charge. But you'll have only yourself to blame if you approach him to talk."

A threat from an elderly woman isn't generally frightening. But Viktor's a decent person—I wouldn't have gotten involved with any other type, either when young and inexperienced or otherwise—so he never made any attempts to come near Misha.

And when Viktor's calculations said Misha had reached adulthood, he went to Ostyor so as to make the acquaintance of an adult person rather than the baby he'd seen all those long years ago.

And here Blyuma was in all her splendor.

Discipline is discipline, so Viktor was in a hurry. You couldn't be especially late for a lecture. People were waiting. Female students in miniskirts and so on and so forth.

I held him back by the elbow, though:

"So you tell me in a word. Does Misha know you're his father?"

"He doesn't know if your mother didn't tell him."

"Viktor Pavlovich, I request of you officially and entreat you as a true mother. Do not show up again in Misha's and my life. Because you'll have work and the labor union and the Party organization to answer to."

He was even shaking:

"Maya, what kind of nonsense is this? Do I really stand guilty before you? You made your own choices. You chose for yourself and chose for Misha."

"That's exactly it. I chose from what I was given. And so you have to choose. Choose what I'm going to give you. Work and love your wife. Do you have other children?"

Viktor sniffled in the negative. He didn't even reach in his pocket for a handkerchief. And he calls himself a cultured person. There was a handkerchief peering out of the small upper pocket of his jacket just the same. Nice and clean and dark blue. Not matching. But okay.

I turned and left. The heels of my shoes clicked. High heels, by the way. Titanium heel tips. They only applied them in two places in Moscow. And not on just any footwear.

Yes. That was my final triumph over Viktor.

Now Lazar and Khasya were left. Along with Motya.

The subject needed to be tightly closed. Like a door.

I needed to unwind and calm down after my meeting with Viktor. My past had been churned up in my soul and was asking to be let out.

I went to Mariinsky Park. The chestnut trees were blooming. With their last color, not like how they bloom at the very beginning. I felt sad. I sat a while on a bench, stood by the railing over the steep slope, and looked at marvelous Kiev from on high. At the Dnieper.

Yes. River crossing, river crossing. Left bank, right bank. Mishenka had studied "Vasily Terkin" in school. He knew about the war from Gilya, not from hearsay.

And what he knew was inaccessible to me. That was the question.

After the lengthy break, it would have been inadmissible to go see Lazar and Khasya without a gift. I went to a food store. And what do you know! I bought a Kiev torte. Without even shuddering. I stood in line and was happy instead of having burdensome recollections.

Yes. Time has a big effect.

I went to the old familiar address. But something unexpected lay waiting for me. Lazar and Khasya no longer lived there. The new residents told me they'd moved a year ago. And they didn't know where. Never in my life had I known where Motya and his family lived. I basically had no need for Motya.

But that's not my point.

The point is that a person is sure of the unchangeability of things. It doesn't matter what. Maybe even a place of residence.

And there were plenty of sources: both Blyuma and Miroslav. But I hadn't asked. And there I was, standing in front of a closed door. With a torte.

My impulse had vanished into thin air. Under the circumstances that had arisen, conversations with Lazar and Khasya seemed unnecessary and even superfluous. Mama knew the true value of these people and wouldn't have entrusted anything important to them.

My momentary weakness passed and new strength led me forward. I sat on a bench in the public garden next to their building. I put the box with the Kiev torte next to me and my whole life appeared before me in plain view.

Mama had carried my past life with her to a deep grave. And it was time to put the matter to rest.

Misha was Misha. And the fact that he wrote long letters in varied handwriting to everybody under the sun spoke of him: anything could happen. Anything could happen with a person like that. There wasn't just one of him. There were four of him. Blyuma had her Misha. Miroslav had his. Gilya had had his own. And I had another.

I stood in line two hours at the train station for a ticket. I bought it for the next day, though it was an early-morning train.

Miroslav and I had tea in the evening. The torte had cracked and crumbled a little during a day of scurrying my way around the city. It was fine over all. Its vendibility remained intact, as they say.

The conversation was relaxed. I told of my lack of success with Lazar and Khasya.

Miroslav started laughing:

"Are you on a farewell tour or something? You aimed to make the rounds of everybody? You should've asked me. After your mother's funeral, when you'd already gone, Khasya made a scene about how you'd been excluded from the relatives, but there you were again. Blyuma told me this. Blyuma stood up to her, said you're the daughter and she couldn't be buried without you. Khasya didn't shut up, but Blyuma brought in the unexpected argument that you'd left them to use the house so now you had the right. Khasya dictated to Lazar how they'd never set foot in that house again and they were leaving immediately and that Blyuma and Fima shouldn't count on their help. As if they were really counting on it, right. You do understand what kind of help they could get from Khasya and Lazar. But Khasya'd warned Blyuma to get ready to move into a nursing home and said she should most likely put Fima in the nuthouse because you and your disposition would definitely show up during the winter and put them out on the street. So instead of waiting, they should take charge of their life in advance. And here's why Blyuma's reaction was so touchy: nobody anywhere would take her along with Fima. Each individually, sure. But together, no. They were differing types, Fima as mentally ill and she as just an old woman. Blyuma was wailing. They called an ambulance. They barely revived her. It was almost a heart attack with a stroke. Blyuma didn't tell you?"

"No. She didn't say anything."

"She doesn't want to worry you. You should give her some sort of written promise that you won't kick them out. It's silliness, of course. But she'll feel more secure."

I nodded. I don't know why, but I did.

Miroslav went on:

"So Lazar and Khasya moved. Motya got an apartment on the outskirts, from Arsenal, in Vinogradar. Khasya and Lazar went there. And Motya and his family apparently stayed in the old place, but they exchanged it for another one. That's just the rumor, though. Nobody knows anything reliable. If you really need to know, you could find out through the information bureau first thing tomorrow morning."

"I don't need to. It didn't work out, so I don't need to. Even so, people's customs do need to be respected: gathering everybody for a funeral and having it out while they're at it. And I didn't invite you to either Gilya's or Mama's. Don't be offended."

Miroslav shook his head:

"You didn't invite me. Misha described how it went in a letter to me. How Gilya courageously died."

I was on my guard.

"Gilya died like a soldier. Without groaning and reproaches. That's what Misha wrote. Misha's not inclined to sentimentality. That's how Gilya raised him."

Miroslav stumbled on his words, realizing he hadn't said the right thing. But I took it. Fine, let it be Gilya, he raised Misha. I'd endured things and was still enduring worse.

Something else hit me. What hit me is that if anything happened to Blyuma, then Fima would land on me like a rock. He wouldn't be taken into any hospital for feeding, watering, and laundering. He was quiet and not dangerous to his environment. And where could he be put?

So I turned to Misha. To Misha because—out of everything—he'd become the neutral topic.

"What did you and Misha discuss all those years without me?"

"He mostly talked with my mother. Listened to her. One time she said to him, 'Misha, you don't know this, but Christ was a Jew. Keep that in mind!'

"Misha didn't understand anything.

"As it happens, you'd moved to Moscow and he was living with Gilya and your mother again. I often took him to my place for Sundays. From Saturday evening on.

"Mama would say, 'You just tell that to everybody who calls you names.'

"Mama was worried Misha's Jewish appearance would get more obvious over the years. Well, I couldn't stand that kind of ignorance. Mama was a simple woman, practically illiterate. In the sense of the current time. And a shut-in besides. When you lie and lie there, everything comes into your head. When Misha wasn't there, I'd tell her, 'Mama, don't put ideas into the boy's head. There's no God now. And there's nothing to talk about.'

"And Mama'd answer, 'Well, there isn't now. But I'm telling him in advance. In case He comes back.'

"It's true, she died well. Quickly. With the hope, you could say, that she'd walk again. It wasn't long before Gilya. I wrote to Misha later, at 'hold for pickup.' As soon as he received his passport, he and I agreed I'd write to him that way. He'd been against the home address before, too. Didn't want to upset you. It's too bad Mama didn't die in the summer, it would have been when he was here. She said before her death, 'Is Mikhailik recorded in your passport? Yes, he is. He's not going anywhere away from you. Don't be sad.' She and Misha used to repeat 'Don't be sad.' He liked that."

So they wanted to connect my son to that death, too. Yes. There were shut-ins and sick people all around him. Shut-ins and sick people. Like some kind of encirclement.

And an occasion had been found to bring God into it. But not for his very own Mama. Though there's always Mama. Mama, whether or not there's God.

But that's not my point.

I asked the main thing that had been torturing me:

"Does Misha know who his father is? Based on your information, does he know or not? Tell me in a word."

"What do you mean in a word! He's not a fool, Mayechka. He figured it out immediately. Fima's his father. Though he's crazy. But he's his biological father. And he loves and respects him as a father. We've talked about Fima, too. Misha's sorry Fima's crazy and isn't in a condition to say much. But love, you know yourself. Blood speaks, not the mind."

"And Misha said that?"

"Yes, Misha. The last time we met. We were sitting at the train station. Silently. He asked me to help Fima and Blyuma. Well, materially and verbally, too. To support them. I help them, don't be thinking anything. I basically hope—just don't be offended— that maybe Misha will move to Kiev after the military. I'll register his residence with me. You have a daughter, too. And I'm alone. What do you think?"

"I don't think anything. Do you remember how I wanted to have a daughter with you?"

"I remember. It's too bad you didn't. So it wasn't on purpose you didn't have a baby?"

"It wasn't on purpose. I have a daughter now, too. Ellochka. A nice girl. Pretty. Smart. She paints. Watercolors. Very talented."

Miroslav nodded joyfully:

"You couldn't have had another kind. I have no doubt. I never had any doubts about you at all. It's just how life shifted. It shifted in an instant. It's silly. Mama had regrets. Did you?"

I didn't answer at all.

We parted warmly, until our next meeting. We no longer had to share Misha. Out of everybody still alive, he's neither mine nor Miroslav's. It works out he's Fimka's.

So much suffering yet again. Why? To establish order inside Misha? But the order of things in there at the current moment is beyond my comprehension. Which is why it's unclear what kind of order needs to be created.

And when am I supposed to have a life? That's the top question and problem.

But that's not my point.

I slept the whole way back. Tranquilly, right up to the Moscow Marshalling station.

The conductor woman shook me:

"Watch your things, woman, people steal when getting off the train."

Yes. Exactly, when getting off the train.

At home, Marik held an inquiry right at the door, asking how long he wouldn't have a mailbox key. The box was full of newspapers he couldn't take. I gave him the key, with a smile.

He was surprised.

"Fine. I was joking. I don't need one."

"You need one, you need one. Everybody needs one. I need to make one for Ellochka, too, so she has a key. It's a responsibility, after all, to pick up the mail. It concerns her, too: there's *Pioneer Pravda* and *Campfire*."

I didn't talk more, I went off to sleep. And slept until evening. Until Ella showed up from her after-school program.

Sometimes things really do come together. Obviously and incredibly.

Beinfest called in the evening. He asked to come visit the next day. The next day was Sunday and there was no reason to refuse. Though I didn't feel like seeing anyone outside the family. Even so.

Natan Yakovlevich arrived with his belated supplemental gift: the chess clock. Marik clutched it with joy and inspired spirit.

We talked about this and that. Among other things, Beinfest politely inquired if I liked the mezuzah he'd given Marik on his birthday.

I was surprised. I knew nothing at all about a mezuzah. In all the confusion, I hadn't asked Marik about Natan Yakovlevich's personal gift, then there was the trip, and Marik himself hadn't said anything.

Natan shook his head:

"It's very regrettable that gifts like that remain without a place in life. But I gave it predicting it would mostly lie somewhere. I understand this isn't the time to hang mezuzahs on doorframes."

Even so, he asked Marik to bring it and show me.

Marik rummaged around a little in his room and brought it about ten minutes later.

Beinfest noticed: "What, did you hide it far away?"

"Far away, Natan Yakovlevich. It's the kind of thing you put far away."

Yes. The mezuzah turned out to be splendid. A silver case, old work, about fifteen centimeters long and three centimeters wide. Inside was a parchment scroll with a prayer handwritten in Hebrew. Natan Yakovlevich briefly explained the essence of the matter.

Ella was hovering here, too. She looked and looked at the mezuzah. And said:

"Where did you get a thing like that, Natan Yakovlevich? Where did you buy it?"

Natan candidly said:

"I didn't buy it. My comrade—a colonel, a pilot—brought it to me from Israel. Back in 1948, he was visiting there on an assignment from our Communist Party and he brought this thingy to me later. I've kept it and I gave it to your Papa and your Mama and your whole large and tight-knit family. Let this be an heirloom for you. It's special because it was presented to my friend by comrade Meir Vilner himself. Israel's main communist! Of course, he's a communist, but for a Jew, something like a mezuzah isn't considered superstition and it has no bearing on Party matters. It's not like that yet here, but that's how it is in Israel."

Then Ella said:

"Uh-huh. I understand. It's for spy information. To stick spy things inside and carry it. Very convenient. A military secret. Well, so your comrade brought you some kind of secret from Israel to keep and now you're spreading it around. And brought it to us. Thank you very much. I'll take it to the police."

Natan Yakovlevich started laughing:

"Your daughter's so cheerful and quick-witted! Ellochka! My comrade was an outstanding communist, it was the Party that sent him, personally. If you want to know, I was planning to go there, too.

As a communist and veteran of the front. It's just that the need for me faded later, so they sent my comrade. You should understand that, you're a smart little girl."

"Uh-huh. I do."

She turned and went to her room. Along the way, she turned around and asked: " 'Natan,' what would that be converted? To Russian?"

Beinfest didn't understand.

I understood immediately, though: "Just so you know, Natan is Anatoly. Go on, go on. Write it down."

Beinfest tossed up his hands in bewilderment: "How old is your little girl?"

"Almost ten. Don't be surprised. She's very mature for her age."

After thinking a bit, Beinfest said:

"You know what, I'm an old fool. Taking apart a mezuzah in front of a child. That's a blow for a child. She twisted the meaning, twisted it. Forgive me. Now you'll have to explain to her, set her head right."

Marik waved him off:

"Don't worry. Our Ellochka has her own special head on her shoulders and there's quite the order established there, like you wouldn't believe! And how! She'll put your mezuzah in its own place. And register it in her mind. We're used to that. Just don't mention Jews in her presence. No reason. For our overall calm."

Beinfest changed the subject, saying:

"You're dear to me, so we should have an especially trusting relationship. Like between a client and an attorney. I'm joking. But there's tremendous truth in every joke. You know that. So, Mayechka. I want to propose something to you since you'll be the primary link in this story. I have a very nice apartment. Not far from yours, on Staromonetny Lane. Two rooms with a huge kitchen.

That's especially important for you to know, Mayechka, as the lady of the house.

"I'll die soon. That's a foregone conclusion. I have a serious illness plus my age. I've consulted with an academician I know and there's no chance. I'll die and the apartment would go to a government from which I have, of course, seen many good things, but even so, that's not enough to make such a lavish posthumous gift.

"This is the plan. A full-on spy plan. Heh, heh. Of course the sham is clear to everybody. But nobody will find fault. You and Marik divorce. You, Maya, will register a marriage with me. I'll register your residence as my wife. And the apartment's yours. I'll live as long as I live and die with my heart at peace because I provided people close to me with the dearest and most important thing: an extra roof over their heads. I've thought about this a long time and can't make a gift like this to anyone but you, so it's straight from the heart and without any hidden agendas. But for you—by all means."

Marik was lost. He asked for time to think. I joined him in that. Gifts like that don't come in every life.

As he left, Beinfest asked us not to drag out our answer since he was pressed for time and could be gone forever at any minute. As he expressed it: *"Zeitnot!"*

The door slammed shut behind him.

I uttered one word: "Well?"

Marik nodded.

That night the future felt as clear and wonderful as a May morning in a song.

Marik and I brought our divorce papers to the Civilian Status Registry Office without delay.

Though it was noted in the declaration that we were in mutual agreement, the procedure had to be conducted through a court because of our child who was a minor: Ella.

Beinfest arranged it on an accelerated schedule. A month later, I was registered at his apartment as his wife.

He announced immediately that he didn't need any help whatsoever from us. It's simple, he said, wait for news. Meaning that he'd died. A housekeeper came to see him every other day. She'd been taking care of things in his family since time immemorial, and would notify us in the event of Natan Yakovlevich's sudden death.

But that's not my point.

A month sped by at a rapid pace.

I didn't write to Misha. There was nothing from him, either.

I didn't see Repkov.

And Ella was just getting mediocre grades. Top grades only in drawing.

I said to her:

"You've completely slipped in your achievement. Are you satisfied with that? Aren't you ashamed of yourself?"

She smirked:

"I'm not ashamed. The after-school drawing group teacher said I have skills for using color. They need to be developed. But you're not developing them. It's you and Papa that should be ashamed."

And then I was ashamed with all my might. If there was even a speck of me in my daughter, that speck had to be pursued all the way. If she had a talent for drawing, then let her go down that road. And have a good journey.

I went to the school the day before the end of the quarter. I met with the drawing teacher: she also taught a painting group and drafting for the older grades. She described to me the promise my girl was showing.

I took Ella by the hand and brought her to the Palace of Pioneers on Polyanka Street right away. The same place Mishenka had once gone. Only it was for a different discipline now: drawing and painting.

The leader—a middle-aged man—took a look at drawings, watercolors, and other sketches in an album and on individual sheets, and confirmed it:

"Let her come. Basically, we take almost everybody. But your little girl for certain. She should have started sooner. She would have already progressed a long way. And now she's probably going to summer camp or to her grandmother and grandfather's, so classes would be in the fall. What grade will you be in?" He looked at Ella as if she were an adult.

"Fourth."

The leader was surprised. Naturally he'd decided she was in at least fifth or sixth. But he was glad. She was beginning age, when it's easy to put in and take out what you want. With art, it's very important to develop taste. That's the first thing. The second is that whatever needs to come will come on its own.

The art group ran during the summer even though most of the children left town.

The group leader's name was Pyotr Nikolaevich Zobnikov. He wrote his telephone number on a slip of paper for me and listed all the necessary items and things for use in learning. Ella already had everything.

She basically already had everything. It was she herself that was lacking.

But that's not my point.

In light of Beinfest, as well as Ella's reluctance to go anywhere for vacation, it lay ahead to spend the summer in Moscow.

I was thoroughly exhausted so was glad of the circumstances. And a family vacation is work, too. Not easy at all, from any standpoint.

Ella went to the Pioneer Palace almost every day. She became friends with one little girl there.

Zobnikov devoted his steadfast attention to group members, gave large assignments, and organized field trips to museums. There were also plans for trips outside the city to make etudes. His method was full immersion in art. Let them draw as they could, learning from nature and their own intuition. The teacher's job was to give direction. Ella conveyed that to me.

I couldn't say things got better at home, but at least Ella wasn't just sitting around under the weight of her own groundless sufferings. Being so busy, she started eating less and lost a little weight. A tiny bit. But the maternal eye always finds something positive in order to be glad for one's child.

My thoughts returned to Mishenka. I wrote a long, warm letter about Ella. I wondered, hinting lightly, when his vacation would be. Not a single word about school. I passed along greetings from Miroslav, Fima, and Blyuma. Without explanations. Just greetings.

I asked Marik to add a few phrases, too. He wrote: "Misha! Come visit soon! We're waiting for you! Your mother's just as beautiful and Ella's growing by the hour, not even by the day."

A nice addition.

Something gave me no peace, though. Of course the situation with Beinfest was only normal at first glance. It actually worked out that we were waiting for his death. Weren't hurrying him, God forbid, but quietly expecting it. We paid him no attention, didn't call, didn't visit. That was in accordance with his request, though somehow that wasn't what normal people did.

I shared my doubts with Marik. He agreed: we needed to go see the old man.

Not for anything specific, but just because. As people.

We didn't bother calling. We showed up without a call. On a Sunday afternoon. I rang the doorbell.

Natan Yakovlevich quickly opened the door. He was happy but not overly so. He's a cultured person.

"You gave in after all. Come in."

Marik stammered:

"We'll leave if you don't want us here. We saw you, that's enough. We'll leave now. Right, Mayechka? We just came for a second."

Beinfest started waving his arms:

"Come in, come in. We'll have lunch together. This is your home. After all."

And he started laughing. Obviously not pretending about anything.

Well, we sat down by the table and were silent. He was silent and so were we.

Marik said:

"So, Natan Yakovlevich, we decided to call on you. Not so much to call on you as so you wouldn't think we forgot about you."

Beinfest said:

"Marik, let's not make fools of ourselves. You're embarrassed that it's as if you're waiting for my death. It's absolutely normal that you're waiting. I myself incited that in you. Provoked it. I'm an attorney and understand what provocation is and how it's cooked up. That's fine. Endure it. You're feeling uncomfortable in this situation. But what can you do? As they say, the human body is full of mysteries. What if I live another twenty years, huh? What, would you be embarrassed all those twenty years?"

Marik was sitting, red, and not knowing how to behave further.

I spoke:

"Yes, what you say is correct, owing to your life and professional experience. Really, live a hundred years. What's it to us? We're all for human relationships between everybody. And we won't dredge up the topic of your departure into the great beyond. Marik's embarrassed out of awkwardness. Men are basically more prone to awkwardness. But I'm a woman. I see the world through eyes, not through words. And I see you're in complete working order at the present moment and don't need our help. That's what we wanted to clarify."

Beinfest leaned curiously in my direction and reached to touch my shoulder with his hand. I was wearing a light dress. The fabric was similar to batiste, but not batiste, and it was modern at the time. With a thin stripe. And cap sleeves. The whole arm was bare. And there were deep triangular necklines in the front and back.

He patted me on the shoulder and withdrew his hand.

"Yes, Mayechka, exactly, you look with your eyes. Exactly. And here's what's interesting. With the exact same eyes. Always the exact same. Have you thought about that question?"

I smiled in response. To give him the pleasure.

He didn't offer us anything, not tea or anything else. Fine.

I inadvertently looked around the apartment, taking a broad view. Nice. Large, bright. High ceilings. Broad windows. Windowsills half a meter wide. Drapes pushed back. And the familiar edge of an Optima typewriter showing. I'd dreamed of one like that when I worked as a secretary at the shoe factory. I had a Moskva. But the Optima's German and was said to run as nicely and smoothly as our government ZiM sedans, effortlessly making six copies.

For old times' sake, I nodded in the direction of the typewriter:

"Why are you keeping it in the window? The ribbon will dry out and the sun and dampness are bad for the metal."

Natan Yakovlevich livened up: "So you understand typewriters, Mayechka? Can you type?"

"I should say so. That was my work at one time. But I could only dream of a machine like that. I pounded my fingers all off on a

Moskva. And my nails broke. And the carriage sometimes recoiled so much it was scary. With a deafening sound, too. The typewriter rang in my ears all the time. It was simply uncontrollable. Like a rocket."

Beinfest asked Marik:

"Bring it over here. Let Maya test its action."

Marik placed the typewriter on the table. It took effort to carry. German metal is German metal.

Beinfest brought paper and carbon paper from the other room.

I stacked sheets of paper with carbon paper as an old typist once taught me: not covering the whole sheet of paper, but so it's peering out about three centimeters on the right side. Then you can pull the carbon paper out nicely, all at once, without having to sort through the sheets.

Yes. Memory. Particularly mechanical memory. My fingers did everything on their own, nicely and correctly.

The men were admiring openly.

I inserted five copies and placed my hands on the keyboard like a pianist.

I said: "I'm ready, Natan Yakovlevich. Dictate."

He looked, keeping silent.

Then he said:

"I have nothing to dictate. I'm dictated out. Take the typewriter for yourself, Mayechka. I made a concerted effort to stop practicing. I have no need for it now. All the cassations have been written. To all the authorities. All of them. And that Optima may yet serve you for a long, long time. I have plenty of paper and carbon paper. Stock up. And there's ribbons. German. Take it."

Marik started refusing, saying it would still come in handy, all sort of things in that vein.

I said directly:

"Thank you. We'll take the typewriter since you don't need it and you're putting it into new hands as a gift, straight from the heart. Does it need to be registered? At the police or anywhere?"

"No. It doesn't. It's unregistered. It came to me by chance. And to you by chance, too. I'll call a taxi now and you'll go home like the wind. Don't haul that heavy thing around on the trolleybus. It doesn't have a case. We'll wrap it in a blanket so it doesn't attract attention."

That's what we did.

Of course we paid for the taxi ourselves, though Beinfest offered his money.

At home, Ella was with her new little friend, Nina Rogulina, from the art group. They were drawing.

I'd decided once and for all not to get involved in her creative work. And she wasn't inclined to showing. But there she was, approaching me with a sheet.

"Mama, I drew your portrait. Take a look."

And she stuck it right under my nose.

I looked and saw Baba Yaga. Matted hair sticking out all over. Hooked nose. Crooked mouth. And big red eyes. In short, my eyes.

Ella bided her time for a minute, so I could react.

"Well then, my little girl. All in all, there's a resemblance. Do you like it yourself?"

Ella hadn't expected my calm. She took the sheet and ripped it to shreds.

The four of us had lunch: Marik, Ella, Nina, and I. Ella was silent and barely chewed. Nina gazed at her and also hardly put anything on her plate. I didn't try to persuade her.

Ella abruptly said: "I'm never going to draw people."

Marik asked: "Why?"

"Because Pyotr Nikolaevich warned me that you have to answer for people. But not for nature. I don't want to answer for anything. I don't want anything at all."

She burst into tears on the last word and ran to her room. Nina following her.

I stayed at the table because I knew full well that what was speaking in my daughter was repentance for her Baba Yaga. I'd need to have a talk with Zobnikov about what he was teaching the children.

When Nina was leaving, I followed after her, as if going out for errands.

I caught up to the little girl and started speaking with her in friendly terms.

"Ninochka, do you like the art group?"

"I like it."

"And do you like Pyotr Nikolaevich?"

"I like him."

"And do you like being Ellochka's friend?"

"Yes."

"And does Pyotr Nikolaevich praise her in class? Tell me the truth. I won't tell Ella."

"Pyotr Nikolaevich says Ella's very capable and could be talented when she grows up. He doesn't praise me, though. But I don't get offended. I'm a top student at school. Ella's a top student, too, she told me. I'm older than Ella. But everybody thinks it's the opposite. I'm not offended. Ella and I decided we'll be best friends now. That's it."

We stood at the trolleybus stop until Nina's trolleybus came. I hadn't learned anything of importance. Other than that Ella lies about her excellent achievement at school. As a pedagogue, I didn't begin to disillusion Nina and speak of Ella's average and below-average grades. I planned to visit Zobnikov on Monday. You have to keep in contact with a pedagogue. It guarantees success.

I took a wild guess on when to go. But I was lucky: Zobnikov turned out to be there.

We spoke very little, monosyllabically. Over all, Zobnikov characterized Ella in a positive light.

This time, though—on closer inspection—Zobnikov made a negative impression. Untidy, unshaven. An unpleasant shirt. And seeing children when looking like that. I kept quiet, though.

He noticed my critical gaze and wasn't embarrassed, instead he defiantly uttered:

"You, Maya Abramovna, caught me not looking my best. I've been a bit unwell. You understand."

Yes. I had an understanding. And he had drunkenness.

I said:

"Fine, fine, Pyotr Nikolaevich. I know artists well, both by character and by nature. Just so long as it doesn't affect the children. The pupils. If anything happens, call me directly, and that's that. I'm a pedagogue, too, I'll understand, and we'll overcome it together."

"I have nothing to overcome with your daughter, though. She should be sent to an uninhabited island so there's nobody around for a hundred kilometers. Let her think a little within herself. She's ten years old, but there's enough jumbled in her head for a full eighteen. I see children like that over and over. She has a pursuit now. I think that will be to her benefit."

Well then, an ally on a child-rearing matter—that's something important. And what other allies were there? Marik? No. And even Zobnikov was quite something. With a hangover, barely able to stand. So it worked out I was still alone and alone again. Zobnikov was only in it for the sake of appearances.

I'd reached the conclusion that the jumble in Ella's head could be overcome.

The girl needed to be pulled out of her usual environment, where her nonsense had already left its mark, and moved into another good place. So she'd have the opportunity to start with a clean slate. She needed another school. It was now summer, just the time.

I told Marik. He approved. We spoke with Ella together, from the perspective that her present school hadn't proven itself and soon she'd start having separate teachers for all her subjects and that would be even worse.

Beyond that, Ella's classmates weren't really right for her.

Of course she was partially to blame, but the class's view of her—as a mediocre student—had already formed. That situation needed to be straightened out right now, while she was seriously involved with drawing.

Ella listened silently. Something was spinning in her head. And quickly spun itself off. I hadn't even hoped.

"Good," she said, "bring me to another school. I'm already tired of it here."

Yes. She was tired of it.

I selected another educational institution. Through clients of Marik's. Kind of far away, but the director was good. And I liked the teacher for elementary classes.

Based on his outward appearance and surname, the school director was Jewish, so I openly hinted that there had been problems regarding the question of nationality. And I hoped that nothing of the sort would occur in the new place.

The director blushed and quickly assured me that international-ism was at the very highest level in their school. There were children of scientific workers, engineers, and so on, including performing artists. They also had extracurricular work, supplementary classes, and interest groups. The broader the development, the broader the horizon, so there was none of the narrowness of perception that constitutes the essence of hostility.

Perhaps I shouldn't have referred to the Jewish question, particularly in the director's office. But if there was internationalism in the school, then why discuss it in a vacuum?

I also noted that everybody wanted to make my daughter into a problem child, but that she wasn't a problem child: the problems were around her and everybody heaped them on one child. As a pedagogue, I could fight that, but it was better to do so within a collective.

He smiled and looked at me with satisfaction.

"Yes, Maya Abramovna. Without a doubt, that's always better within a collective."

I recalled myself as a child and couldn't find parallel lines connecting me to my little daughter. It's a different generation. A different atmosphere. And I still felt like living a little, without her nerving me up.

Our whole family entered September with good hopes.

Several letters arrived from Misha. He didn't mention vacation. Or future studies, either. Alive and well, period.

I recalled my efforts regarding the oil institute with sadness. But that sadness was radiant.

Repkov and I met extremely rarely. And that was only outside, during his lunch break. We looked at the river from the granite embankment and didn't talk. Only once did Sasha wonder how my son was. I answered that he was fine. Couldn't be better. And that he likely wouldn't go to the oil institute.

Repkov sighed:

"Too bad. Such prospects are opening up. The whole country's turning to oil. And your son doesn't want that. What, did he set his sights on another place?"

"I don't know. And don't want to know. I served him the school on a platter. It didn't interest him. He's an adult. Let him set his sights where he wants."

Without any transition, Repkov said: "Maya, it seems to me that our relationship is over."

I turned away from the water and said, right into Sasha's eyes: "It seems that way to me, too."

It didn't *seem* that way to me. That's how it was.

Repkov knew too much about both me and my inner life. That impeded our relationship. Like it or not, that always impedes.

And now there was something completely different in me and Sasha was pulling me backward, to what he knew.

But that's not my point.

Regarding the typewriter.

I'd made up my mind that it would be good to have something to keep me busy.

Household management isn't the be-all and end-all for a woman. There needs to be something to put the rest of your soul into. And so I sat down at the typewriter. And immediately found my mainstay. Rapidity returned to my typing and a knack reappeared in my fingers and my gaze.

I retyped pages of texts from books for practice; I practiced with the radio since it's a completely different matter typing from a voice instead of paper.

In short, I started taking on work. Marik asked around among his acquaintances and then students started coming with their term papers, like a chain reaction. Not a lot, but I didn't need a lot.

I could retype a page several times. Some typists strike over an error so it comes out as a bold letter in one spot and the mistake is visible anyway. Or they glued on postage stamp paper (it comes in very handy, there's glue on the back). I knew those tricks. But why bother? I needed neatness and flawlessness. My heart was happy when the printed letters stood in even rows.

But the main thing was the sound. The loud keys imprinted something on me, one little stroke after another. Firmly, very firmly.

Ella didn't disturb me. Marik either. Not one thought was left in me. Just rat-a-tat.

Repkov called once. He probably had intentions, but I pretended not to understand and naively asked if he had any potential type-writing clients. He readily said their typist pool wasn't keeping up and so they were hiring people to do piecework. I asked him to get more detail.

And so I immersed myself in tables. People paid more for tables because usually nobody liked to type them so they off-loaded them on each other, with mistakes, too. But I loved tables. I'm a mathema-tician after all, so figures were more understandable for me.

But that's not my point.

My gratitude to Beinfest had grown.

Why had he given his apartment to me and Marik in particular? Naturally that would be in the future, but he'd given it.

I asked Marik, who shrugged.

"Old people have their quirks. He was a friend of my uncle's. And a relative, besides. Albeit a distant one."

"And what, he doesn't have other friends and relatives who are also in need? We have an apartment; we don't have a material need. But he gave us this imperial gift. And we're neither compensating nor taking care of him. You have to agree it's strange."

Marik threw up his hands: "People all lose their minds in their own ways."

Well, yes. They do. And I did know how people lost their minds.

The parents' meetings at Ella's school went decently. Not a single bad word about anyone. Apparently, everybody was good. My Ella was good, too. Her grades were bad, but she was good.

I stayed with the teacher after a meeting and asked: "Are there any complaints about Ella? Tell me the truth."

"No complaints."

"But she gets mediocre grades."

"Those are grades, too. On the other hand, she draws the newspaper for the bulletin board."

"How's her relationship with her classmates?"

"There isn't one. On the other hand, she sits quietly and takes things in, just takes them in. I see it in her eyes."

The teacher was looking at my shoes as she talked. I'd just, just bought them near House of Shoes on Lenin Prospect, from a profiteer woman.

Yes, women always do find something in common.

"Elena Vladimirovna, you and I are the same age, isn't that right?"

"Well, yes."

"Let's be candid all around. As a pedagogue, do you see what's in my little girl's soul? How are things for her there? Is there a ray of hope?"

The teacher kept looking at my shoes. She looked and looked.

"Maya Abramovna. It's rough in Ella's soul. I understand her. And you yourself acknowledge how it can be for a little girl's soul in a family where she's adopted and scolded for every little offense. She told me this with tears in her eyes. Now don't you be thinking I'm rebuking you. The secret of adoption and all that is protected by law. But keep in mind that I'm not leaving this unchallenged. Yes, you're adoptive parents, but have you no shame and sympathy? Indeed, it was Fyodor Mikhailovich Dostoevsky who spoke of a child's tear. One tear. And Ellochka pours out so many tears. She holds on at school. But she cries and cries. Cries and cries. And that's all without witnesses. So as not to upset anybody yet again. She told me. But somehow all the children in class know and pity Ellochka. And give her extra food. An apple from one, a pastry from another."

I was dumbfounded.

"What adopted daughter? Ella thought up this claptrap and you believed it. Have you looked at the documents? I'll bring you her birth certificate so you know who to believe. She's my birth daughter! She resembles me! Have a closer look! And she resembles her father, too! Stand them together! The gait, the motion. She only cries when there's nobody to see it. You couldn't squeeze a child's tear from her! You couldn't! Not for anything!"

I felt like I was falling into the depths and the waters were closing in over me. As if I were giving birth to Ella backward.

All I could ask as I sank to the floor was, "Some water!"

Elena Vladimirovna came back with a dampened handkerchief, and wiped my face.

"Hold on, now I'll run to the teacher's room for a glass. There aren't any here."

And she ran out.

I was sitting on the floor, rubbing mascara all over my face, rubbing. It got in my eyes; stinging. Tears flowed. Yes. One could kill over one tear from a child. But who should be killed for my tears? There was no answer. There wasn't.

What documents should I bring here to wave around? Well, passports, birth certificate. After all, they were only pieces of paper.

Pieces of paper!

But there was a divorce from Marik and a marriage to Beinfest in my passport. And I was registered in another place. Without Ella. It was all grist for her mill, literally all of it.

I drank some water and washed up in the teacher's bathroom.

Elena Vladimirovna and I were sitting across from each another.

There it was. Two pedagogues. And one little girl. Who wasn't even present. There was no presence, but there was treachery.

Elena said: "I don't know what to do. How to handle her further."

Nor did I know.

One thing was clear: Ella couldn't be touched. Either from my side or the school's.

That was the condition I was in when I called Beinfest: he was dying, he was an intelligent person, and he needed to transfer his intelligence to someone, so let him transfer it to me.

Natan Yakovlevich greeted my call unenthusiastically, but I said: "An issue of life and death is being resolved."

And I left without waiting for an answer.

Yes. Beinfest's days were already numbered. He was emaciated and pale to the point of blueness. It didn't smell of medicines in the apartment. I noted that specially. The thought even occurred to me that he wanted to do himself in.

Natan Yakovlevich was dressed in fine style, wearing a suit and necktie. About three sizes larger than he needed now, but he wasn't looking for wardrobe updates. This was the sort of situation where you wear out the old. You can't deceive yourself.

"What happened, Maya?"

"Excuse me, Natan Yakovlevich. I myself don't know why I showed up at your house. I want to share some thoughts. Hear your opinion."

He sat down across from me and placed his hands on a pink jacquard tablecloth that was probably from before the war.

He said: "I'm ready to listen."

I told him about Ella. About her general behavior and her idiotic fabrications. About my own condition.

He heard me out silently, without interrupting.

Then he said:

"Mayechka, did you come to me as an attorney? Of course not. You came to me to see a smart old person. Well, yes. I'm smart and old. But I don't know what to say to you. What clause to use to orient you. I'll just say this: Ella truly is adopted for you. It's as if she's not a stranger to you, but she's also not completely yours. It's that kind of generation. I've thought about this. She's embarrassed of her Jewishness. She doesn't want to answer for it. Because there's nothing Jewish in her. And there's already none of it in you now. But you and Marik do at least answer for your parents, who did have it. And if someone asks Ella for that, she shouldn't have to answer for anything about anything. Nobody wants to answer if there's no guilt."

I didn't understand what he was getting at.

"This is what you should do, Mayechka. Step aside for a while. Let Ella think up whatever she likes. Let her spread, as it were, her panicked moods. She's little, she'll recover from that panic. Everything always makes children scared. And she's scared. She's scared because she ended up Jewish. All children are afraid of the dark. And Jewishness is akin to the dark for children if they don't engage with it. It's useless to explain. Trust me and just step aside and wait silently until the light starts blinking on its own. And it's best if you bring back the mezuzah I gave you. Tomorrow. There's no use for it in your apartment. Return it to me."

He said that and went silent. He was breathing as heavily as a horse.

To ease the tension, I said with a smile:

"Is it true you were acquainted with Grigory Ivanovich Kotovsky himself?"

He didn't answer anything, he just started brushing dust specks off the tablecloth with his hand. But there weren't any dust specks.

His last words to me were:

"I can't even tell you what a treasure your visit is for me. I can have a last look at you, Mayechka, and no longer wait for anything else. Go home and don't fear anything. And don't fear your Ella. And Misha. And Marik. And, first and foremost, don't fear yourself. Go."

There you have it. He'd left me in the dark. What was it to him? It was nothing to him.

At home, I searched a long time for the mezuzah. I finally decided to ask Ella.

Ella immediately admitted, proudly, that she'd given away the "Jewish piece of metal," as she expressed it, for scrap. At the very first metal recycling event at her new school.

Just the silver was worth hundreds of rubles. In prices back then. Not to mention the historical value.

I didn't say anything. My tongue was tied. As Beinfest ordered, so it was tied. I had stepped far, far aside. And it was best not to ponder what side that was.

But that's not my point.

Beinfest's housekeeper called in the morning with a notification: Natan Yakovlevich had died.

As the deceased had ordered, neither I nor Marik went to the funeral.

His housekeeper—an ordinary village woman—dropped by our apartment, bringing keys, payment stubs, and the death certificate. She said goodbye as if she'd dropped in to sell a pitcher of milk, then she went off in a direction forever unknown.

But that's not my point.

Nina Rogulina came to our house almost every day. She and Ella had become very good friends. Ella bossed her around and Nina obeyed.

Marik worked in the workshop on Arbat Street and at home in the evenings.

He'd finally fixed the chess clock. He boasted.

I tapped on the typewriter, not hearing anything around me. And I kept quiet.

Early one morning, I heard Ella shouting:

"Mamochka! Mamochka! Help! Save me, Mamochka! I'm dying!"

I rushed to her, half-asleep.

Ella was sitting on the bed. Her fat legs were apart so I could see she was all covered in blood. So I thought at first that Ella had spilled ink. Maybe on purpose, maybe by accident.

She was speaking quickly, in a loud whisper:

"I didn't do anything there. Honest. It happened by itself. There's blood coming out of me. I'm dying, Mamochka. I'm dying. I wanted to go to the bathroom to pee. Just to pee. And it happened by itself. And my tummy aches, and my back, too."

Ella was talking like a little girl. Like in the times when I was happy with her at the sea and she was thin and pretty.

I shouted to Marik to call for an ambulance.

"Calm down, daughter. It's nothing awful. The doctor will be right here."

I thought about an infected appendix, about some sort of perforation, who the hell knows what I thought about. But I didn't think about her period.

The ambulance came quickly. There weren't any traffic jams back then.

They examined her and calmed us.

The doctor was an old women; she took me aside and said:

"The little girl started early, nothing awful. It happens. Early puberty. Explain it to her as a woman, as a mother."

I apologized for what worked out to be disturbing her for nothing. But the doctor lady assured me:

"It's better to disturb someone unnecessarily. And you know, she'll remember the fact of it. After all, it's an event in the life of every woman. A dividing line."

I lay down next to Ella on her bed. Right on the stained sheet.

I pressed the girl to myself and said:

"You're going to be completely different now, daughter. The past went away along with the blood. It leaves every woman. And it will leave you."

Ella was lying next to me, as if she were just embracing me around the neck, but as if she were strangling me.

"Oy, Mamochka, I love you so much! I love you so much! I'm going to tell the other girls in the class, they won't believe it. We've talked about this, but some said not everybody has it. That it's only the pretty ones who'll get married and lie down with a man in bed. So they can make children later. I already know everything."

I attempted to move away, but Ella held me firmly with her whole arm, bent at its chubby elbow.

My whole life focused on letters and numerals. I wasn't buying myself new clothes, although decent money unreported to anyone had made its appearance. I didn't feel like spending it.

There was no news from Ostyor.

Brief notes from Misha, with insignificant content, came about every two weeks.

A year passed like that.

Nothing from Ostyor.

Then another year.

Not one line from Ostyor.

I wasn't worried since I understood that somebody would tell me if anything happened. Somehow people always tell you if anything happened.

Misha didn't come home for vacation.

He wrote that he'd refused it for a valid reason he wasn't allowed to explain, because of military considerations.

We awaited his return in the autumn of 1971.

He wrote, though, that he and a friend were headed to Murmansk to get work on a fishing boat—they were expected there.

Yes. The winds of distant travels.

Marik went to parents' meetings at Ella's school and brought me terse pieces of news: "Fine."

What's fine? Who's doing fine?

Okay.

Ella drew day and night. Sometimes I peered into her room and watched.

I didn't understand anything. But Zobnikov called from time to time and praised her. He and I had settled into a strange relationship. He would hold telephone conversations, but only after he'd been drinking. For some reason I listened to him.

One time we ran into each other on the street by the bread shop across from our house. He was eating a high-calorie roll. He was embarrassed when he saw me.

I reassured him with a smile and was the first to speak:

"And so we meet. It's always by telephone, then by telephone again. How's my Ellochka? Any new successes?"

"Wonderful successes. Find her a good private tutor. She needs to go to art school. She has a future," he stuffed the unfinished roll in his pocket and wiped his hand on his jacket.

"And what, you're not a tutor, Pyotr Nikolaevich?" I wanted to continue in a joking manner, but Zobnikov went gloomy.

"What kind of tutor am I? She needs to establish an in for herself, even now. She needs a member of the Artists Union, somebody with connections. But I don't have connections."

"Then help us, find someone, make a recommendation."

"I'll try."

And he bowed, as if I were someone higher ranking and had set a task.

I started laughing. Not from merriment, but from pity. A middle-aged man eating a roll on the street. A soiled jacket. Shoes unevenly worn down. Wrinkled shirt. And yet he was teaching about beauty. How did he feel about looking like that?

"Let's have a walk, Pyotr Nikolaevich."

I offered with the hope he'd refuse. He didn't refuse.

We strolled for a long time along Pyatnitskaya and Ordynka Streets. We were silent.

On Ordynka, Zobnikov said:

"I have a pal from the academy who works here. A restorer. Let's stop in now, I'll introduce you to him. He won't be able to resist when he sees you, Maya Abramovna. And he's famous. He'll find someone for Ella."

We entered a wrought-iron fence. A former monastery and church. Everything was rundown and peeling.

That same friend and restorer was in one of the little rooms.

Zobnikov introduced me.

And that's how I became acquainted with a marvelous person.

Yury Vasilyevich Kanatnikov came into my life like a whirlwind. He conquered me with his attentiveness, culture, and broad range

of interests. As Zobnikov had foreseen, Yury fell in love with me
practically at first sight. Despite his not-so-young age.

Of course, he had a wife and children, even a grandson. But our
hearts hungered for one another despite day-to-day and family
complications.

In this case, there were no problems at all about where to meet.
Beinfest's apartment became our quiet harbor. We made no plans.
Even though as a woman, I did want to hear plans.

As far as Ella went, Yura truly played a good part in the fate of her
talent. He rated it highly. Especially color. He found a teacher. Ella
grew creatively.

If I were to speak of happiness, then I was fully happy. Despite the
fact that Marik immediately guessed the reason for what could be
considered my rebirth. But he pretended. I didn't pretend, though.

The exhaustion that had been accumulating in me for so many
years but hadn't found a reliable outlet had boiled away.

There was only a green light ahead of me.

Not every woman has the occasion to become deeply close
with a genuine artist. Naturally, I asked Yury to paint my portrait.
Not immediately. Roughly a half-year later.

He answered tersely: "I'm a restorer. I don't paint portraits."

"You can't even do mine?"

"Especially not yours."

By virtue of various circumstances, Yura and I were isolated from
the outside world. He was forced to hide from the general public so
all our meetings took place behind closed doors. I wanted to walk
arm in arm through exhibit halls. Travel with him to the Artists'
House resort.

I won't hide that there are women who use a baby to divorce a
man from his old family. I didn't belong to their numbers.

My age still presumed the possibility of giving birth to a child. I was only forty-two years old. But wasn't getting pregnant.

And then one time, in a fit of desperation, I said to Marik:

"There's no point in us dragging out our joint residence. I'm registered in another place. So I'll live there."

Marik cited Ella as an argument. A little girl without a mother. And so on.

I said Ella had spurned me long ago. She had her little girlfriends instead of a mother. Nina Rogulina would do her laundry and cooking. That was a little girl growing up completely without parents. With her grandmother. And she was fine.

Marik kept quiet.

Yes. Repairing mechanisms is one thing, but regulating your own life within your own family and closest circle is something else entirely.

I told Ella that a lot of typing work had piled up so I was moving temporarily to another place so as not to disturb anybody.

I packed a suitcase with clothes for the season. So I wouldn't drag over junk for all occasions right away. The taxi driver helped me carry out the typewriter, in Beinfest's same blanket.

The typewriter was for show. After all, I did feel sorry for Ella. I didn't feel sorry for Marik, though. I'd given him my best feminine years. Beyond that, part of the apartment on Yakimanka was mine, too. An integral part.

And so I'd ended up alone. The telephone was silent. I covered myself with someone else's blanket, used someone else's dishes. Good quality, but someone else's.

Beinfest had left his accumulated things so they seemed like they shouldn't be touched.

Those things hadn't meant anything when I'd been here with Yura. But now they were catching and catching my eye.

I called the restorers' studios to revive myself. Yura wasn't there. I waited until evening for him to call. Then all night. Then in the morning, I called him at home at around eight. I had his number, in case of something urgent.

His son picked up the telephone. His voice was tense.

I asked for Yury Vasilyevich.

"Who's speaking?"

"It's his acquaintance Maya. Maya Abramovna."

"Ah, Maya Abramovna! Do you know what, Maya Abramovna? Please don't call here. My parents went to Palanga on vacation, to the Artists' House."

"How could they go to the Artists' House if just yesterday nobody was planning to go anywhere?"

"He wasn't planning on it yesterday, but today he was. Do you understand Russian?"

And then a dial tone.

Yes. That meant that I hadn't marked a new life for myself by leaving my own home, it was something different. Completely different.

I lay for three or four days without food and water.

I took a look at myself in the mirror. My face had thinned a lot, but had become even more beautiful. My cheekbones had become prominent, like Sophia Loren's. My nose was slightly large and over all I somewhat resembled that actress. Especially with the thinness.

I called Marik: "How are things at home?"

"Things are good."

"How's Ella?"

"Ella's good."

The conversation ended with that.

Only four days had passed. That's why things were good.

I called around to several of my old clients asking if they had work. It turned out they did. One woman brought a doctoral dissertation, something about rodless pumps.

I remembered that because I had the impression at the time that air was being pumped and pumped out of me, just pumped and pumped out. And nothing was being pumped into the freed-up space.

Yes.

I made a vow to myself: I wouldn't go out into the world until I'd typed that up. Except to go for essential food.

I pounded at the keyboard with all my heart. With all my womanly soul.

In the end, I'd done the most important thing for Ellochka: she now had an excellent tutor and the firm hope of being admitted to art school and, after that, into a post-secondary institution or specialized high school.

Even if she couldn't appreciate that now, I didn't need her appreciation.

Misha didn't appreciate me and neither could she. That's a mother's fate.

And so I pounded and pounded, either imitating Morse code or something that was figurative, too. And a thought was growing in my head: "It can't be that nothing has happened in Ostyor for so long. Something's not right. Misha's not asking about Ostyor, either. He sends little notes with the return address 'Murmansk, hold for pick up.'"

And then I realized there was a pattern.

Ella and I had mailbox keys. I'd specially given her a key so she'd have a family task. And since after a certain point I couldn't have cared less about the mail, I didn't go near the box. Ella pulled out the newspapers and everything else early in the morning: for her this was something like an athlete's pursuit of speed. Her hoofs clattered on the stairs, waking up everybody on our stairwell. And she always gave me Misha's letters opened.

She'd say:

"I couldn't wait, I tore it open so neatly. Misha's life is excellent. He's sailing and sailing. And I plod off to school every morning."

I quit typing in midword right there, broke my sacred vow, and went to Yakimanka.

Ella was still at the after-school program. The apartment was empty. The only thing audible was clocks ticking in Marik's room. Out of sync. Each on its own. I stood a bit and listened a bit—I wasn't exactly listening, but gathered my thoughts a little and then went to see Ella at school.

As it happened, she was on her way out. It was winter and she didn't have a hat; there was a scarf tossed over her shoulder.

A boy, probably an upperclassman, was carrying her satchel. She was looking at him with amorous eyes. He was looking down on her. But in a nice way.

Yes. First love.

There it was, everybody's loved. Those who are beautiful and those who weren't loved at first sight. By the way, though, an age difference is dangerous.

I politely said: "Hello, Ellochka. I'm here to get you."

Ella was surprised: "What happened? Zhenya and I were planning to go to the movies. Right, Zhenya?"

The boy was flustered.

I said: "Fine, you'll go another time."

And I decisively took Ella's satchel from Zhenya. He took one look, then another, muttered apologies, and just ran off.

Ella was getting ready to shout, something she knew how to do.

But I cut her off: "If you start yelling now, I'll hit you in the yap in front of everybody. Knock it off with the show. We're going."

If there was one thing Ella always had, it was an animal instinct. She could sense in advance when she'd have to pay for some misdeed she'd committed.

We walked beyond the corner of the school. I turned her by the shoulders so she faced me, then I asked her one question without letting her go: "Where are the letters from Ostyor?"

Ella answered right off: "I threw them away."

"You read them?"

"I read them. I re-e-e-ad them."

Ella started whimpering. But I didn't notice any tears. Just slobbering.

"Let's go home. Fast."

We rode in silence.

At home, we sat on the sofa as we were, in our coats.

"Tell me."

Ella told.

The first time, she opened an envelope from Ostyor because it had very funny names on it: Blyuma and Fimochka.

There was a photograph in the envelope. Based on Ella's description, it was undoubtedly Blyuma and Fima. There was an inscription on the back: "For dear Mayechka, Marik, and Ellochka Faiman from Blyuma and Fima Surkis." There was nothing out of the ordinary in the enclosed letter: they asked for money since the roof needed repair.

My gut noticed they hadn't included Mishenka in the list of Faimans. Blyumochka had jabbed me there, too.

Ella read the letter and brought the photograph to school, to have a laugh with her little girlfriends. And then it became a game for her. A letter would arrive from Ostyor and she'd read it and throw it away. Read and throw away.

"Why did you throw them away? So you read them. Damn you. But give them to who needed them!"

"They asked for money there. First for the roof. Then for the hospital and medicines. And it was written so funny I always brought them to school and everybody laughed."

"And did you laugh?"

"I was the first. If you're the first to laugh, then it's not like it matters to you."

"Ella, you acted like an enemy. Beyond the fact that you were reading someone else's letters, you laughed at them. And there was the question of health there. Do you realize health is the most valuable thing a person has in the world? When was the last one?"

"There hasn't been one in a long time. They'd only been coming three times a year anyway. There was a letter when Misha came out of the military and went to Murmansk. They wrote they were glad how Misha's life was coming along. And nothing more. Honest."

I passed the verdict:

"Ella, you have neither honor nor conscience. I'm your mother and I'm ashamed to have this kind of daughter. Did you at least give me all Misha's letters?"

"All Mishka's, yes. What was there in those to show anybody?"

"Ella. I have another question for you. What's your relationship with that boy Zhenya?"

"Relationship? He's chasing after me. And there's lots more of them chasing after me. And you thought they were only after you?" Ella giggled smugly. "Can I take off my coat? It's hot."

Ella slowly unbuttoned her insulated coat and unwound her scarf. She lifted her shoulders repulsively, like a country woman, and the coat flopped to the floor like a sack. She picked it up and dragged it to the hallway, to the coat rack.

Blyuma. She was a replica of Blyuma.

And that was where I finally came to my senses.

That was how all my dear ones returned. Blyuma and Fimochka and Mishenka. Ellochka was mixed up in their company, too. And Marik had also found himself a place there. I didn't know which side they were coming from. But they were all one bunch.

I had to go to Ostyor to resolve the issue.

But what had to be resolved?

The house in Ostyor stood, boarded up. I hadn't boarded it up, driven in the nails, and shuttered the windows. Somebody else had done that for my benefit.

And so there was this.

The neighbors told me Blyuma'd complained: she was writing and writing to me in Moscow with tactful requests and I was silent, just silent. But she had her pride and the world certainly wasn't lacking for good people. And she had diabetes, in addition to her nerves and all that. And the house needed something. And Fima needed something. And she had no energy.

She waited for Mishenka: first for him to come home for vacation, then from the military. She wrote to him, with unconcealed pretensions directed at me. As soon as Misha was demobilized, he started sending regular money transfers, moreover for large sums. Blyuma bragged that Misha was earning well on some ship.

Then Blyuma died in the garden over the potatoes. She was digging and died.

She'd told the neighbors before that if anything happened, they should send a telegram to Misha at "Murmansk, hold for pickup." She hadn't given my address.

They sent Misha a telegram but it was no use. He was out at sea.

They buried her. The neighbor apologized that it was without the Jewish priest and they'd lowered her in the hole on embroidered towels, the custom for Ukrainians. And sprinkled snowball tree berries on the coffin, all of them the best of the best. I praised them. He said that wasn't done for my gratitude, but for Gilya's sake.

Misha received the telegram, but with a delay.

He came for Fima.

Where had he taken him? Where would he register him? Misha himself was without house or home. I didn't know. Nobody knew.

The neighbors tidied and boarded up the house.

And then I myself showed up. As if I'd had a hunch.

Yes, a close heart is a soothsayer.

I was sitting in the house. And the thirst for activity wasn't letting me go. After all, I'd come here to do something.

I cleared junky old things out into the yard. I broke stools and little chests of drawers with my bare hands. I piled what I could into a mountain.

It was cold. There were stars in the sky. And the sky was dark, dark blue. A deep, deep sky.

I set fire to some newspaper and stuck it inside that mountain.

It immediately went up in flames.

It burned a long time.

The neighbors ran over in droves to look: they were afraid it was a house fire.

No, I said, it might be a house fire for somebody, but not for you. Thank you for everything! Don't be afraid. It's not a house fire.

I watched the flame and the sparks, and I whispered, as if I were praying:

"There's your partisan campfire, Gilechka; there's your light, Natanchik; oh, how it burns, it burns in all twenty-five degrees below zero, it burns for all Ostyor."

The neighbors thought it was dangerous to leave me by myself. They started trying to convince me to go inside. They said they'd put out the fire themselves. Sprinkle it with earth. What earth, though, if it's frozen solid two meters deep?

In a word, they put it out without me.

Nothing else happened later in my life.

Of course Ella grew up. She's not here.

Of course I outlived Marik.

I haven't seen Misha again—it's been forty years. A long time. Though not for the maternal heart.

Comparing the past and the future, I can't help but say I'd want to set certain things right.

I'll do just that when I end up in the same place as Mama, Gilya, Fima, Blyuma, Natan, and many others. But may they, too.

May they, too.

R

RUSSIAN LIBRARY